"Thought I'd stop just because CTU did?" Jack said. "You don't know me very well."

"I'll work on it," Tintfass said, more hopeful than anything.

"You don't have the time."

A quick flick of the gun sent the other four card players scraping their chairs away from the table.

"We don't know you at all, man," one of the others, the dealer, said nervously. "I don't think we want to."

Bauer glanced at them. "You left the game early. Tintfass stayed behind to clean up, make a phone call, like that. None of you saw what happened after that."

The dealer nodded in complete agreement. "I'm in bed an hour ago."

The others nodded, too, though the man with the paunch hesitated a little. "I'm . . . I gotta be dreaming."

"Don't remember this one," Jack said as he laid the sights over Tintfass's thick chest and pulled the trigger.

24 DECLASSIFIED Books
From HarperEntertainment

CHAOS THEORY
VANISHING POINT
CAT'S CLAW
TROJAN HORSE
VETO POWER
OPERATION HELL GATE

DECLASSIFIED

CHAOS THEORY

JOHN WHITMAN

Based on the hit FOX series created by Joel Surnow & Robert Cochran

HarperEntertainment
An Imprint of HarperCollinsPublishers

This is a work of fiction. Names, characters, places, and incidents are products of the author's imagination or are used fictitiously and are not to be construed as real. Any resemblance to actual events, locales, organizations, or persons, living or dead, is entirely coincidental.

HARPERENTERTAINMENT
An Imprint of HarperCollins*Publishers*
10 East 53rd Street
New York, New York 10022–5299

ISBN: 978–0–06–084229–1
ISBN–10: 0–06–084229–6

First HarperEntertainment paperback printing: June 2007

Printed in the United States of America

Visit HarperEntertainment on the World Wide Web at www.harpercollins.com.

10 9 8 7 6 5 4 3 2 1

After the 1993 World Trade Center attack, a division of the Central Intelligence Agency established a domestic unit tasked with protecting America from the threat of terrorism. Headquartered in Washington, DC, the Counter Terrorist Unit established field offices in several American cities. From its inception, CTU faced hostility and skepticism from other Federal law enforcement agencies. Despite bureaucratic resistance, within a few years CTU had become a major force in the war against terror. After the events of 9/11, a number of early CTU missions were declassified. The following is one of them.

24™

DECLASSIFIED

CHAOS THEORY

PROLOGUE

Three Weeks Ago

Bauer kicked in the door and let his SigSauer lead the way into the back room. The five men at the round wooden table gawked silently, and the only sound in the room was the battered door whining as it bumped the wall and swung back. Jack stopped it with his foot.

"Tintfass," he said.

They'd been playing cards, and four of them were statues now, including the dealer, who held one arm out, a card waiting to be flicked to one of the others. But one of them, an older guy with wide-set eyes, a paunch, and probably a little more to lose, was less comfortable staring at the downrange end of the Sig. He turned his head toward one of his partners. The Sig slid smoothly over to cover the one he'd looked at.

Adrian Tintfass was short and round, but bulky rather than fat. His head was bald on top and stubbly around the sides. His cheeks were chubby and soft, but his eyes were quick and bright, like a rat's. Behind the cherub face his mind was racing.

"Thought I'd stop just because CTU did?" Jack said. "You don't know me very well."

"I'll work on it," Tintfass said, more hopeful than anything.

"You don't have the time."

A quick flick of the gun sent the other four card-players scraping their chairs away from the table.

"We don't know you at all, man," one of the others, the dealer, said nervously. "I don't think we want to."

Bauer glanced at them. "You left the game early. Tintfass stayed behind to clean up, make a phone call, like that. None of you saw what happened after that."

The dealer nodded in complete agreement. "I'm in bed an hour ago."

The others nodded, too, though the man with the paunch hesitated a little. "I'm . . . I gotta be dreaming."

"Don't remember this one," Jack said. He laid the sights over Tintfass's thick chest and pulled the trigger.

1 *2* *3* *4* *5* *6* *7* *8* *9*
10 *11* *12* *13* *14* *15* *16* *17*
18 *19* *20* *21* *22* *23* *24*

THE FOLLOWING TAKES PLACE
BETWEEN THE HOURS OF
8 P.M. AND 9 P.M.
PACIFIC STANDARD TIME

8:00 P.M. PST
Federal Holding Facility, Los Angeles

"Bauer, you're up!" the corrections officer barked.

Jack sat in the gray plastic chair, shackled to the hard seat, which was bolted to the concrete floor. He was bent forward, his elbows resting on the orange pants legs of his prison jumpsuit.

"I'm not calling anyone," he said.

"Someone's calling you. Get the damned phone."

Jack stood up and walked toward the phone cubicles on the far side of the community hall. He wasn't expecting a call. He walked past a few rows of other inmates, all dressed in identical orange. Most kept to

themselves, waiting for their turn to reach the outside world, to talk to the lawyer or the girlfriend that
was supposed to care about them on the inside. A few
glared at Jack as he passed. These were the ones who
had nothing else to do, the ones who had no lawyer
but what the county paid for, and whose girls had left
them for guys who hadn't been collared. Jack glared
back at them as he passed.

He hadn't met this corrections officer yet. He was a
big man, with the broken nose and lumpy eyebrows
of a former boxer now gone to fat. He pointed to an
unoccupied cubicle.

Jack sat down in another molded plastic seat and
picked up the phone. "Yeah," he said.

"Jack, you okay?"

Peter Jiminez. Jack was surprised he hadn't called
days ago.

"Considering," Jack said with a shrug. He had no
interest in long conversations with Jiminez. No good
would come of it. CTU didn't recruit the naïve, but if
anyone in the Counter Terrorist Unit could be called
wet behind the ears, it was Peter. Somehow his three
years in Diplomatic Security Services and five years
in the CIA had failed to stamp out the young man's
quixotic notions.

"You're going to beat this, Jack, I know it," Peter
said. "It's bullshit what they're doing, it's bullshit that
they didn't back you about Tintfass in the first place,
and I'm saying it to their faces right now."

Right now. So Henderson was in the room, and
probably Chappelle. That was fine with Jack. He was

happy to have Henderson listen to the conversation, and as for Chappelle, well, he was what he was.

"It's all going to be fine, Peter," Jack said into the phone. "I did my job and I'd do it the same again."

"Chappelle says they have a witness."

Jack thought of the man with the paunch. His name was Arguello. "That doesn't matter. No one's arguing about me pulling the trigger. We're talking about cause."

"You had cause," Jiminez said. "I know you did. Two months on the job and I already know that about how you work. They shouldn't let bureaucrats judge field agents."

Jack heard a squeak in the background and recognized the familiar note of Regional Director Ryan Chappelle's disapproval. "Tell Chappelle I'm having a good time. I wish he was here."

"Jack, is there anything—?"

Bauer cut him off. "I'll be fine." He heard a voice behind him calling time. "I have to go." He hung up.

"Showers!" the broken-nosed guard said. "Let's go."

"Let's do it tomorrow!" an inmate yelled.

"Screw that. You stink," called another.

Jack knew they wouldn't wait until tomorrow. The prison had a schedule to keep, even if overcrowding had pushed the schedule back. Showers, meals, everything was late due to the number of inmates packed into the jail.

He moved away from the phone and fell into line with the other prisoners.

8:11 P.M. PST
CTU Headquarters, Los Angeles

Peter Jiminez put the phone down and glared at his superiors. Regional Director Ryan Chappelle was accustomed to receiving those looks from everyone, and his pinched face remained impassive. Christopher Henderson, Director of Field Operations and Peter's direct boss, shifted uncomfortably.

"He okay?" Henderson asked.

"He's in jail, sir," Jiminez replied, biting down hard on the *sir*. Two months under Jack Bauer's wing had taught him a lot, but the forced politeness of the Diplomatic Security Services remained.

"Where he belongs," Chappelle sniffed.

No one, not even Jack, denied what he had done. Jack had barged in on a poker game in the back room of Winston's, a dive bar in the Fairfax District, and shot Adrian Tintfass in the chest. There were witnesses; there was video. Those facts were not in dispute. But the *why* of it was everything. Tintfass was a connector, a middleman who made his cut by putting together people who could use one another. Three months earlier, the CIA's listening stations had plucked his name out of the air in a conversation between a Ukrainian arms dealer and a known terrorist named Hassan, recently escaped from an Afghan prison. Tintfass, it seemed, had put the two men together, and since Hassan had publicly promised to "turn the streets of America into rivers of blood," or something like that, Tintfass immediately graduated to the Counter Terrorist Unit's A-list. Jack tracked him down and brought him in for questioning. Tintfass broke easily under interrogation, but most of CTU became quickly convinced that he had little or nothing to do with Hassan. He'd had some semi-legitimate business dealings with the Ukrainian, and everyone was convinced that he'd never met or spoken with Hassan.

Everyone, that is, except Jack Bauer. He'd continued to push the investigation, insisting that Tintfass was not only complicit, but pivotal to Hassan's next plot. When no one at CTU would listen, Jack did what Jack was known for: he solved the problem on his own.

The problem was, no one at CTU could back him up. As far as Ryan Chappelle was concerned, Jack had murdered an innocent man in cold blood. He'd been handed over to Federal agents immediately, and he'd been stuck in a Federal jail for the past two weeks. No judge in his right mind would give bail to a suspect with Jack Bauer's skills and resources, so there he sat, waiting for his trial.

"Did he say anything?" Henderson asked.

Peter looked at the Ops Director. Henderson had a hard face, but blue eyes that softened when he was truly concerned. They were soft now. Peter knew that Henderson had helped recruit Jack into CTU, and that the two men had been friends.

"No, he wanted off the phone."

"That's Jack." Henderson nodded. "He'll shut it all off. Undercover inside his own skin."

Chappelle smirked. "You sound sorry for him. He's a murderer."

Peter stiffened. "From everything I've heard he's saved our asses more than once." He walked out.

Chappelle's little eyes watched Jiminez's tense shoulders as he left the room. "Hero worship," he said as if the words tasted bad in his mouth.

Henderson considered Chappelle. He didn't share Jack's visceral dislike of the Regional Director, but there was no love lost between them. Chappelle was a cog in the machinery, no more or less than he or Jack. "You're just as committed the other way. You've already tried and convicted him."

Chappelle shrugged. "I know exactly what Jack Bauer did."

Henderson checked his watch, looking for a way out of the conversation. "Threat assessment meeting at eight-thirty, I need to prep. I'm going to need coffee for this. You want coffee?"

"Sure," Chappelle said.

8:18 P.M. PST
Federal Holding Facility, Los Angeles

The shower room was like showers Jack remembered from high school—a long room with tiled floors and walls tiled six feet up. The tiles were dirty beige and the grout was gray. There were shower heads along the walls, and in the middle of the room a long pipe ran the length of the room about seven feet off the ground, with more shower heads sprouting from either side. The room could shower thirty or forty men at once, and often did.

There were only twenty in Jack's group. Following a routine, they all entered the adjoining room carrying another orange jumpsuit, underwear, T-shirt, and socks, put this folded pile on a shelf. Then they undressed and dropped their dirty clothes in a wheeled laundry cart with canvas sides and marched into the shower room. They were an ugly assortment of bodies, as far from the human ideal as was possible: mostly slouch-shouldered, hairy, spotty, with folds of belly drooping over their hips.

Jack found an open shower nozzle, turned it on, and stepped under the jet of water. There was pressure and heat, which was something to be grateful for. Warm water pounded his head, massaging it, then poured down his face and neck. This was the only pleasurable experience allowed in the Federal jail. There was a small plastic bottle of liquid soap on the wall. Jack squeezed some out and scrubbed it into his hair.

As much as he allowed himself to enjoy the moment, Jack had not let his guard down from the minute he'd stepped inside the jail. His instincts told him something was wrong even before his brain had assessed the details. The shower room was filled with a low roar of twenty or thirty shower nozzles, and steam clouded the air. But the room was empty. The other inmates had turned on their showers, then all of them had left.

Not all.

Three inmates, all Latino, stepped into the shower fully clothed. There was no way for them to hide so they strode toward Jack. The one on the left was stocky, with a barrel chest and huge arms. The middle one was the tallest, thin and wiry. Jack noticed the shiv, a sharpened toothbrush, in his right hand. The one on the right carried the most bulk, but it was mostly fat, and he looked least confident. They didn't say anything. If they had any message to deliver, it was carried in the point of the shiv.

Jack grabbed the soap dispenser off the wall and smashed it against the tiles. The plastic didn't shatter, but it split diagonally across the side of the bottle, and soap poured out onto his hand. Jack threw the bottle down, the motion flicking a thick stream of soap off his hand and onto the floor now running with water from the showers. The thin man with the shiv stepped over the bottle, grinning at Jack as he held up his weapon. The sharpened toothbrush was crude, but Jack knew it could kill him as easily as a bayonet if he let the man stab him. He reached up, caught the shower nozzle for balance, and kicked the thin man in the chest. The kick was awkward, but it made enough impact to make the attacker step back. He snarled and tried to come forward again, but slipped in the soapy water at his feet and hit the deck with a curse.

The stocky one lunged forward. Jack kicked his feet back, feeling his bare feet jam painfully against the tiled corner behind him, jamming his forearms against the man's shoulders to hold him off. Jack just glimpsed the ornate tattoo on the side of the man's neck that read "Emese" in gothic lettering. Jack pivoted sideways and used his arms to slam the man into the tiled wall. Jack was counting on a slow reaction from the fat man, and he was rewarded. He spun to find the third attacker only now bracing himself to punch. Jack stunned him with a left to the nose, then cracked his jaw with an overhand right that snapped his head back. He went down heavily and did not get up again.

The thin man was already on his feet, though, moving tentatively on the slippery surface. "You getting fucked up, *ese*," he promised. He jabbed with the shiv and Jack slid back.

The muscled gang-banger came up faster than Jack expected, slamming into him with a bear hug that caught one of his arms and nearly took Jack off his feet. With his free hand, Jack grabbed one of the shower nozzles across the middle of the room. If he went down it was over. Bracing himself against the overhead pipe, Jack didn't bother to regain his footing on the slippery tiles. Instead he wiggled his trapped hand down, grabbed the gang-banger's groin, and twisted. The tattooed man let out a scream and a curse all in one and forgot about the bear hug. Jack kneed him in the stomach, then the face, then released the overhead pipe, and brought an elbow down on the back of the other man's neck.

The thin man hesitated. He glanced at his shiv, which suddenly seemed smaller and less dangerous now that he was alone. Jack took a step toward him.

At the same time, whistles blew. The thin man threw the shiv into a watery corner as a squad of prison guards flooded into the shower room, grabbing them both, slamming them against the walls. Jack watched, and as they handcuffed the thin man, he saw an MS–13 tattoo crawling up his forearm.

8:29 P.M. PST
Beverly Hills Fight Camp, Los Angeles

Beverly Hills Fight Camp was nothing like its name implied. Far from being the "Beverly Hills" of martial arts schools, it was a cramped, one-room training gym with a weedy asphalt parking lot, patched-up mats that smelled of stale sweat, and a boxing ring with frayed ropes and a sagging floor.

It was, however, home to some of the greatest full-contact fighters in the world, champions of the growing sport of mixed martial arts that combined boxing, kickboxing, wrestling, and other martial arts. The sport had migrated up ten years ago from Brazil, where it was known as *vale tudo*, or "anything goes." During its first few years in the United States it had been called no-holds-barred fighting, but before long savvy businessmen got hold of it, realized that no-holds-barred was both untrue and unpalatable to an American audience, and started touting "mixed martial arts" fighting. The hard core of the fights remained, but some of the rough edges were smoothed over, and suddenly MMA was a multimillion-dollar business.

Those millions, truth be told, rarely trickled down to the fighters who bled in the ring. The best of the best made money, but like boxers, MMA fighters climbed a high, hard mountain to reach the pinnacle of success.

Beverly Hills Fight Camp felt miles away from that pinnacle at the moment. The gym was empty except for a lone fighter, himself a mountain of a man now compressed down to the size of a small hill, hunched over a thick training pad, smashing it with elbow strikes repeatedly, then checking his balance, then returning to pound the pad. Picture frames hung on the walls bearing photographs of former and current champions who had trained at the fight camp. He felt their eyes judging him and finding him wanting. His name was Mark Kendall, and seven years ago he had been the Extreme Fight heavyweight champion of the world. Only for three months before he lost the title, true, but he'd been there, and he was determined to get there again.

Mark pounded the pad. Fight magazines had asked him why he was making a comeback.

"You're getting older," they said, which was as unfair as it was true. No man should be "older" at thirty-six, but fighting was a young man's sport.

"The game's grown past you," others implied. Equally unfair and equally true. He'd earned the heavyweight belt back in the days when size, strength, and some college wrestling were enough to make a champion. The game had become tougher, with fighters cross-training and become adept with their hands, their feet, and their groundwork as well. He admitted that, but it didn't faze him. Those skills weren't secrets. They were out there for anyone to possess, if he put in the work. And Mark Kendall was a hard worker.

"Why would anyone so battered and beaten choose to go back into it?" everyone asked.

That one was easy, Mark thought. There was no choice involved. There were the medical bills piling up, the doctors always saying there were more tests to be done, and there was that three-year-old's face looking up at him asking him to make it all better. There were all those things, but there was no choice.

Mark Kendall hit the pad again.

8:42 P.M. PST
Federal Holding Facility, Los Angeles

"Why were you causing trouble, Bauer?" the broken-nosed guard said as they led Jack, handcuffed, back to his cell.

"Bored," Jack quipped. "So when those three gang-bangers walked into the shower with all their clothes on for no reason, I jumped them."

The broken-nosed guard's laugh was a wheeze, like a car engine failing to turn over. "They say that shiv's yours. You pulled it outta your ass, huh?"

"That's what I do with everything," Jack replied. The guard wheezed again.

They reached his cell. The guard opened the barred door and he stepped inside. Knowing the routine, Jack waited for the cell door to close, then stuck his cuffed hands backward through the rectangular opening on the bars. The guard freed his hands.

"Serious," the guard said, glancing around and dropping his voice a little. "You know those boys are—"

"MS–13."

"You watch yourself." He nodded and walked away, keys jangling down the hall.

"MS–13? What about them?"

Jack's cellmate sat up on his bunk, a suddenly worried expression on his face. His skin was light brown under his jumpsuit, and he wore a pencil-thin mustache that he'd managed to keep neatly trimmed even in jail.

"What's this about MS?" he asked again.

"A couple of their guys jumped me in the shower," Jack said simply, and sat down on his bunk. With both of them sitting on the edge of their bunks, their knees were scant inches apart, and they could walk the depth of their cell from door to back wall in four short steps.

His cellmate, whose name was Emil Ramirez, blinked. "Three? And you, you're—"

"I'm good," Bauer said, lying back on his bunk.

"You gotta watch your back. You mess with them, maybe?"

Jack shrugged. The MS stood for Mara Salvatruchas and the 13 was a number associated with California gangs. The gang was started by immigrant
Salvadorans in the streets of Los Angeles, and had
grown into one of the most dangerous gangs in the
country. Bauer had had one or two run-ins with them,
mostly by accident. He'd be surprised if they remembered him, and he certainly hadn't done enough to
trigger some jailhouse vendetta.

He tilted his head to study Ramirez, who was
still staring at him with a look of deep concern. But
Jack knew it wasn't empathy. Ramirez was afraid for
himself.

"You know about MS–13, too," he stated. "Have
you worked with them? Is that why you're in here?"

Ramirez hesitated, as though he hadn't heard Jack
at first. Then he shifted his eyes and his trance was
broken. "Me? No! I didn't grow up in the barrio. I
wouldn't mess with those guys. But I know a guy who
does. He used to be one of them. Now they work for
him sometimes."

He stopped, clipping off the end of his last sentence
and focusing on Jack. He was clearly afraid that he
had just said too much, but Jack didn't show much
interest. "What are you in for?" he asked.

Ramirez had been tight-lipped since Jack had
moved into the cell a couple of weeks earlier, and
Jack hadn't pushed it. Asking people for information
was often the surest way of making them shut up.

"Embezzlement," Ramirez said. "I'm an accoun-
tant."

"No way," Jack said. "You wouldn't be in this place. Not a Federal facility for an embezzlement charge."

Ramirez grinned boyishly. "Well, embezzlement is how it started," he admitted. "But the guy caught me. We got into a fight, and then"—he winked—"this big glass trophy I got as an award, it fell off the shelf and landed on his head."

"I hate when that happens," Jack said dryly. "And you? Why here?"

Jack shrugged. "A big glass trophy might have fallen on my guy's head, too, except I shot him first."

Ramirez laughed, impressed with Jack's bravado. "Me, I hope the charges don't stick, but the DA says the trophy fell on him nine times. They say that's not possible."

"I never took physics," Jack replied, sounding bored with the conversation.

"Still, I gotta say it's lucky. Even if that charge sticks, it's lucky. They could get me on worse."

More boredom. "Yeah?"

"Yeah." Ramirez leaned in, determined to impress Jack. "The guys I work for, they got something going. It's . . . well, it's pretty big shit."

Jack sat up. "If you say so. What is it?"

"Uh-uh," the other man said, smoothing his already smooth mustache into place. He leaned back coyly, the very picture of a tease who was satisfied now that he'd captured Jack's interest. "I'm not telling. But you'll hear about it soon enough. This time tomorrow, you'll know exactly what it is."

· ·

THE FOLLOWING TAKES PLACE
BETWEEN THE HOURS OF
9 P.M. AND 10 P.M.
PACIFIC STANDARD TIME

· ·

9:00 P.M. PST
Federal Holding Facility, Los Angeles

The thin gang member was named Oscar Cisneros, and he was annoyed at losing his shiv. It took a long time to grind down the toothbrush to make a good weapon like that, and he hadn't even stabbed one person with it. He would have liked to stick it in that blondie, partly because he was getting paid to do it, and partly because he just didn't like white boys. Now, of course, he was determined to get blondie because the *pendejo* had broken Ricky's jaw and smashed in Pedro's teeth with his knee.

These were the thoughts going through Oscar's

mind. He wasn't concerned at all about the trouble he'd get into for fighting in jail.

"Hey, Petey-boy," he said, leaning against the bars of his cell. There was no one in the hallway as far as he could see, but after a minute he heard footsteps and a corrections officer appeared, a middle-aged white guy with a face like bread dough and a big lower lip that hung down like he was pouting. "Petey-boy, I need to make a phone call."

The dough-faced guard frowned and shook his head. "You know that's not going to happen."

Oscar smiled. "I know it is going to happen, home-boy, just like last time. 'Cause all I want to do is make a phone call, and all you want to do is keep your little wifey and daughter over in Simi out of trouble."

Pete's face turned purple as he replied in a low, angry voice, "You're going to push me too far, you little shit."

"But I'm not," the Mara Salvatrucha said with that same smile pasted on his face. "That's why we get along, homes. I'm never gonna ask for too much, 'cause if I do it's bad on me. And you're always gonna do what I ask, 'cause if you don't, it's bad on you."

Pete stood there silently turning a darker shade of purple. He hated this goddamned job. Most of the jail-birds were easy enough, and even the majority of the troublemakers were easy enough to handle if you were careful. But some of these gang-bangers were better organized than the Mob, and way more ruthless. Pete had worked up in Chino before moving to the Federal side, and he knew a guy there whose sister got raped when he wouldn't help some Salvatrucha soldier on the inside. *Goddamn*, he thought, *it's not worth it.*

He opened the door and let Oscar out.

The gang-banger practically led the way down to Broadway, the main thoroughfare through the prison. A few inmates in their cells watched them curiously. Oscar felt like waving at them or flipping them off, but that would be rubbing it in Petey's face and he didn't want to do that. Extorting the guards was a tricky game, and there was no point in pushing it when he'd already gotten what he wanted.

Pete led him through three levels of security and back to the phone room, then backed away as Oscar picked up the phone and made a call to the number he'd been given.

A voice picked up before the second ring. "Is it done?"

"No, *ese*," Oscar said. "That *cabron* messed up my homeboys. I'm gonna stuff his—"

"I told you he would put up a fight!" the man on the other end of the phone snapped. "Go back and get it done."

Oscar considered. "Okay, homes, but the price is going up. I want—"

"Shut up and listen," the man said. "You'll do it for what we agreed on, or I'll make sure you and your friends go down in flames, you understand me? You'll get buried so deep your own fucking mother will forget you."

Oscar's smile turned wistful. Yeah, that's what it was like in the extortion business. Sometimes you just didn't have the power, and then you had to bluff or back off. Oscar knew when to back off. "Okay, *jefe*. We'll do it."

"Do it *now*," the man insisted. "I've got a backup plan already, but you do your goddamned job." The line went dead.

9:13 P.M. PST
CTU Headquarters, Los Angeles

Tony Almeida was only a third of the way through his threat assessment when he thought, *Jesus, Chappelle's already bored.* The Regional Director was staring off into space, his eyes glazed. At the far end of the table, Nina Myers looked bored, too, but he was accustomed to the sardonic look she sometimes wore. A few other CTU agents sat around the table, dutifully upright and attentive, but more out of respect than interest.

"In any case," he continued his report, "the Governor's meeting with the representatives from Southeast Asian countries started tonight with the reception, and the meetings start tomorrow. We're considering that a primary target for any activity."

Henderson walked back in, carrying two cups of coffee. He sipped one and put the other down in front of Chappelle. "You wanted more, right?"

"Hmm?" Chappelle said hazily. His eyes focused on the coffe and he said, "Oh, yeah. Thank you. Go on, Agent Almeida."

Tony pressed a button and a large screen changed from a picture of the Chairman of the Federal Reserve to a collection of three candid black-and-white photos, all of Arabic men in their late twenties. "I'm keeping these three on our watch list even though they're probably not in our region. They still got released in connection with one of our cases, so I figure—"

"It wasn't our fault," Nina Myers said. "We were solving the case. We weren't the ones who caved to terrorist demands."

Tony nodded. It was an old case that had been wrapped up, but in a related incident, three suspected terrorists had been released. All of CTU was irked that they'd gotten away. He moved on.

"Presidential candidates from both parties are making campaign stops in and around Los Angeles in the upcoming months, ramping up for the primaries. The advance teams know to contact us, and communication is good." The agents nodded and scribbled notes.

Henderson spoke up. "But we don't have any likely suspects? I'm asking, not telling. Is that right? We don't have any hard evidence of any terrorists having infiltrated the country."

Tony agreed. "Nothing to set off alarm bells, which is a good thing."

"Then why are we here so late?" Henderson asked.

"I wanted it," Chapelle said as if no further explanation were necessary.

Tony continued. "Our data analysts"—he gave a nod to Jamey Farrell, who tipped her imaginary hat —"have pulled up some information on locals with possible connections to Jemaah Islamiyah. It's thin, but I'm going to follow up."

"Good," Henderson said. "Well, that wraps it up, ladies and gentlemen, I—"

"Chappelle?" Tony said, looking past Henderson.

The Regional Director's eyes hadn't just glazed over. They were rolling back in his head, and his face had gone gray. A bit of drool seeped from the corner of his mouth, and by the time Henderson turned to check on him, Chappelle was falling out of his chair. Henderson caught him and laid him gently on the ground as the others crowded around.

"Chappelle!" Henderson said, tapping him lightly on the cheek. "Ryan! Call security, get medics," Henderson said with authority, but the team around him was already on the move. "Get them here quick. He's not breathing!"

9:19 P.M. PST
Federal Holding Facility, Los Angeles

The broken-nosed guard was named Adam Cox, and Adam Cox was looking forward to getting the hell off work, slogging his way through traffic, and putting his feet up in front of SportsCenter. Viv would probably ride him for not finishing the weather stripping on the garage door, but hell, it wasn't going to rain any time soon.

Adam checked his watch as the inmates filed past, joining the chow line. He stood with his back to the wall, near the double doors that led into the mess hall. His eyes scanned the room as they had four days a week, every week, for the last seven years, stopping at each guard position to make sure his guys were okay, then moving on. Lately he'd been halting his gaze on that new inmate, Bauer, watching him for trouble, but tonight Bauer was being fed in the library because of the attack.

Mind off Bauer, Adam told himself. *You got plenty of other mad dogs in this yard.*

Even as Adam thought that, Big Ferg walked by. Big Ferg had been in the Federal Holding Facility for up on a year now, waiting for his trial on weapons charges. He was a leader of the Aryan Bloc. Truth was, he didn't seem to cause much trouble himself, and he and Adam had formed a kind of grudging respect for each other. But in a jail full of blacks and Latinos, a white supremacist was a trouble magnet, and Adam had been forced to break up a dozen fights that Big Ferg hadn't started.

Adam's eyes were on Big Ferg, so he was the first to see the black inmate move toward him. He didn't know the guy's name—he was a new arrival. But he was as wide as a truck and nearly as tall, and he moved through the crowd at the chow line like a semi roaring down the road. He and Big Ferg were on a collision course. Adam was on the move, raising his hand in a signal to the other guards.

Adam got there just as the black man threw his first punch. Ferg, though, was no dummy, and no big black man approached without him knowing it and getting off his heels. He ducked the punch and put an uppercut into the other man's ribs. He might as well have hit a side of beef for all the effect it had. The black inmate slammed both hands down and Ferg dropped to one knee.

"Break it up!" Adam roared, stepping between the two fighters, facing the truck-sized newcomer to shield Ferg. "Get the hell back!"

He didn't feel the first stab. He was only aware that he'd been shivved in the back when the blood seeped out, warm and then suddenly cold against his skin. He felt Big Ferg's bulk against his back, holding him with one arm so he couldn't spin around as the other arm pumped forward, backward, forward, backward, over and over.

"Sorry, dude," Ferg whispered. "Just business."

Goddamn, Adam Cox thought as his legs seemed to disappear beneath him.

9:23 P.M. PST
Federal Holding Facility, Los Angeles

Jack sat at a library table closest to a wall. He didn't like having his back to a room under normal circumstances, so in this place his caution was even more extreme. At the warden's orders, the guards had brought food to them in the library.

Ramirez had been brought along, too, simply because it was easier for the guards to keep track of both of them. Ramirez lifted a clump of gray, dripping food halfway to his mouth and grimaced. "I knew the food in here would be bad, but Jesus—"

Jack wolfed his food down without tasting it. He didn't expect to like it, but he knew he needed the nutrients while he was locked up in this place. He wasn't sure how long he'd be here, and he needed his strength.

"Salt," Ramirez said. "I gotta have salt. Guard, is there any salt?" He turned around in his chair to look at the spot where the guard had been standing. There was no one there.

"The minute you want one of those guys to do some work, they're gone," he muttered. He stood up, but Jack grabbed his sleeve, his face going hard and his eyes narrowing.

"Stay here," he ordered.

Jack knew what was coming the minute the guards disappeared. This MS–13 gang had some connection with the guards, or some hold over them, otherwise they'd never have been able to clear out the showers the way they had. Now they'd done it in the library, too. Jack cursed himself for allowing the isolation, but then he figured it wouldn't have mattered. In a crowd, he wouldn't see it coming. At least here he had some warning. Jack stood up and went to the nearest bookshelf. He scanned the books—not the titles, but the sizes—finally finding a short, thick one that fit his hand nicely. He stepped out of the aisle and back to his table just as they appeared.

The thin Latino—Adam Cox had called him Oscar—was there again, this time with three thugs to back him up. Ramirez squeaked and backed up, bumping against the chair behind him.

"You didn't think we was finished, did you?" Oscar said, sauntering closer. One of his thugs disappeared down one of the aisles, meaning to flank Jack.

"Your two guys seemed finished to me," Jack said. "You'd have been finished, too, if the guards hadn't saved you."

"You gonna want those guards this time, *ese*," Oscar said. "We gonna—"

Jack threw the book at him. It wasn't heavy enough to do much damage, but it made him flinch, giving Jack time to step forward and kick him in the groin. The kick landed hard, lifting Oscar's feet off the ground, and the thin man doubled over with a cough. Jack grabbed him by the orange collar and shoved him at the two thugs on his left, then bolted right, down the stack of books. He didn't like that third man hiding in the stacks, and wanted him neutralized.

"Javie, he's coming!" one of the other gang-bangers shouted.

The Salvatrucha Javie jumped out from behind a corner and was surprised to see Jack already on top of him. Jack punched him in the face and drove his forehead in right behind the punch, feeling the crown of his head connect with a cheekbone, splitting it. He grabbed Javie's collar and put a knee into his ribs. Then, stepping past him, he kicked his legs back, sweeping the gang-banger's feet out from under him. Javie hit the ground hard. Jack raised his knee and stomped on the man's face.

He walked back down the aisle to the table. Oscar was still curled up on the ground. The other two were on top of Ramirez, one holding him and the other punching him in the face. They were bullies, not soldiers. They had pounced on the weakest member rather than focusing on the real threat. Their mistake.

As soon as Jack reappeared, the puncher turned on him. He was fast, and probably tough, but not skilled. He came at Jack with a killer sneer and two big, flailing hands. Jack threw two straight punches right down the middle. He felt one of the Salvatrucha's punches box the side of his skull, stinging but doing no damage, while both his punches hit the man in the throat. He gagged. Jack ducked low and put a left hook in the man's liver. The man stood back for a minute, blinking as though Jack's punch had no effect. Then his knees buckled.

The last attacker was faster. He'd already thrown Ramirez off, and before Jack could turn he grabbed him from behind, lifted him, and slammed him onto the table. Jack felt his left shoulder go numb and hoped it wasn't broken. The Salvatrucha tried to lift him again, but Jack dropped his weight, going heavy, then spinning around inside the man's arms. He dug both hands into the gang-banger's face and eyes, not just pushing but tearing at the flesh. The man gave a strangled cry and tried to push Jack away, but Jack forced the man's chin up, then drove it backward and down, doubling the inmate over. Jack released one hand and punched him in the face.

He paused, gasping for breath. His heart was

pounding, but his senses were alert. He scanned the room, searching out additional threats. Finding none, his eyes settled on Ramirez, who was staring at him in utter astonishment.

"Holy shit," the man said. "Who are you?"

"The guy you want on your side."

"No kidding." Ramirez looked at the four men, two unconscious, two groaning and quivering in the middle of their own misery. "Who, what do these guys want with you?"

"I don't know," Jack said truthfully. It couldn't be that old event, could it? He'd needed some information from an MS–13 member, but the case itself had little to do with the gang, and once he'd gotten his information, Jack hadn't touched them again. He couldn't believe they'd hold a grudge for that, especially against someone they knew to be law enforcement. But he couldn't think of any other reason. He certainly hadn't attracted their attention inside the jail.

"You okay?" he thought to ask.

Ramirez's face was bloody. The punches had surely broken his nose, and his cheek was cut open. A huge mouse was already forming under his right eye, and his teeth were smeared with blood from a cut inside his mouth. "I'm not much of a fighter. And these . . ." He shook his head at the four men. "They don't stop. I know that about them. They never forget, and now they're not going to forget me."

"They weren't after you," Jack said, still wondering what they were after.

"No, but now I'm part of it. Jesus! I heard a story

about them once, that some gang member talked to the Feds and went into the witness protection program. They lost him for seven years. Seven years! He didn't even testify against them, he just got out. Then one day he turned up dead, the skin peeled off his hands. They cut his throat." He shuddered.

"You don't like them, but you said your boss uses them."

"Not my boss," Ramirez corrected. "Just a guy I know."

"Right. This guy who's got something planned for tomorrow. If MS guys like these are involved, it's probably not going to go well."

Ramirez pinched his lips closed. He used his sleeve to dab the blood off his cheek and nose. "You wondering about that little thing tomorrow, huh?"

Jack shook his head. "I have enough of my own problems. Just curious about these." He kicked Oscar with his toe. "Hey, you," he said. "What are you after? What am I to you?"

Oscar looked up at him, tears in his eyes. "A dead man."

9:37 P.M. PST
CTU Headquarters, Los Angeles

Less than twenty minutes had elapsed since Ryan Chappelle had collapsed in the CTU conference room. Five minutes after he'd fallen, the medics were there, and ten minutes after that—ten minutes full of CPR, three applications of the defibrillator paddles, and several medications to stabilize him—a medical team moved Ryan Chappelle out of CTU and toward a waiting ambulance. A moment or two after the defibrillator had restarted his heart, Chappelle had actually opened his eyes. His eyes rolled for a moment, unfocused, and finally settled on Henderson's angular face.

"Don't . . ." he mouthed. The word was barely audible.

"Just relax, sir," the medic said, putting a hand on his shoulder.

Chappelle pushed the hand away weakly. "Don't . . ." he said again, his voice a faint breath slipping out of his body, ". . . let . . ."

Henderson leaned close, with Tony Almeida beside him.

Chappelle shuddered. ". . . Bauer . . ." he gasped. "Don't . . . Bauer."

He passed out.

"Crashing again!" the medic yelled. He snatched up the defibrillator paddles again and shouted, "Clear!" He barely waited for the others to step back before shocking Chappelle's heart again. Chappelle's body convulsed, and his heart beat faintly in the portable monitor. "Okay, go!" the medic ordered.

"Do we go with him?" Tony asked.

Henderson nodded. "I'll follow."

"What was he saying, about Bauer?"

"I don't know."

"What does he think we're going to let Jack do while he's in jail? Don't let him what?"

"Delirium, probably," Henderson guessed.

Tony paused. "You know, no one's been talking lately about Jack."

Henderson watched the medics wheel Ryan Chappelle out the front door. "This may not be the time, Tony."

"Yeah, but now's when it's come up. There's no one here that thinks Jack Bauer really killed an innocent man in cold blood. Is there?"

Henderson turned back toward Tony. They were opposites in appearance—Tony had a soft face with sad eyes, a sharp contrast to Henderson's steel blue gaze. But underneath, both men were made of the same hard, dark material.

"You're asking if I believe it," Henderson said. He paused for a moment.

"You have to think about it," Tony said disdainfully. "You and Jack, you've been on bad terms since Internal Affairs started looking into that missing money."

"That's nothing," Henderson said dismissively. "It'll go nowhere. No, I'm wondering what I've done to make you think I'm that much of an ass. I brought Jack Bauer in here. I've stuck my neck out for him before. No, I don't think he's guilty of murder. But that guy getting rolled out on the stretcher did, and I have a feeling that a jury is going to see it that way, too."

9:46 P.M. PST
Federal Holding Facility, Los Angeles

The guards returned to the library, conveniently, when the fighting was done. One of them, a squishy-faced guard with an oversized lower lip, was the same guard who had disappeared just before the Salvatruchas appeared, but he was accompanied by a platoon of officers headed by an older black officer with the blasé look of a man who'd seen everything one could see inside a prison. His name tag said "Lafayette" on it.

"Get the four-pieces," Officer Lafayette said with a slow Louisiana drawl. "Hook these boys up and get 'em into isolation."

The platoon produced four-piece steel wrist and ankle cuffs, connected by chains, and began to fetter the four gang-bangers. Oscar was still doubled over and could barely walk from the pain in his groin. Jack was sure he'd ruptured something and wished the Salvatrucha a slow and unsuccessful recovery.

"You gonna get fucked, blondie," Oscar said as he was led away.

"Well, you're not gonna be doing it," Jack said. The guards tugged Oscar out the door.

Lafayette turned to Jack. His low-slung posture and heavy sigh told Jack he didn't expect to get much information. "You gonna tell me what happened?"

Jack believed the guard hoped to hear a no. "Your guy, the one with the swollen lip, took a coffee break right about the time these four showed up. They tried to kill us, but we took them down first."

Lafayette leaned to the side, looking past Jack at Ramirez, who was still slumped against the table. The guard looked back at Jack and chewed the inside of his mouth. "We, huh?"

Jack decided he needed to get some help. "Look, I don't know why these guys have come after me twice, but I've had enough of it. I need to speak with Officer Cox right away."

Lafayette shook his head. "That ain't possible."

Jack insisted. "If you talk to him, he'll explain everything, even if you have to call him back in to the office. I promise you, he'll want to know."

"You ain't gettin' me, son, it ain't possible. Cox took a shiv under the ribs not half an hour ago. He didn't make it."

Jack felt a firm, cold pressure start in the bottom of his chest, a sense of some danger long present but only now discovered. "Then the warden. He'll want to talk to me if you tell him my name."

"Can't do that, either. Warden took sick this afternoon. He's in the hospital."

The pressure built up into Jack's lungs, tightening them, though he showed no emotion whatsoever. "Then call him there. Trust me, he'll want to know this—"

"He ain't takin' calls. What I heard, he's had a heart attack or something."

The pressure reached Jack's heart, nearly freezing it. He looked around him, and for the first time in three weeks, he felt as if he were in jail.

1 2 **3** 4 5 6 7 8 9
10 11 12 13 14 15 16 17
18 19 20 21 22 23 24

. . . .

THE FOLLOWING TAKES PLACE
BETWEEN THE HOURS OF
10 P.M. AND 11 P.M.
PACIFIC STANDARD TIME

. . . .

10:00 P.M. PST
Bauer Residence

Peter Jiminez knocked on the door. The woman who opened it was lean, with short-cropped hair. She was pretty in a homey sort of way, but dark circles hung heavily below her eyes.

"Mrs. Bauer? Peter Jiminez, I worked with your husband. Sorry for the late hour. We've actually met twice, once right after I came on and a couple of weeks ago when—"

"Yes, I remember, um, Peter. How are you?"

Peter shifted a little uncomfortably. "Well, ma'am, I just, I wanted to stop by and talk to you. I just can't get my head around Jack being in jail."

Teri bit her lip and looked past Peter, as though expecting to see someone else there. "Come in, Peter."

Teri stepped back and let him enter, feeling as she did as if she was allowing the CTU agent to cross some sort of boundary. Her relationship to Jack's work was, by nature, distant and difficult. At the moment it was also tragic.

Peter looked as uncomfortable as she felt. He had a boyish look for a CTU agent, with a plump face and a ruler-straight part in his thick black hair. He wore a blue suit and dress shirt, but no tie. This Peter Jiminez might have been a young movie executive or a banker, but Teri knew from experience that he would have a gun slung under his arm, and probably another hidden somewhere.

"Can I get you something?" she offered, motioning him to sit on the living room couch. She took a seat in a chair across from the table.

"No, ma'am, thank you," he replied. "I don't want to trouble you. Truth is, I'm not even sure why I'm here. Do you mind if I just jump right in? Here's the thing: when my chance came to join CTU, I jumped at it, because I wanted to work with your husband."

"Did you know him?"

"Not him personally, but his reputation. CTU guys don't talk much about their work, that's true of a lot of agencies, of course. But word gets around. I was in Diplomatic Security Services when they started the CTU program. We did protective services—bodyguard stuff, but we don't like using the word *bodyguard*. I was too young to get in, but this is where I wanted to be. So I jumped from DSS to the CIA. In the CIA, of course, I heard all kinds of stuff about what CTU was doing. I've got to tell you that Jack's name came up a lot."

"I'm sure it did," Teri said wryly.

Peter laughed. "Well, there was some colorful language attached to his name sometimes. But he also had a reputation for getting the job done. So I jumped into CTU the first chance I got. Two months on the job, and now this happens."

Teri pulled her feet up and crossed her legs in the chair. This Peter Jiminez was very sincere, but she was confused. Did he want her to be his counselor? If so, he had another think coming. She had a daughter whose father was in jail for murder. "Agent Jiminez, is there something you need from me?"

"I just don't think he did it, ma'am," Peter insisted. "Not without a good reason. But there's no one looking into it on his side. CTU has just written him off. I figured"— he fixed his eyes on her to let her know how serious his statement was—"I figured I'd see what I could do on my own to help out, and I thought I'd start by asking you if there's any direction you might point me."

So it was an investigation. Teri folded her arms across her chest. She wasn't sure if Jiminez's schoolboy demeanor was an act or his true persona, but she'd been around Jack long enough to recognize a good-cop interrogation when she saw one.

"Agent Jiminez," she said, her voice hardening ever so slightly. "You have to know that there were lots of things about Jack's work that he didn't discuss at home."

"Of course, ma'am. It's just that . . . well, to be honest, a man will sometimes tell his wife things that he won't tell anyone else."

Teri laughed, but it was a small thing, with a bitter sound in it. "There are probably more things a man *won't* tell his wife."

Jiminez actually blushed. He really was a schoolboy. "Maybe you're right, ma'am. But if you don't mind me saying so, you seem like someone to trust. I'm wondering if there was something going on at the agency that Jack didn't like. Something he might have confided in you. Maybe someone else was out to get him?"

"You think he was set up."

Peter held his hands up, warding off the suggestion. "I'm not saying anything for sure, ma'am. I'm just wondering if he said anything to you about trouble with anyone else at the agency."

Teri shook her head. "You may or may not know that my marriage with Jack has had some pretty rough patches, and pretty recently."

Jiminez fidgeted in his seat, but nodded. "Ma'am."

"There've been times when we've barely spoken and when we did, it wasn't about his work. There are times when he's gone for days at a time, and he comes home without a single word about where he's been or what he's done. For all I know, he's saved the world from a nuclear bomb. Or maybe he's just been in somebody else's bed. I never know. So no, he's never told me about any trouble at work. But I will tell you one thing I do know." Now it was her turn to fix her eyes on him. Her gaze bored into him in a look she had long practiced. "The one thing I do know is that Jack is capable of anything."

10:11 P.M. PST
Federal Holding Facility, Los Angeles

Jack followed Ramirez back into their cell, escorted by Lafayette and two other guards. As soon as the door was locked, Jack turned to the officer. "I need to get in touch with someone on the outside. Can you make a call for me?"

"Call tomorrow," Lafayette drawled lazily. The trouble was over for now, and he wanted to move on before this became something that required paperwork.

"I can't wait," Jack said. "This gang will keep coming at me. Look, all I'm asking is for you to make a one-minute phone call."

Lafayette frowned at him. He was fit for a man in his early fifties, but he wore all those years in the lines of his face when he frowned. "You know what it'd be if I made a one-minute call for every bird in this cage?"

"They're not all getting killed. Come on, thirty seconds."

The lines on the guard's face deepened. "Awright. I

make this call, you forget all about this fight tonight. Then I don't have to do paperwork."

Jack agreed. He gave Lafayette the number to CTU. "Tell them you're calling for Ryan Chappelle. Tell them it's an emergency. When you get Chappelle, tell him you're calling because things are going south. Say exactly that, okay?"

Lafayette had been reluctant at first, but he also didn't like too many fights on his watch. A scuffle here and there between inmates was all right—hell, sometimes it was downright entertaining—but he didn't like what was going on with these Salvatruchas and Bauer. There was some bad sauce on those ribs, like his mama always said. He locked Jack back in his cell and moseyed down to the guard's office behind its Plexiglas walls.

Lafayette had returned a few minutes later. "You're having a bad day," he said to Jack. "Or maybe it's everyone around you's having a bad day."

"Did you tell him? Jack had asked eagerly.

"Nope," the corrections officer said. "Couldn't. He's in the hospital, too."

Lafayette had walked away, his job done. But Jack clutched the bars of his cage, squeezing until his knuckles turned white.

But it wasn't in him to panic. He let go of the bars and watched the color flow back into his fingers. Observe. Assess. Act. That was how battles were won. He had suddenly become a target of MS–13, and since MS–13 was a major force in Los Angeles, and ran a crime syndicate that violated dozens of Federal laws, this Federal jail was crowded with Salvatruchas. They'd keep coming at him from different angles until they put him down. Adam Cox, who was more valuable to Jack than anyone in here knew, was dead. The warden, whom Jack could have turned to, was out of commission, maybe dead, too, for all Jack knew. And now Chappelle. It was certainly no coincidence that the three people he could turn to had all been neutralized.

He was in trouble. What kind of trouble, he didn't yet know, and he would certainly never find out by waiting around inside for MS–13 to kill him.

By 10:16 Jack had made his decision, and by 10:18, he had a plan.

10:18 P.M. PST
Bauer Residence

The truth of it was that Peter's schoolboy style wasn't an act. He'd been raised in Glendale, Arizona by his maternal grandparents, and they'd trained him up to be polite with a combination of what his grandma called "beatings and sweets," rewarding good behavior and smacking the sass out of him when necessary. *Sir* and *ma'am* came naturally to him, and so while his aw-shucks habits weren't an act, he was conscious of their usefulness during interrogations. He was an instinctive good cop.

He walked out of Jack Bauer's house sure that Teri Bauer knew more than she was saying, but equally sure that she had no information about any personnel conflicts inside CTU. He'd watched her closely while they talked. When she'd mentioned that Jack never talked to her about what he'd been doing, her eyes had moved up and left, an indication that she was accessing the creative side of her brain. When she claimed that he never mentioned personnel conflicts her eyes flicked down and right, usually suggesting use of the brain's factual side.

Peter got into his car and drove away in the fading twilight. He hadn't gone more than two blocks when a Crown Victoria pulled up beside him. The window slid down, and a man in sunglasses flashed a badge and motioned for him to pull over. Peter complied, rolling to the curb. He was tempted to get out of the car, but he knew that if he was on the job and pulled someone over, even another Federal agent, he'd want them to stay put. Common courtesy.

Two men got out of the Crown Vic, both wearing half-decent blue suits and inexpensive, comfortable dress shoes. They split off, one to each side of Peter's car. The one on the driver's side, who looked Japanese, showed his badge again. FBI.

"Agent Jiminez, I'm Jason Fujimora, FBI, and that's Special Agent Holmquist."

"You want to see my ID?" Peter asked.

"We know who you are, Agent Jiminez," Holmquist said, making Peter turn his head to look the other way. "We just wanted to pass on a quick word."

"Lay off the Bauer case," Fujimora said.

Peter swiveled his head again. "That's five. Words, I mean."

Fujimora ignored that. "There's nothing for you to find there."

Peter smiled a friendly smile. "Well, fellas, if there's nothing to find there, there's no harm in looking. Nothing wasted but my time."

"Wouldn't want you to waste the taxpayers' money," said Holmquist. This time Peter didn't bother to look. "Bauer's in jail for good reason, and he'll stay put. Understood?"

"Not really," Peter replied. "Why you guys? Was Tintfass involved with the FBI? Informing for you, maybe? You guys pissed that Bauer offed him?"

"Bauer's in the zoo where he belongs," Fujimora leaned in a little, resting his hands on Peter's window frame. "Just don't disturb the animals too much. No one wants to get bitten. Good talking to you."

10:21 P.M. PST
Intensive Care Unit, UCLA Medical Center,
Los Angeles

Kris Czikowlis plucked a blue pen out of the pocket of her white medical coat and began scribbling on a notepad. It was standard stuff, but she always felt better when she made notes: *Get medical history. Seizures? Family history. Strokes?* She used layman's terminology because it prompted her to use the same words with the family.

The patient lying on the bed in front of her was a male, mid-forties, Mr. Ryan Chappelle. Some sort of government employee or cop. Not overweight, although of course that didn't rule out some sort of heart condition. No prior signs of distress, until he'd collapsed less than an hour earlier. By the time he arrived at UCLA Med he was comatose.

History of drug use?

He wouldn't be the first government employee, even police officer, to use drugs, and the right drugs in the wrong hands could turn the brain off like a light switch.

A man in a gray suit walked into the ICU, tugging at his tie. He saw the patient and then Kris. His eyes slid down her body and then back up to her eyes. But he did it quickly, and that passed for politeness these days.

"You're his doctor?" the man said, offering his hand. "Chris Henderson."

Kris replaced her pen and shook his hand. "I'm Dr. Czikowlis. Are you family?"

"No, colleagues. I was there when he collapsed. Do you know what happened?"

"Not yet," she said. "He's stable now, but comatose. Did you give a history to the paramedics?"

Henderson looked at Chappelle. On his best days the Regional Director looked thin. Lying in the ICU he was practically skeletal. "As much as I could. We're not that close, really. But he always seemed to be pretty healthy."

"We'll find out what's going on," Dr. Czikowlis

promised. "I'm ordering blood work and a few other tests."

"What will the blood work show?"

"Anything in his system, drugs, like that."

Henderson handed her a card that listed him with the Department of Homeland Security. It was official enough to look important, without giving away any classified information about CTU. "It's fairly important that we get him well as soon as possible," he said. "Also, it's standard procedure for us to keep track of any information that goes out. Please let me know where the blood work is being sent." She wrote it down for him.

"Thanks," he said. "Will you call me the minute you know anything?"

"Of course," the doctor said. "Is he . . . Look, I don't know what you guys do, but is this related to his work? Was he doing something . . . Is he a spy?"

Henderson chuckled. "No, he's a bureaucrat. But he's an important bureaucrat, so please try to get him better."

10:30 P.M. PST
Union Station, Los Angeles

He came up from San Diego on the Pacific Surfliner and sighed as the train rolled into L.A.'s Union Station. He loved trains or, more specifically, he had a love-hate relationship with them. When the trains ran on time, their precision was a thing of beauty and, as

Keats had said, *A thing of beauty is a joy forever.* But the trains often did not run on time, and the result was discord. Disharmony. Chaos.

He liked train stations and subways more than airports because they usually displayed maps of the tracks, concise representations of the elaborate systems of paths, cars moving on paths, people getting on cars moving on paths.

The web of our lives is of a mingled yarn. Shakespeare, which play?

He stepped off the Surfliner and into the crowd of travelers. A family composed of a man, a woman, and two twin girls of about nine years passed. The girls were pulling matching pieces of Coach luggage on wheels, and he noticed instantly that the woman constantly looked back to the girls while the man looked to the train schedule. Fulfilling their roles: father-leader, mother-protector. Those were their roles in this situation, but change the situation, he thought, and see how quickly their roles change. Grab one of the girls, smash her head with his fist, and then suddenly the father becomes the protector and the mother becomes the guide, leading them away from danger. Comfortably predictable.

A man in a respectable black suit saw him standing still in the middle of the crowd and mistook him for someone lost. Mistook him for a sheep. The man approached and held out a pamphlet called *The Watchtower.* "Have you heard the word, my friend?"

He smiled. "I have heard seven from you, and will probably hear more."

"If you're looking for guidance, you'll find it here." He indicated the pamphlet.

He was enjoying this. He had learned long ago to find pleasure in minor distractions, rather than being annoyed by them. "Will it show me how to get to the Staples Center?"

The man in the black suit laughed. "No, but it'll show you the word of God."

"Ah," he said, pretending only just now to understand. "To die for a religion is easier than to live it absolutely." That was Borges.

It suddenly dawned on the Jehovah's Witness missionary that he was being toyed with. "Huh?"

"I'm going to make things easier on you. Enjoy the rest of your day."

He walked away, feeling the eyes of the Jehovah's Witness on his back for a few seconds. Then the man turned away, passing out more of his pamphlets. His stack contained roughly forty pamphlets, and the traveler estimated quickly that it would take him another fifteen minutes to pass out those pamphlets.

The train exploded ten minutes later. The traveler had just gotten into a taxicab and was driving away when the sound of the explosion roared out of the entrance to Union Station.

It was not a big explosion, and did not cause extensive damage. A truly large explosion would have brought attention that the traveler did not want, so this one was made to look like an explosion of diesel fuel, which was combustible at 105 degrees Fahrenheit. It was not, as the traveler had already reminded himself, big enough to cause extensive damage. But it was big enough to stop the train service at Union Station which, at that particular time of day, would cause a ripple affect, disrupting the service of Los Angeles's Metro transit system, as well as train service in Santa Barbara and San Diego, and, to a lesser extent, delaying train service as far away as Santa Fe, New Mexico, and Chicago, Illinois. The family with the Coach luggage would not be injured but, in some small way, their lives would be changed forever by the ripple effect of his actions. He smiled happily.

"Where you headed?" the taxi driver asked.

"Staples Center," he said.

"Got it. I don't wanna lose a fare, but you know you coulda taken the Metro right from Union Station. Drops you off right at Staples."

The traveler glanced back. Wisps of smoke drifted up out of the Union Station building, barely visible in the streetlights, and he could already hear sirens. "I think they're having trouble with the trains."

The drive was a short one, directly across the downtown area of Los Angeles, the only place in the suburban sprawl that simulated the "downtown" feel of New York or Chicago, with concrete canyons formed by skyscrapers looming over streets. Oddly enough, these streets were cast almost completely in shadow during the day. At night they were bright with light pouring out from the buildings. A quick run down one of these canyons and the taxi emerged on the south side of downtown, where the Los Angeles Convention Center and Staples Center together covered whole acres of land.

The taxi pulled to a stop in front of the Staples Center and the traveler got out, paid, and walked toward the north side of the building. There were small crowds moving in and around the center for some event or concert that was of no consequence to the traveler.

He spotted Francis Aguillar before Aguillar saw him. This was to be expected, because the traveler changed his appearance quite often. Aguillar, too, had changed his appearance, but the traveler looked past the new van dyke and the longer hair. Aguillar's posture was the same, his habit of standing with the weight on his left leg was still obvious, and the tilt of his chin was the same.

"Francis," he said.

"Oh!" Aguillar said. "You shaved your head. Bald suits you. Are you wearing contacts?"

Zapata nodded. "I have always envied the green eyes of others. And in public, I am Charles Ossipon. Remember that technology has made the dreams of the ancients come true."

Aguillar nodded, though Zapata could see from his face that he did not understand. To Zapata, the comment was quite clear. Ancient shamans and wizards believed that names held power: to know the name of a thing gave one power over the thing itself. Modern technology turned the shaman's fantasy into the police officer's reality. A single name, entered into the right database, laid a man naked before the powers that be.

"Everything you asked for is ready," Aguillar said.

"Good. We have a little time. Let's get something to eat."

But instead of walking, he stopped as he had done in the train station, and looked around. In his mind's eye he saw this spot, then suddenly his vision pulled back from it, expanding to encompass this whole city, and then the state, and then the United States. Every point within the scope of his vision was connected like the stops on a train station map. All interconnected, all interdependent. Choose the right spot, identify the nexus at just the right place, well, then one bomb, even a small bomb, could affect the lives of millions. By this time tomorrow, he would have done just that.

He smiled happily.

1 2 3 **4** 5 6 7 8 9
10 11 12 13 14 15 16 17
18 19 20 21 22 23 24

. . . .
THE FOLLOWING TAKES PLACE
BETWEEN THE HOURS OF
11 P.M. AND 12 A.M.
PACIFIC STANDARD TIME
. . . .

11:00 P.M. PST
Van Nuys, California

The building was large, constructed right on the main thoroughfare of Van Nuys Boulevard in the San Fernando Valley just north of Los Angeles, and because it was so obvious it was completely and utterly anonymous. A person might drive by that building five days a week for ten years and never notice it. Most of the building was owned by Barrington Suites, an executive rental company that specialized in leasing office space to small businesses, who could use a common receptionist, common conference rooms, copy rooms, and the like. According to the data Jamey Farrell and her people had gathered, there were more than thirty small businesses renting executive suites from Barrington in that building.

One of those small businesses was called Mataram Imports, owned by a Riduan Bashir, a naturalized citizen of Indonesian origin.

Tony Almeida reached Bashir's office door a minute after eleven. He didn't see the urgency in this investigation, but Chapelle had insisted. He had the license plates for two cars registered in Bashir's name and one was in the parking lot, so he expected to find the man at work. The door itself was not welcoming—a solid wood door, locked, with a small sign reading MATARAM IMPORTS on the wall beside it, hung over a doorbell. Tony pushed the bell. He heard nothing, but a moment later the door clicked and buzzed.

Almeida pushed the door open. The office inside was humble—a small reception area that opened onto an equally small office strewn with papers. Through the opening, Tony saw a wall map and a large dry erase board with a hand-drawn calendar grid, covered in notations.

Riduan Bashir was getting up from his desk and walking toward Tony, his face open and unsuspecting, his manner unguarded.

"Yes, may I help you?" the man asked. His English was musical, though as he spoke further Tony found his speech gently clipped with the uninspired "K," "T," and "P" of the Malay accent.

"Tony Almeida," he said, handing over a card similar to the one Chris Henderson had used at UCLA. "I just have a few questions for you."

The official seal on the business card put Bashir immediately on edge. Tony noted this, but reached no conclusions. He was the government, and the government always put people on edge.

"You work late, Mr. Bashir. I tried your home and they said you were here."

"I am at the mercy of Indonesian time, sometimes. Am I in some sort of trouble?" Bashir asked. Like most Indonesians, he was dark-skinned, and Tony could not tell if he had blushed or lost color. But he was definitely nervous.

"No, sir," Tony said, falling easily into a spiel meant to put the subject at ease. "This is fairly routine. I'm sure you know that we're always following up on information we get from all kinds of sources. Most of the leads go nowhere, and most of the people we question are just innocent bystanders like you. But we have to be thorough because that's what we're paid for."

The phrase "innocent bystanders like you" acted like a tonic, washing tension from Bashir's body. "Well, of course. Would you like to sit down?" He indicated his office.

"Why not here?" Tony pointed to the small couch and visitor's chair in the reception area. Bashir would feel less secure if he wasn't sitting behind his desk.

They sat, and as soon as Bashir was settled, Tony said easily, "Are you familiar with Jemaah Islamiya?"

Bang. The question was like a cannon shot. It was a hurry-up version of a classic interrogation technique: make the suspect feel like he is not the suspect, then surprise him with a hard question.

This one certainly threw Bashir off-balance. "Jemaah . . . ? Yes, well, of course. From the news."

"Then you know Jemaah Islamiyah is a terrorist group operating in Indonesia, and that they were responsible for that bombing in Bali that killed 202 people and injured hundreds more? They also claimed responsibility for the truck bomb that blew up a Marriott."

Bashir shook his head sadly. "I remember the newspaper. Not just the *Times* here. I get several papers shipped over from Indonesia. It was terrible."

Tony sifted through the papers he had brought with him. He only had one pertinent question, but he wanted Bashir to think he had reams of information. "Do you recall making a trip to Jakarta in May of 2002?"

Bashir leaned forward with his elbows on his knees, clearly anxious, but clearly trying to look helpful. "I travel home once a year, and sometimes twice. I don't remember the dates exactly, but May sounds correct."

"Business or pleasure?"

"Both, of course."

"Sure. While you were there, you met with Khalid Ismahuddin, a member of Jemaah Islamiyah."

Bashir uncrossed and recrossed his legs. "Is that a question?"

"No."

"Well, yes, I met with Ismahuddin. But not because of Jemaah Islamiyah. He runs a shipping business out of Jakarta and I was looking for lower prices for my own merchandise."

"Hmm," Tony said as though dissatisfied, but he was only fishing. Bashir's statement jibed with the information he already had. Ismahuddin was on watch lists at CTU and the CIA, but he wasn't considered a major player. He really did run a legitimate shipping business, and was only on CTU's radar because he donated some of his profit to radical Islamists in the Indonesian archipelago.

Bashir shifted again, literally and figuratively. "Look, Mr. Almeida, I don't know if I'm a suspect in any of this, but I assure you I have nothing to do with those people. I think everyone should consider Islam, even you, but I have no interest in blowing people up. I do not know how to make a bomb and I certainly would not drive an exploding van into a hotel. Ismahuddin offered me competitive prices for my business so I met with him. I would do business with him tomorrow if it gave me a chance to expand." He waved his arm around the tiny office. "As you can see, I can use all the help I can get."

Tony nodded, closed his folder, and stood up. "I understand, Mr. Bashir. We're aware that Ismahuddin's business is legitimate, even if his intentions aren't always good. Like I said, we just have to be thorough."

He offered his hand, which Bashir accepted with relief and genuine warmth.

"I appreciate your efforts to keep people safe," Bashir said, opening the door and ushering him out.

As the door shut behind him, Tony's smile fell away.

11:19 P.M. PST
CTU Headquarters, Los Angeles

"Jamey Farrell."

"Jamey, it's Tony. Can you do a quick search for me?"

"What I'm here for. What do you need?"

"Look at that Marriott bombing in Jakarta from a while back. The local police report and the Indonesian government's published investigation. Also whatever briefs the CIA put out to us and anyone at other intelligence agencies."

Jamey was already at her computer, her fingers bouncing over the keyboard. "Okay, but what am I looking for?"

"If I remember it right, the Indonesians put a plant in that story?"

"Hold on."

Jamey buzzed through several reports in her database before coming back on the line. "Yes," she said finally. "It wasn't much, though, because so much of it was public. But the official report said that the bomb was delivered by a truck that exploded in the parking lot."

"Did the news media pick that up?"

"Hold on." Again, there was a pause. "I'd have to take more time to give you a comprehensive answer, but most of the outlets reported the story as is."

"Truck bomb."

"Right."

"When the vehicle was really a—"

"A van," she finished for him.
"Thank you."

11:26 P.M. PST
Staples Center, Los Angeles

His real name, if he had been willing to admit it to anyone, was Jorge Rafael Marquez, and he was a genius. This wasn't a boast. He had known it from an early age as surely as one knew one's gender. The same way a little boy knows he is different from a little girl, Jorge knew he was different from all the children around him, different even from the adults. In the little school in the Chiapas province of Mexico where he grew up, when the teacher was trying to teach addition to the others, he was already mapping out multiplication tables, and without knowing its name, he used algebra and calculus to help his father map out his soybean farm to produce its maximum yield.

He read, and anything he wished to commit to memory, he remembered forever. When his uncle showed him a guitar, he had memorized the chords in a single day, and though he himself denied that he had mastered the art of music, the science and organization of music he understood with ease.

Because the real gift of Jorge Rafael Marquez was in patterns. He recognized them easily, and could project them forward to their logical ends based on any changes he was presented. He still remembered the day he was handed a Rubik's Cube, battered, some of the cubes chipped. It was a gift from an older cousin who had made the long migration to El Norte and come back after several years. In America, he had said, there were lots of geniuses, and all of them could solve this puzzle.

Rafael, twelve years old, had stared at the cube for a moment without touching it. His cousin laughed, thinking he was intimidated. His father patted him on the back. "Don't worry, Rafael," he had said with a laugh. "If your gift helps me farm, it's enough for me!"

But Rafael hadn't been intimidated. He had been spinning the cube in his mind. In the few seconds of his cousin's laugher he had identified three different methods of solving the puzzle. Finally he picked it up, his hands spinning the cube faster than his cousin's eyes could follow. He put it down, each side a solid color, thirty-seven seconds later.

The next day he had started out for America.

These days he left the name of Marquez far behind, and his associates knew him as Zapata. He had come to the United States on this trip under the name of Ossipon, guessing correctly that no one who heard the name would know or recall the name of the anarchist in one of Joseph Conrad's books.

Zapata and Aguillar walked freely into the Staples Center—the concert, whatever it was, was nearly over. No one would bother entering the event now. Zapata had only a small bag with him. He took a camera out of the bag and handed it to Aguillar. "Put this around your neck."

They walked around the wide promenade that ringed the actual center, passing rows of concession stands, upscale bars, and kiosks that sold food and souvenirs to a few people, all of whom seemed eager to get back into the concert. Zapata ignored them all. At one of the kiosks, Zapata stopped near a large pot that held a small tree. He glanced around to make sure no one was looking, then dug into the plant, placed a small package there, and covered it with soil.

They continued until they came to a set of double doors that read, "No Admittance."

11:33 P.M. PST
Federal Holding Facility, Los Angeles

Ramirez was reading a book picked up from the library. Jack went to his bunk and dug his fingernails into the seam of his mattress. With a tug, the seam parted. He stuffed his hand inside and came out with a shank. Unlike a shiv, which was any weapon made of nonmetal, a shank was a makeshift knife. This one was a razor blade embedded into three plastic knives that had been melted together for added strength and to hold the razor in place. The Federal Holding Facility was a maze of metal detectors, so shanks were impossible to move around. Impossible for other people, but not for Jack.

"What's up?" Ramirez asked, looking up over the edge of his book. "Jesus!" he yelled, as Jack slashed his left palm with the blade. "Stop it!" Ramirez shrieked as Jack made a second cut along the side of his own neck.

"Help!" he shouted. "Goddamn Christ! Help!"

A guard came running. "What the hell's wrong . . . Holy shit!" He saw blood all over Jack's hands and face, his appearance made worse by rubbing his hands over his shirt and face to spread the blood.

"Open her up!" the guard shouted. "Call the infirmary!"

"He cut me!" Jack yelled, making his voice high-pitched and panicked. "He's loose on the block and he ran by and cut me!"

"Who's loose?" the guard said. "Somebody's loose."

"Yes," Jack said. He punched the guard in the face, putting him back on his heels, and before he could react, Jack was behind him, holding the razor to his throat. "Don't struggle or you'll end up looking a lot worse than I do."

Jack turned to Ramirez. "Come on, you're going with me."

Ramirez was stunned. Thirty seconds ago he'd been sitting quietly reading his book. "Me? What?"

"I'm not going to let those gang-bangers kill me, and you said yourself they'd come after you, too."

"But—"

"Come on!" Jack dragged the guard out of the cell and down the hall. By the time he got to the choke point at the edge of the block, the guard behind the Plexiglas could see him.

"Open it!" he said, brandishing the razor blade.

The guard hit an alarm and sirens sounded. But the door remained closed.

Everything depended on fast reactions, sudden movements, drama. It was like using the element of surprise to attack a larger force. Move fast, strike hard, don't let the enemy's training kick in. Jack cut his hostage across the scalp. The wound was all but harmless, but the scalp gushes blood, and it had the desired effect. Gouts of blood dripped over the guard's face, and he screamed. "Do it!"

The guard panicked and slapped another button. The security door buzzed and Jack pulled it open. Now he was inside. Before the second guard could say or do anything, Jack kicked him in the stomach. He doubled over, and Jack kicked him in the head. He went down and didn't get up. Jack scanned the room; there were riot batons but no firearms, not this deep inside the facility. He did, however, have another weapon.

He threw the switches that opened all the cells, and spoke over a loudspeaker. "Free time, everyone. Come out and play."

He heard the first whoops before he saw anyone move. Jail was, he had noticed, an oxymoron. If society was the establishment of procedures and organization, then prison was a much more efficient society than any neighborhood or town. It was, in that sense, the epitome of society. At the same time, it was far closer to the edge of disaster than any other social group. Prison was routine, routine, routine, all just one step away from riot.

Jack was satisfied to note that Ramirez had followed him. Tentative, shocked by what Jack had done, but compliant nonetheless.

"You're fucking crazy!" the cut guard gurgled, his throat compressed by Jack's forearm.

"Yeah, so don't try to reason with me," Jack said. "Look." He turned the guard toward the Plexiglas. They could see down the cell block, where prisoners were now appearing in ones and twos. Some were already jumping up on the railings, or running into the cells of other inmates. One deck below, where the bunkhouse slept twenty to a room, a fight had already broken out.

"They'll be coming this way in a minute. Most won't touch you, but I bet there's one or two that'll take a piece of you before this gets shut down." Jack saw a glint of fear in the guard's eye. "So let's all of us get out of this block before it goes insane."

Jack passed through the guard station into the next corridor. One more station and he would be in the open. There was another door here, but this one required a code. Jack pointed at it.

"I can't do it," the guard insisted.

"You're going to lose your fingers for sixty thousand a year," Jack threatened. "It can't be worth it."

Alarms sounded farther off. The whole jail was awake now.

Jack held up the razor blade. "Open that door and I'm someone else's problem."

That was enough to convince the guard. He punched in the entry code, and the door opened. Jack sealed his arm around the guard's throat, putting him in a carotid choke. The man gasped and flailed, but Jack held on until he went limp. He laid the unconscious guard gently on the ground.

"Come on!" he ordered. Ramirez followed obediently.

Jack knew he'd never get out of the final layers of security without help. He needed to create more diversions. The more chaotic he could make the jail, the harder it would be for the jailers to stop him.

11:41 P.M. PST
Staples Center, Los Angeles

They passed through the doors and descended two flights of stairs. Below the Staples Center was a miniature city, a maze of storerooms, maintenance rooms, and other rooms. Zapata seemed to know exactly where he was going. They arrived a few minutes later at a door with no markings, but with a small black man wearing a windbreaker that said "Security."

"I help you gents?" the man said amiably.

"We're here to talk to see one of the fighters," Zapata said. He held up a notepad and pointed at the camera hanging from Aguillar's neck.

The man nodded and let them through.

"How do you do that?" Aguillar whispered. "How did you know that man would just let you in?"

"People like it when their expectations are met," Zapata replied casually. "This place is out of the way.

That man is bored. He would like to do his job, but he doesn't want to do real work. He wants to check people who come his way, but he does not want trouble. We met his expectations."

The room beyond was a storeroom that had been converted into some kind of athletic training area, with mats on the floor and a boxer's heavy bag hanging from an iron post with a heavy base. On the far side of the room, two fighters were rolling on the ground, but only practicing, while two or three men stood around them giving comments.

Much closer, a man stood by himself, slowly removing cloth wraps from around his hands. He was huge, at least six feet, five inches tall, with shoulders as wide as Zapata and Aguillar standing together. His hair was shaved very close to his head. His ears were swollen and misshapen, and his nose was bent to the left.

"Excuse me," Zapata said boldly, "are you Mark Kendall?"

The man looked at them. "Yeah. Did I have another interview set up?"

Zapata smiled and shook his head. "No, I'm not a reporter. I am a man with a proposition for you."

Kendall stopped unwrapping his hands and looked down at Zapata. "Not sure I like the sound of that. What kind of proposition?"

"One that will probably save your daughter's life."

The big fighter's eyes narrowed. "What the fuck are you talking about?"

Zapata spoke softly. "This is what I'm talking about. I want you to kill someone for me. Tomorrow night. You're going to lose your fight, probably in the second round. When you lose, you'll be washed up. No one is going to give you another chance. Except me. After the fight, you'll have an opportunity to kill someone that I want dead. If you do that, I will pay for your daughter's medical treatments, and she will live a happy and healthy life."

Zapata delivered his proposal so quietly and casually that it took a second for Kendall's brain to process it. And when he did, he looked around for cameras, or practical jokers giggling in a corner somewhere. When he saw nothing else that might explain this bizarre little man's speech, he had no choice but to turn back to him. "What the fuck are you talking about?" he repeated.

"I'm completely serious," Zapata said.

"Well, this—you little shit, who do you think you are!" Mark yelled at him.

"Calmly, sir. You are getting angry," Zapata said. The amiable quality of his voice changed, strengthened, demanding more attention. "You'll get even angrier in a minute. Before you attract too much attention, you need to hear me. This proposal is sincere. I have more than enough money to take care of your daughter, and your wife. You will go to prison, probably for life, but your daughter will be pain-free."

Kendall looked around again. "This is some goddamned practical joke. You think I'd say yes to something like this? I'm not going to lose!"

"Yes, you will, probably in the second round. Which means you won't get the big purse, and you won't have an opportunity to fight for the championship. You probably won't get any more fights at all."

"Get the hell out of here!" Kendall yelled loud enough to attract attention from the fighters across the hall.

Zapata nodded. "I'm leaving. But remember, you don't need to decide now. You don't even need to decide before the fight. If you win, then I'm wrong and nothing matters. If you lose, then you can make your decision. You'll have the chance to kill the man I want dead. Here. Take this." He handed Kendall an envelope. "This will tell you everything you need."

The anarchist wheeled around, dragging the startled Aguillar in his wake. They passed through the double doors with the security man calling behind them. "Short interview?"

"I got what I wanted," Zapata said over his shoulder.

11:49 P.M. PST
Federal Holding Facility, Los Angeles

Alarms blared in every hallway. At each corner, revolving sirens flashed. The jail was in full-scale riot. An inmate ran shrieking past Jack, pursued by three other inmates intent on exacting some kind of revenge.

"We're gonna get killed!" Ramirez said, cowering against the wall of the corridor.

Jack grabbed him by the collar of his orange jump-suit. "Listen. By now they'll have set up a perimeter inside the jail. They'll have called for outside help. We only have a few more minutes to get out before the place is sealed and they hold everyone in."

Bauer had visited the facility often enough to inter-rogate prisoners. They had reached the last ring of security. Beyond this, there was only the courtyard and then freedom.

A group of inmates had reached this hallway be-fore them. A door burst open and two prisoners appeared, dragging a guard, who struggled against them. One of the inmates raised a hand and stabbed downward with some kind of shiv, jabbing the guard in the chest.

Jack lunged forward, planting his shoulder in the inmate's chest and throwing him backward. The other one looked at him, dumbfounded, as Jack hit him with an uppercut that doubled him over. Jack grabbed the prisoner by his stringy hair and slammed his head against the wall.

The guard, bleeding from his chest, looked at him in shock. "Th-thanks . . ."

"It's not deep," Jack said of the wound. "Barricade yourself until the riot team comes." He shoved the man back into the room. "This way."

11:54 P.M. PST
Sepulveda Pass, Los Angeles

Tony was driving on the 405 Freeway over the Sepulveda Pass, which connected the San Fernando Valley to the west side of Los Angeles. There was traffic in Los Angeles, even at this hour, but it wasn't bad—just enough to allow him to follow Bashir without being noticed. He kept his eyes on the taillights of Riduan Bashir's vehicle about three car lengths ahead.

His phone rang. "Jamey, go."

"He's very accommodating," the data analyst told him. "There's no way he's worried about surveillance. He's on his cell phone and we're tracking him. There's nowhere he's going to go now."

"Good." Tony dropped back far enough to avoid being noticed, but close enough to keep good visuals. "I'll let you know if I lose him."

"Probably best to keep your eyes peeled, but we can tell you where he's going," she replied. "He's meeting some guys at a place called Little Java. It's on Atlantic."

11:56 P.M. PST
Staples Center, Los Angeles

Aguillar had trouble finding his voice. "I . . . I can't believe you just did that."

Zapata looked disappointed. "I thought you knew me."

Aguillar nodded, and shook his head, and nodded again, unsure how to respond. He had worked with Zapata several times before. He knew the man's methods . . . or, really, he understood Zapata's absolute lack of methods. But this was beyond belief. "Do you . . . will he . . . is he going to do it?"

"I think so. Of course, he doesn't know he's going to do it. He won't know it until after the fight tomorrow. He probably won't decide until right at that moment. But he'll do it."

"What if he wins?" Aguillar countered.

Zapata looked at him as if he were insane. Hadn't he already said Kendall would lose?

Aguillar sighed. "You could make a fortune betting on sports."

Zapata shrugged. "I have a fortune already."

11:58 P.M. PST
Federal Holding Facility, Los Angeles

Jack burst through the doors and into the outer courtyard of the holding facility. There was a flood of inmates rushing out of other doors from other wings, all with the same idea: safety in numbers. Gunfire crackled from above. The courtyard was surrounded by high walls, and someone had positioned snipers up there. A man next to Jack stumbled and fell.

A chain-link fence at one end of the courtyard was just now swinging shut. Whoever had been smart enough to call out the snipers had been too slow to seal the exits.

"Run!" Jack yelled. Ramirez was next to him, alternately panting and yelping at the gunfire all around him. Inmates roared and shoved, a mass of orange bodies churning toward the gate. No one had gotten out yet, and two guards were bravely trying to roll the high chain-link fence closed. Three or four layers of men stood between Jack and the exit, and they were stalled now, jammed in by the two guards. Another near Jack yelped and went down as something small and hard bounced off him and tapped Jack on the shoulder. Rubber bullets.

Grabbing Ramirez by the collar, Jack shoved his way through the crowd of men. He bladed his body when he could, and kneed, scratched, and clawed when he had to. It helped that some men were now cowering under the rain of rubber bullets from above. Jack reached the fence.

"Get back in there!" one of the two guards yelled. He jabbed his riot stick at Jack.

"Sorry," Jack said. He grabbed the stick, pulling the guard into the half-closed fence and hitting his head on the metal frame. The man went down, and Jack stepped over him quickly. The other guard swung his stick. Jack ducked, then came up and punched the guard in the jaw. At the same moment something jabbed him in the side. He was sure the rubber bullet had cracked a rib.

Cursing, Jack dragged Ramirez through the fence, then kicked an inmate away and shoved it closed so no one else could escape.

"Run!" he yelled.

THE FOLLOWING TAKES PLACE
BETWEEN THE HOURS OF
12 A.M. AND 1 A.M.
PACIFIC STANDARD TIME

12:00 A.M. PST
CTU Headquarters, Los Angeles

Jamey Farrell rushed into Chris Henderson's office, her eyes wide as saucers. "You're not going to believe what Jack Bauer just did."

12:01 A.M. PST
Little Java Café, West Los Angeles

Tony turned the corner on Atlantic and found a parking space a block away from the Little Java. He was in no hurry now. CTU had brought the full power of its surveillance to bear, and Bashir had been tracked through his cell phone, through traffic monitors, and with visuals from Tony himself.

Almeida got out of the car and walked casually past the restaurant and around the back. There was a back door that led out into the alley where the cooks and dishwashers took the trash out to the Dumpsters. Tony walked through that door into the dishwashing room, where two Hispanic men in white aprons and rubber gloves loaded gray trays of dirty dishes into the automatic dishwasher. He ignored their inquisitive looks and walked past them to the small kitchen where two men were cutting and prepping over a hot grill. They didn't even look up.

Tony reached a swinging door with a round window in it. Looking through the window he could see most of the small restaurant, and he spotted Riduan Bashir almost immediately. The man was sitting at a corner table with two other men, both most likely Indonesian as well. Neither of the two men looked familiar, but Tony hadn't done much work on Jemaah Islamiyah, so he wasn't likely to recognize even its top members except by name.

He studied their body language for a few minutes. Although Bashir was doing most of the talking, it was clear that he was reporting, not dictating, and his slumped shoulders and open, expressive hands suggested that he considered himself the other man's inferior. The third man seemed to speak only infrequently, and then in suggestive, supportive ways to the man in the middle.

Tony knew that whatever Bashir was, he wasn't a key player. With the exception of his annual trips to Indonesia, he led a sedentary life, and he spent most of his time at home, where he made no suspicious phone calls. But this other man intrigued Tony. He wanted to know more.

A busboy in a white coat and a hairnet barged through the swinging door, which Tony had to dodge. "Hey," Tony said, flashing his badge. "I need a coat like that. And a hairnet."

The busboy, wanting no trouble from anyone with a badge, helped him into a white coat from the storeroom. Tony slipped the hairnet over his head and used it to pull his hair back from his forehead. There was a mirror in the employee bathroom. He looked into it and hunched his shoulders. To him, he looked like himself in a hairnet. But to a man who'd just met him and spent only a few minutes while viewing him as a figure of authority, the hunched-over busboy with the hairnet might not be familiar.

Tony walked out into the restaurant and took a tour. It was a small place, no more than ten or twelve tables, but they were all occupied. Out of the corner of his eye, Tony watched Bashir's table. The man in the middle took a sip of tea from a small cup. They were speaking in some Malay dialect.

"Excuse me." Tony realized a man at a small booth was talking to him. "I dropped my fork. Get me another."

Tony bristled at the rude tone, but held his tongue. He simply nodded, and looked around. There was a bussing at the back. Taking the dirty fork, Tony walked back and saw a drawer full of clean silverware. He also saw a stack of porcelain teacups. Tony first reached into his pants pocket and retrieved a small digital recorder he carried whenever possible, and turned it on. Then he wiped the dirty fork off on his coat but picked up a clean one, then returned to the booth and laid the same fork on the table. The man there ignored him. Tony turned just as the man with Bashir took another sip of his tea, finishing it, and laying it down. Exhaling slowly, Tony walked up, set down the new teacup, and picked up the old one. He lifted the teapot off the table and filled the new cup.

"Thank you," the man next to Bashir said without looking at him.

Tony said nothing. He walked back to the kitchen, holding the teacup delicately so as not to disturb the fingerprints he would find there.

12:19 A.M. PST
CTU Headquarters, Los Angeles

There was an emergency meeting at CTU Los Angeles. It was a moment for sobriety, but Nina Myers began by saying with a shrug, "Jack Bauer escapes from prison. Does this surprise anyone?"

Chris Henderson was livid. "This is no time to be glib, Nina. Do you have any idea how bad CTU is going to look after this?"

"You sound like Chappelle," she observed.

"How is he, by the way?" asked George Mason. There was a hint of electricity in the air when he spoke to Henderson. They were on decent terms, but both men had been considered viable candidates for the position of Director of Field Operations. The fact that Henderson currently held that post created a rivalry between them, though Mason would never admit it. While the command structure at CTU was always clear, promotions and assignments were sometimes fluid as cases sometimes took personnel out of the office for extended periods. And there had been rumors, none stated publicly, having to do with Henderson and the transfer of funds.

"Comatose," Henderson replied. "I haven't heard more."

Peter Jiminez shifted impatiently. "I'm sorry to speak up, but if Jack went to the trouble of escaping, he had a good reason."

"Yeah," someone smirked, "he didn't want to go to prison for the rest of his life."

"Or he's trying to prove his innocence," Jiminez replied.

"Hell of a way to do it." Henderson, standing, frowned down at Jiminez. "We need to put aside the hero worship for a minute. This could cost Jack, and cost us, and cost CTU a lot if we don't help solve this thing. I want to put our resources into helping to find him. Some of us know Jack pretty well."

"I'll say," Nina agreed.

"I want each of you to put together any notes on

any cases you've done with Bauer. Contacts he has, informants he's used, safe houses. Everything. Give it all to Peter."

"I'll take it," Nina offered.

Henderson overruled her statement. "I want Peter. I want someone who hasn't worked with Jack as long to go over the list. Fresh eyes."

"Give it to me, Chris," Mason offered. "I know Jack —"

"It's Jiminez," Henderson said in an I'm-the-director tone of voice. "Start putting your lists together now."

12:22 A.M. PST
Los Angeles

Jack and Ramirez were in the back room of a thrift shop. Jack had kicked in its back door, and by some miracle, as he pointed out to Ramirez, the alarm hadn't gone off. Jack had dumped their orange jumpsuits and found pants, shirt, and shoes that fit well enough.

Sirens went by, but didn't slow down. They seemed to have lost the police, who were more occupied with containing the several hundred inmates still trying to get out of the jail.

While Ramirez continued to look for clothes, Jack crept up to the phone at the front of the store and dialed.

The telephone in the middle of the conference table rang. Henderson leaned in and slapped the call button irritably. "No calls, I said."

"I'm sorry," said one of the receptionists who fielded general calls. "But it's—sir, it's Jack Bauer."

The entire CTU team looked at one another. Only Nina Myers, who knew Jack well, seemed unsurprised.

Henderson blanched. "Okay."

The line clicked in. "Uh, Jack?"

"Chris." Jack's voice came on the line "I need to speak with Chappelle."

"He's not available," Henderson said. "And you need to turn yourself in."

"Chappelle first. How is he?"

"Not well. Jack, it's George," Mason called out to the speaker. "Where are y—?"

Jack interrupted. "Listen, everyone. I need Chappelle. This whole thing's been a setup and—"

The line went dead.

Jack hung up the phone quickly as Ramirez approached him dressed in baggy jeans and a Kobe Bryant basketball jersey. "Best I could do. Who was that?"

"I tried to call some contacts I have, but I couldn't get through," Jack lied. "I didn't want to hang on too long in case it was traced." He had not wanted Ramirez overhearing what he was saying to CTU. He needed Ramirez's cooperation, now more than ever, and the last thing he wanted was for the other man to get nervous about who was on the other end of the line.

"So this job you did before you went in," Ramirez asked. "You worked for the government?"

"Yes. I was an investigator. I shot someone."

"Did he deserve it?"

Jack shrugged. "Most people do, for something or other."

They sat together in silence, each of them taking a moment to release the stress of the last hour. Silence was not uncomfortable for either of them. They had shared a cell for the past three weeks, and in such close quarters silence and privacy were precious.

Jack considered his next move. He could go to CTU, but the chances of anyone there helping him were slim. In their eyes he was guilty, and anyone who assisted him would be aiding and abetting a suspected felon.

Ramirez broke the silence. "Why'd you decide to break out? Your case that bad?"

"It wasn't good," Jack admitted. "I had nothing to lose anyway. No way was I getting my job back after the accusations anyway, so there was no reason to ride it out. And not with those gang-bangers after me."

"You still haven't said what that's about."

"I still don't know. I've got one more call to make."

Teri answered on the third ring.

"It's me," he said quickly. He would have liked more privacy, but to send Ramirez away would have aroused his suspicion. "Have you checked the news?"

"Ja— the news? No."

"You're going to hear a few things," he warned her. "Just bear with it. I'm okay, and everything's going to be okay. I need you to do something for me."

Her concern was palpable over the phone line. "Tell me."

"The bicycles hanging from the racks in the garage. On mine there's a small bag, it looks like a saddlebag. I need you to get that and drop it somewhere for me. You remember that place we went to, where we had the big argument?"

She laughed, but he could hear tears in her laughter. "You have to be more specific."

"The one where I tried to make the big exit and smashed into the waiter with the water glasses."

More tearful laughter. "Yes."

"Drop the bag off there, anywhere hidden. I'll find it. Just have it there by two A.M." He hung up without saying goodbye.

"Here's the story," Jack said to Ramirez. "I have contacts all over this city, but all of them are burned. Anywhere I go, my people will be looking. So we need to go to your people."

Ramirez balked. "I don't have anyone we can go to."

"Everyone's got people. Someone. You had business associates you worked with. The deal you were involved in, the embezzlement thing. Who was on the other side of that?"

Ramirez tugged at his new Lakers jersey. "There was . . . I mean I killed the guy."

Jack shook his head. "On the other side."

Ramirez wriggled now like an insect stuck on the end of a pin. "We couldn't do that. I couldn't do that with you."

Jack shrugged. "Think about it, because right now I'm all you've got. Without me you'll be picked up in ten minutes and put right back in there." He softened his tone. "In the meantime, I'm going to lay low for a while and let the search pass us by. Then I'm going to hot-wire a car and go pick up something useful. You're welcome to come."

12:36 A.M. PST
Federal Holding Facility, Los Angeles

Dan Pascal ambled up to the gates of the Federal Holding Facility, his six-foot, four-inch frame just big enough to hold his girth, even if his belt wasn't. Pascal was a U.S. Marshal, and with his size and his square, flat-faced head, he was born to it. The courtyard beyond the fence was quieter now, but by all accounts there'd been all hell of trouble here not long ago.

Pascal turned to Lafayette, the senior officer on duty during the breakout. "Only the two got out?"

Lafayette gave two, slow, deliberate nods. "Bauer and Ramirez. Had a hell of a time keeping the others in but—" He clucked loudly with his tongue.

"But what?" Pascal asked.

"You can watch it on the video. Pretty clear that Bauer got out, then turned around and shut the gate."

Pascal grunted. "That was stupid. More inmates that got out, more trouble it would make for us. Pure chaos."

"That's what I'm saying. He had to push some of those boys back to close it. I don't think he wanted them out."

Pascal turned to one of his own people, Emerson. "That guy here yet?"

Deputy Marshal Emerson put a radio to his ear. His lips moved, then he listed. "Two minutes, Marshal." They all called him "Marshal," even though he was a deputy marshal. But he looked so much like Marshal Dillon from *Gunsmoke*, and he fit the profile of an old-style marshal so much, that no one could resist.

Pascal nodded. Right around midnight he'd gotten two calls right in a row. The first had been from his own commander, the actual marshal of this judicial district, informing him that there'd been a prison break at the Federal Holding Facility and that he should take charge of the manhunt for two escapees. The second call, so fast it had actually beeped into the first, was from someone at someplace called the

Counter Terrorist Unit, telling him that they were sending someone to talk with him. How they learned that he'd been assigned to the manhunt even before he did, he meant to ask them.

Pascal looked at Lafayette. "You from Louisiana?"

Lafayette nodded. "N'awlins. Born and raised."

"Accent's still with you a little bit. You ever do any manhunts down there?"

"Couple."

"Me, too. At least there are no bayous here."

Lafayette spit through his two front teeth. "But there's a world of people here. Bayous might be easier."

Pascal looked out at the buildings, lit dimly by their lights, stretching for miles in every direction. He decided Lafayette might have a point.

A man approached them. His suit fit well and his thin hair sat nicely on his head. "Deputy Marshal Pascal? George Mason."

"Yes, sir," Pascal said, looking down politely. Mason looked a little too neat for him, but he had a good handshake, which said a lot, and Mason also looked him right in the eye, assessing him. Pascal liked that. "You have some information on the fugitives?"

"One of them." Mason eyed the others and suggested they step apart for a moment. Pascal complied. When they had put some space between themselves and the others, Mason said, "One of the men who escaped is one of our people. A field operative for CTU."

"I'm afraid I don't know what CTU is."

Mason explained briefly about the Counter Terrorist Unit's mandate and Jack Bauer's background, and phrases such as "Delta Force," "covert operations," "counterintelligence work," "subterfuge," and "survival tactics" rolled off his tongue. With each new phrase, Pascal's broad shoulders settled a little deeper into a determined, unhappy slump. Mason painted as clear a picture as he could of Jack Bauer's capabilities without divulging any classified information.

When he finally finished, Pascal heaved a huge sigh. "Well," he drawled at last, "I figure he was got once, we'll get him again. Come on, Emerson," he added with a wry look on his face, "we got to go catch Captain America."

12:47 A.M. PST
CTU Headquarters, Los Angeles

Tony walked back into CTU carrying the glass delicately in his hand. He dropped it off with the forensics team, already bleary-eyed from some other task that took them past midnight. "This is a priority," he said. "I need to know whose prints these are. Now."

He walked into the heart of CTU, the computer stations where analysts worked, often around the clock, digging up information and analyzing data for the field agents to act on. Jamey Farrell was at her own station with her eyes, apparently beyond the need to blink, fixed on her screen. "Jamey, I need information on a group."

Jamey didn't look up from her screen. "Seth Ludonowski. New guy, very good. Not going to last long. Take advantage of him now."

Tony went down to the other end of the row of stations to a young man with short, bleached blond hair and pale skin. He might have been an albino but for his blue eyes and freckles.

"Seth?" Tony asked.

"Agent Almeida," he said. "We haven't met, but I picked your name up. What can I do for you?"

"Jemaah Islamiyah. I need everything you can tell me about them. I'll be at my desk."

Tony walked over to his own desk, and by the time he got there, Seth was already feeding him information. Tony began to scan it closely. Jemaah Islamiyah was an Islamic fundamentalist group operating out of Indonesia, with the same mission that most such groups pursued: to establish a fundamentalist Islamic theocracy, in this case in Indonesia, Singapore, and other Southeast Asian states. Jemaah Islamiyah (Seth had already translated it simply as "Islamic group") had bombed hotels in Bali and the Australian embassy in Jakarta. The degree to which JI lusted after American blood was uncertain, since they limited their activities to the Asian Southeast, but they had targeted tourist sites that catered to Westerners, both Australians and Americans. California's decision to host a Southeast Asian trade conference gave JI a logical new target, combined with the fact that an émigré from Indonesia had met with a JI supporter, created a trail that demanded exploration. Riduan Bashir didn't strike Tony as much of a terrorist threat, but the fact that he'd identified the vehicle as a van when the published report—and Tony's own comment—declared it was a truck, suggested that he had slightly more intimate knowledge than the average person.

Tony wasn't sold yet—the comment could have been an innocent slip, and his late night meeting with the other Indonesian men could be nothing more than it seemed. The fingerprints would—

His phone buzzed and he saw Seth's extension. "We've got a match."

"Already?"

"Hey, we're professionals. I'm sending it over now."

Tony leaned forward in his chair as the information flowed top to bottom down his computer screen.

"Goddamn," Tony murmured to himself.

Riduan Bashir had just had an evening meal with Encep Sungkar, third in command of Jemaah Islamiyah.

1 2 3 4 5 **6** 7 8 9
10 11 12 13 14 15 16 17
18 19 20 21 22 23 24

. . . .

THE FOLLOWING TAKES PLACE
BETWEEN THE HOURS OF
1 A.M. AND 2 A.M.
PACIFIC STANDARD TIME

. . . .

1:00 A.M. PST
CTU Headquarters, Los Angeles

Tony touched the call back button on his phone. "Seth, I've got more work for you."

"Hey, I'm just getting started."

Tony smiled, and at the same time understood what Jamey had meant about this one not staying around long. The data analsts at CTU were a unique breed: brilliant, inexhaustible, and quirky. Seth had a little too much liveliness in him to fit the job entirely. He'd love it for a while, and then burn out and look for a job that allowed him to see the sunlight directly, rather than through videotape downloaded from a traffic camera. Still, he'd be a godsend while he was around. "I want you to track down credit card receipts coming out of a restaurant called Little Java." He recited the address. "Start digging for anything that looks out of the ordinary. I'm after an alias for Encep Sungkar, an Indonesian terrorist I think got into the country somehow. I'm guessing he's got a full alias, and I need to know it."

"Coming right up!"

1:02 A.M. PST
Los Angeles

There are two ways to evade a search: stay ahead of its expanding perimeter, or lay low and let it pass you by. Jack had chosen the latter, and so far it had worked. He slipped out the back door of the thrift shop with Ramirez trailing him. The sirens had died out, though the police were surely out in force looking for them. He had to get out of here, not only to retrieve the package Teri would leave him, but to put distance between himself and his previous location. The more random his movements, the more chaotic they seemed, the harder he would be to track down. The police would look for patterns, follow leads, try to establish a path that Jack was following. He knew, because that's what he would do if he were on the hunt. He had to avoid the trap of falling into just such a pattern.

The alley was dark and lined with large metal

Dumpsters that stank of food from nearby restaurants. The alley itself smelled of urine. Jack kept to the sides, ready to melt into the deeper shadows at the first sign of approaching headlights. During the day, he would have walked in the open, trying to appear as natural as possible. But at one o'clock in the morning, anyone walking down an alley would attract attention, so it was better not to be seen at all. Five buildings down, the alley intersected a side street, a residential strip with cars parked at the curb. He turned right and walked quickly down the sidewalk, checking the windshields of the cars.

"What are we doing?" Ramirez asked, swiveling his head like an owl as he looked nervously about him.

"Looking for a car with a permit."

"Why?"

Jack spotted one, a dark blue Nissan Maxima with a white and gray tag hanging from the rearview mirror. The permit suggested a resident, and a resident was most likely someone who wouldn't come out to look for his car until seven or eight o'clock. By that time, Jack would have ditched this car for another.

Next, he searched the ground and found a head-sized rock on someone's front lawn with the word "Serenity" carved into it. The rock was nestled into a cluster of morning glories now closed up for the night. Jack plucked the rock out of the garden and, without hesitation, heaved it through the back seat window. Immediately the car's alarm blared, the tone and rhythm of the alarm changing every three or four seconds.

Ramirez panicked. "What the fuck! Someone's going to hear!"

Jack's expression showed his annoyance. "When was the last time you heard a car alarm at night and came running outside?"

Ramirez realized that Jack was right, of course. He reached inside the car, careful not to cut himself on broken glass, and opened the back door. A moment later he had the driver's door open. Lying down across the seat, Jack reached underneath the dash and, in a few seconds, stopped the alarm and hot-wired the ignition.

"Get in."

Ramirez got in and Jack drove off. A block away, they passed a black-and-white police car cruising in the opposite direction.

1:14 A.M. PST
UCLA Medical Center

Megan Wallen spun around on her swiveling stool in the med lab at UCLA's Medical Center. As she completed a full circle her knees came around and bumped the counter where the tests were being run.

I bet if I tuck my knees in I can make it a seven-twenty, she told herself. She pushed off again and spun around, sliding past the counter once and almost coming around again before losing her balance and slipping off the stool and landing heavily on her hip.

"Ouch. Damn!' she said, picking herself up. "Stupid. Kill myself while killing time."

Nights at the lab got long, even when there were a lot of tests to run. She got through most nights trading e-mails and IMs with Tim and Martina or doing med school homework, but Martina was out of town and Tim was working, and her eyes were bleary enough from tests. She didn't feel like reading.

The lab phone rang, making her jump. It had been a quiet night, except for one test brought down from the ER, and in the silence the phone sounded demanding.

"Lab, this is Megan," she said.

"Megan Wallen, right? This is the security desk up in the lobby. Listen, there's someone here who says they need to see you. Wants you to come up."

"Me? Who?"

"They, uh, they say it's a surprise." The caller's voice dropped. "Look, I don't want to ruin things, but I got a clown here with way too many balloons. Can you just—"

A surprise? Balloons? She wondered if it was a prank of Tim's. "I'm coming."

Still rubbing her hip, she opened the door and walked down the hall. Behind her, the door closed slowly, pushing gently toward the frame by the spring in its hinge. But before it closed completely, someone walked out of the stairwell and calmly stopped the door. The figure slipped into the lab and walked up to the same counter that Megan had just vacated. On the counter stood a vial of blood that read "CHAPPELLE, RY." The intruder reached into his breast pocket and pulled out an identical vial, also filled with blood. Carefully, carefully, he peeled the recently applied label off the original vial and put it on his new one. Then he dropped the new one into the rack, took the original, and left.

Megan returned a few minutes later, carrying a bunch of metallic "I'm Sorry" balloons and a mystified look on her face. She wondered what Tim had to apologize for. She figured she'd find out soon enough. In the meantime, she had blood work to run.

1:23 A.M. PST
CTU Headquarters, Los Angeles

Tony had just finished reviewing data on three names that were likely aliases for Encep Sungkar. The new guy Seth had done good work, including providing rationale for eliminating four other names. He was relieved—the odds could have been much worse. He was so engrossed in his review that he didn't notice Jamey standing over him until she cleared her throat.

"Oh, hey, what's up?" he said, rubbing his eyes. It was getting late.

"What's up is Jack Bauer," she said. "Did you know he called here?"

Tony stared at her blankly.

"Oh, crap, let me start again," Jamey said. "Did you know Jack Bauer broke out of jail and then called here?"

Tony sighed through clenched teeth. "Oh, shit. Did anyone get hurt?"

Jamey shrugged. "The news isn't all in, but there was a riot at the jail, so I'm sure some of it was ugly. Word is that Jack cut a guard across the forehead. The other word is that he stopped some inmates from escaping after he went over the wall."

Tony stood up, the sleep suddenly gone from his eyes. "Unbelievable, unbelievable," he muttered. "Are we on it?"

Jamey sat on the edge of his desk and put her hands in the air in a universal sign of perplexity. "Search me. Chappelle's out of commission and Henderson seems to be in watch-and-wait mode. He sent George Mason over to liaison with the marshals. But—" she stopped, scrunching up her face in an unhappy look but saying nothing.

"But what? Come on, I don't have time—"

"Tony, we should have been on this one. I mean, it's Jack Bauer. The guy friggin' never even read the rule book. But kill a guy for no reason? Come on. And we never even looked into it. Shouldn't we do some homework?"

Tony rubbed his temples vigorously enough to wear holes in them. Jamey was right. It had been weeks since Jack had shot that Tintfass character, and with the exception of some cursory cooperation with the Federal prosecutor, CTU had had almost no involvement. That was Chappelle, of course. The man was a bona fide tool and hated Bauer. He probably relished the thought of Bauer behind bars. But that wouldn't have stopped Bauer from digging deep into the story, and it shouldn't have stopped them.

"Okay," he said. "But I've got a problem. I'm on a lead that might be important. Jemaah Islamiyah is in our neck of the woods."

Jamey was quick. "That Southeast Asia thing is tomorrow," she said.

"It's tomorrow. I'm sure they're going to hit the meeting, but I don't know how and I'm only just learning who. I need to stay on it. You should dig into it, though."

"Any suggestions on where to start?"

"At the beginning," Tony said.

1:29 A.M. PST
The Metro, Los Angeles

It was a hot afternoon in Los Angeles. Jorge ran down the alley, over the fence into the Gonzalezes' yard, zigzagged around the piles of rusted car parts and stolen bicycles, then through the chain-link gate and down the street to the Olivera house. He ran through the door and up to his room as Juan Olivera leaped from the couch and followed him.

"Jorge!" He heard Juan's overweight steps on the creaking stair. Fourteen steps to the top. Seven steps to Jorge's door (including the three little shuffling steps to square himself up). Approximately four pounds per square inch of pressure applied rapidly and repeatedly with fist.

"Jorge!" The door opened and he watched Juan, his belly rolling out over the top of his belt, barely

contained by the white wife-beater shirt. "What are you doing!"

"Sitting on my bed," he said, which was true.

"In that gang!" Juan thundered. "I don't want you in that gang! I don't care if you are Sofia's cousin. I don't care if you're her brother! No gang members in my house!"

Jorge's eyes flashed. He hated Juan's pathetic, imperious tone, the regal pontification of a petty emperor. He despised all authority as dictatorship. He resisted the urge to snatch up a pen from his little bleach-wood desk and poke it into Juan's stomach. But he was only fifteen and in no mood to pay for his own room and board. Besides, he was reacting to the concept because of the presentation. He could not abide a dictator. But to argue would not address the point. "Okay."

Juan raised his finger to scold, then stopped. He grunted and hitched up his pants. "Okay?"

"Okay."

It was hardly a concession. Jorge had just run home from quitting the gang—run, because one did not quit those gangs and survive. Either the gang killed you, or rival gangs learned you were weak and killed you. Jorge, though, did not think his compadres would try to put him down. He'd already shown them how to take their pathetic, bloodthirsty little crew and transform it into a viable and growing criminal empire. They would leave him alone.

But as much as he could foresee their growth, he could also foresee their limitations. The gang was

*another Rubik's Cube: nearly infinite combinations,
one result clearly to be seen, and no way out except
to put it down.*

*Jorge already knew which puzzle he wanted to
pick up next. He had been reading a great deal about
the growing popularity of connected personal computers. The next morning, he would wake up early,
throw his few possessions into a blue Adidas bag,
and run away again.*

Zapata leaned back into the faux leather seat of the
Metro, heading away from the Staples Center. They
could have walked to the hotel from the Staples Center, of course, but he was as intrigued by the Metro as
he had been by Amtrak. He was mildly disappointed
that he couldn't bomb it, but after his Amtrak prank,
another minor disaster would attract too much un-
wanted attention.

Besides, the hour was late, and a bombing now
would affect so few people.

To take his mind off the various ways he could disrupt the workings of the Metro, Zapata was about to
speak to Aguillar, who was nodding sleepily across
the way, but a one-sided conversation at the far side
of the car caught his attention.

A man sat there, a man in his forties with a cherub
face and short, straight brown hair with a perfectly
straight part. He was round and harmless-looking,
and he was chatting with a young lady of about sev-
enteen whom, Zapata deduced, was traveling home
from her job working at one of the concession stands

at Staples. He further deduced, with equal certainty, that the middle-aged cherub had also come from Staples.

". . . I thought it wasn't their best concert," he was saying confidentially, as though whoever they were, they might be listening. "Did you see the one last year?"

The young lady, dark-haired and dark-eyed and uncomfortable, shrugged. "I didn't work there then."

"Oh, take my word for it, you would have liked it better," he said with a wink. "More people, too. Can you believe we're about the only two people on this train. A couple of night travelers, us."

The young lady smiled politely. The cherub seemed to perceive her discomfort and sympathize. He didn't change his seat, but he shifted away in his own, giving the impression of more space between them. "Sorry if I'm so chatty, I just end up riding the train a lot at night, and it's usually all lonely."

She nodded. "Yeah, I guess so."

Zapata tapped Aguillar with the toe of his shoe. "Are you listening?" he said.

Aguillar's eyes had been drooping, but they popped open. "Hmm? To them? Sort of. Why?"

Zapata leaned close. "Watch. In a moment he will make a suggestion that they walk together. He intends to rape her."

Aguillar pivoted his shoulders as though to stretch his back, and in doing so was able to look at the cherub. When he turned back, he looked skeptical. "Him? I doubt it."

Zapata spoke, as he often did, in the voice of mentor, though he kept it low and quiet, as though he and Aguillar were hidden behind some blind in the forest, observing wildlife. "The technique is classic. He has already established a connection, created an 'us' where it did not exist. He is imposing himself on her."

Aguillar continued to disagree. "He's sitting back, away from her."

Zapata shook his head reproachfully, playing the disappointed tutor. "Would you sit next to a woman at this hour and speak to her?"

Aguillar considered. "I guess not. It would make her uncomfortable."

Zapata nodded. "A harmless man not only does not make her uncomfortable, he goes out of his way not to. That was her warning sign."

Aguillar had long ago accepted his role as the student and had never ceased to be amazed by his instructor's insights. "So why didn't she—"

"She is not allowed," Zapata interrupted. "I mean, society doesn't allow it. It's rude. So instead of doing the smart thing and getting away from a man who is imposing on her, she sits there to avoid being rude. This is why the society must be destroyed."

Aguillar inclined his head skeptically toward the cherub and his prey. "This?"

"An analogy. A microcosm," Zapata said, intercepting his doubt. "The machine is broken and needs to be dismantled."

The Metro train squealed and then slowed to a

stop. "Come on," Zapata whispered. "We'll get off here."

"Our stop is next."

"Here," Zapata said again.

The two men stood as the train doors slid open and walked out. Zapata indicated that they should hang back for a minute as the young lady and the cherub exited the doors nearer to them. The cherub smiled and said good night, then laughed as he discovered, to his mild embarrassment, that he was walking up the same set of stairs.

"You still have your stun gun?" Zapata asked.

"Of course."

The stunner was small, a black device about the size of an electric razor. It looked like a laser weapon from a science fiction movie. When Zapata pressed the trigger, an electric current crackled between the two prongs at its end. Zapata held him back for a moment, then nodded, and the two men walked up the same set of stairs the other two had taken. The stairs went up a flight to a landing, then turned and continued to the street above. The cherub had stopped the girl on the landing, and though he had not touched her yet, he was now clearly standing between her and her exit.

". . . had a connection," he was saying, "and I could tell you felt it, too."

The girl folded her arms across her chest. "I really have to get home."

"I can just walk you. I bet it's on my way." The man smiled.

"I'm sure it's not." Zapata spoke firmly. He was not a large man, nor very muscular, but he had force of will, and the shaved head helped him to look tough.

The man turned, his pudgy face caught halfway between expressions of predation and fear. "'Scuse me?"

"No." Zapata shot him with the stun gun.

The cherub squealed and his knees gave out. Zapata looked at the young woman, who seemed suddenly far more afraid of Zapata than of the brown-haired man. "You're afraid of the wrong thing," he said. "Get out of here. Next time, listen to that voice telling you something is wrong."

The young lady nodded wordlessly, inched her way past Zapata and Aguillar, then hurried up the stairs.

The cherub climbed back to his knees. "What the fu—?"

Zapata shocked him again. "Oh, I'm sorry. Did I interrupt?" To Aguillar, he ordered, "Grab his arms. Cover his mouth." When Aguillar had secured the man, Zapata pressed the stun gun to the inside of the man's thigh and pressed the trigger, holding it there. The cherub screamed, the sound partially muffled by Aguillar. They held him down as he bucked under the shocks. Zapata shocked him three more times on the genitals, the neck, and the stomach. The chubby man whimpered.

"That's for the ones you've already hurt," Zapata said. "If you hurt more, I'll find you." He stood and walked up the stairs without looking back.

Francis Aguillar released the man, who remained

curled on the landing in a fetal position. Aguillar looked from the cherub to Zapata as his employer walked away, confident that he had done right. Aguillar could not be so confident.

He rested his foot gently on the man's hand. "Were you going to rape her?"

The man sobbed. "No."

Aguillar pressed his foot down.

"Yes, okay, yes!" the cherub squealed. "Yes!"

Aguillar caught up to Zapata where the stairs fed out onto Flower Avenue. He was almost positive that his employer had already put the sexual predator out of his mind. He had been like this for all the time Aguillar had worked for him. He observed people and claimed to know them almost instantaneously. Zapata paid as well as any other criminal activity that he might have chosen, but it wasn't the money that influenced Aguillar. Aguillar had simply never met anyone as smart as that man before. Not graced with great intellect himself, Francis still possessed enough in himself to appreciate it in others. He knew almost nothing about Zapata except that he was brilliant, an anarchist, and incredibly wealthy. Aguillar believed he'd made his money in another life, working in computers. Now he devoted his life to anarchy.

Aguillar caught up with him. They walked together in silence until Francis said, "You're always right."

Zapata nodded and said objectively, "Yes, I'm always right."

1 2 3 4 5 6 **7** 8 9
10 11 12 13 14 15 16 17
18 19 20 21 22 23 24

· ·

**THE FOLLOWING TAKES PLACE
BETWEEN THE HOURS OF
2 A.M. AND 3 A.M.
PACIFIC STANDARD TIME**

· ·

2:00 A.M. PST
UCLA Medical Center

Chris Henderson followed Dr. Czikowlis into Ryan
Chappelle's hospital room.

"I don't understand how you can't know anything,"
he was saying.

"Me neither," the doctor replied frankly. "He's sta-
bilized, but he's still in a coma. At first I suspected
some kind of barbiturate overdose or poisoning."

"Poisoning?" Henderson said, surprised. "Chappelle doesn't do drugs. But poisoning? Did you test
for it?"

She nodded, picking up his chart and reading it for

the fourth time. "His blood work came back negative. Nothing in his system."

Henderson stared at Chappelle, inert on the hospital bed, air tubes running up into his nostrils. Cruel
as it seemed to think it, Henderson had to admit that
Chappelle looked better in a coma than he did in real
life. There was an aura of peace around him that was
the opposite of his effect on people when conscious.

"Please keep at it," he said firmly. "In the meantime, I don't want to alarm you too much, but there
is a fugitive on the loose. I'm going to station a uniformed security guard on this door."

"A fugi— security guard? Here? Are you saying
this fugitive might come get my patient?"

Henderson held up a hand to calm her. "It's not
very likely. But the fugitive made a call and asked
about Chappelle. I can't imagine he'd get anything
out of coming here, but better safe than sorry. The
armed guard starts immediately."

2:07 A.M. PST
West Los Angeles

Jack and Teri had once argued at La Strada, a nice
Italian place on the north side of San Vicente Boulevard in West Los Angeles. The argument had been
over nothing, or everything, depending on how you
looked at it: Jack's work schedule, Teri's feeling that
she was competing against the needs of a country at
risk. He couldn't remember how it had started—it

might have just been the continuation of a previous argument that had never been settled—but he did remember her saying, "Whatever you're doing at work, it can't be more important than our marriage."

And he remembered himself saying, "Yes, it is."

That hadn't gone over well.

Now, just after two A.M. this Saturday morning, he was returning to the scene of that crime. San Vicente was deserted, and La Strada, which took up half the street level of an office high-rise, was pitch black. Even the neon sign in cursive writing had been turned off. The entrance to the restaurant was an apse carved out of the corner of the high-rise, with several large potted trees and a stone bench with carved lions for legs.

Jack parked the Maxima a half block away, on a side street perpendicular to San Vicente with a clear view of the corner. He waited there for a while, holding up a hand to keep Ramirez quiet. He wasn't looking for anything in particular—there were too many places to hide—but he wanted a general sense of the area. A car drove by once, at fairly high speed, but there was no other activity. Jack got out of the car and motioned Ramirez to follow. He walked up to the corner, again keeping close to the walls and away from the streetlights. Trees lined the parkway between the sidewalk and the curb, so it was easy to stay relatively hidden until he reached the corner. He stopped short under the shadow of a blossoming pear tree. La Strada was right across the street.

"What are we waiting for?" Ramirez whispered.

Jack ignored him and studied the restaurant's facade, wondering where Teri had hidden his package. He needed to move quickly to get the package, without fumbling around the storefront, so he wanted to guess correctly. She had three obvious choices for the stash: each of two potted trees, and the space under the stone bench, between the two lions. One tree stood thick with glossy leaves, though he didn't recognize the tree itself. The other, though the same species, was frail, with fewer leaves and several branches no more than sticks. The lions stood there impassively, their jaws opened to roar.

Jack thought he knew where to look.

He walked quickly across the street, feeling immediately naked and exposed on the bare asphalt with streetlights and traffic lights laying bare his every move. He half expected to hear screeching tires or gunshots, but all he heard was the faint echo of his sneakered feet on the ground. He reached the far side and hurried into the apse, straight for the withered tree.

It was there, nearly invisible in the dark: a navy blue zipped pouch. Jack opened it and pulled out a thick wad of bubble wrap, then tore at the bubble wrap until its contents were visible: a spare SigSauer, three full high-capacity magazines, and a box of ammunition, along with new identification for Jack. The minute he slammed a magazine into place and racked the slide, he felt better.

His stomach dropped away a second later when he felt a hand on his shoulder.

2:20 A.M. PST
Los Angeles

Dan Pascal squeezed his girth into his government-issue Crown Victoria with the unhappy growl he reserved for this daily and inconvenient event. Once upon a time they'd issued him a Bronco, which was paradise for the big man, but Homeland Security had commandeered all those, so now he was back to packing his frame into the Vic.

To make matters worse, his cell phone was ringing. With an additional grunt, he shifted and stuffed a hand into his pocket, pulling out the phone with some difficulty.

"Pascal," he announced.

"Marshal, Sergeant Mike Santomiere, LAPD."

"Yes, Sergeant?"

"Not sure this is much, but we don't have a lot. Thought you'd want to know that someone just reported a car stolen. Parked on DeLeone Avenue. It's a pretty long sprint from the Fed Facility, but it's doable."

Pascal took down the make, model, and license plate number.

2:21 A.M. PST
West Los Angeles

Jack whirled and swept away the hand that held him, trapped it, and clamped his hand across his attacker's throat. Only then did he recognize Teri Bauer's face.

Her eyes were now bulging and her face had contorted into a mask of sudden terror.

Jack released her immediately and pulled her into the shadows of the apse. "Jesus!" he hissed.

"Jesus yourself!" she shot back. "Your face, I didn't recognize you for a minute." She was shaking. His expression had shocked her far more than his physical movements. His blue eyes had gleamed ferociously, and his lip had curled into a snarl. She had known for years that her husband was capable of killing people; that he had, indeed, killed people when necessary. But not until that moment did her thoughts reshape themselves into something more definitive. *My husband is a killer.*

"What are you still doing here?" he asked, immediately sorry that his tone was so accusatory.

"I waited to see if I could help," she replied. "I was just about to go."

He forced his voice into a slower, more soothing tone, though his heart was still racing, his muscles still coiled for a fight. "That would have been better. There's, there's a lot going on right now."

"Who's this?" Ramirez asked. He had been surprised by Jack's sprint across the intersection, and then had hesitated, not sure if he should follow or not. But he disliked being left alone.

Teri Bauer spotted the look of caution in Jack's eyes. "A friend," she said vaguely.

"Are we staying with her?" Ramirez said. "We need a place to—"

"No," Jack snapped, before Teri could respond.

"We're not that good of friends," Teri followed up.

Either she was pissed at him, or she was good at this. Jack decided it was probably both. He caught the dull roar of a car shifting gears as it came around the corner. The others seemed not to notice.

"Damn," Ramirez said, kicking one of the planters with the toe of his stolen sneakers. "I'm exhausted. We need someplace to—"

"Down!" Jack commanded. He smothered Teri with his body and grabbed Ramirez by the back of his Lakers jersey, nearly strangling him as he pulled the other fugitive to the ground. At the same moment, the air around them exploded with sound: shotgun blasts and semi-automatic pistol reports, whining bullets, shattering glass. Shards of glass rained down on Jack's head as he leveled his Sig at the car—a black Chrysler 300C that screeched to a halt. They couldn't see Jack or the others in the shadows under the apse, and most of their shots went high. Jack's did not. He put two rounds right through the front passenger window, and a silhouette there vanished. He swiveled a few degrees to the rear window, but Ramirez struggled underneath him and the shots went low, punching holes in the door frame. Someone inside the Chrysler screamed, and the big car roared away.

"Oh my god, oh my god," Teri whispered over and over.

"Got to move now," Jack stated. He jumped up and hauled her to her feet. "Get out of here," he commanded. "You were home. If the phone rang or anyone knocked, you didn't hear it because you were asleep. Go." He shoved Teri toward the corner. Before she could protest, he grabbed Ramirez by the arm and half-dragged him across the street. Teri was going to hate him for that, but she'd be alive to hate him.

"Who the hell was that? And who the hell was *that*?" Ramirez asked, his brain still addled by gunfire, referring to both Teri and the shooters.

"She was no one in particular. They were more of the same from jail." Jack didn't know it for sure, but the guess was a good one. The hit was gang-style, the car was gang-style. MS–13 was still after him. This couldn't be a gang vendetta, which meant he didn't know why they were after him. And what was more, how had they found him?

Jack didn't release Ramirez until they reached the car, and he didn't say a word until they were driving away. Two blocks down the street he pulled over and parked at a meter, now dormant for the evening. He killed the engine and the lights. "Get low," he said to his companion. They both slid low in their seats. A minute later sirens wailed and two squad cars hurried by, lights blazing. Jack calculated. If CTU cooperated, LAPD would run ballistics on the SigSauer and track it back to him. He had to stay ahead of the law, stay ahead of the pattern.

"What the hell did you do to MS–13 that they come after you?" Ramirez asked.

"Nothing," Jack said truthfully. "Maybe it's you."

"I've got nothing to do with them!" the other man protested.

"Either way, we need cover. A hotel is out because neither one of us has ID," which was a lie because the navy blue pouch had included some cash and a driver's license and credit cards under the name of

John Jimmo. "You said you might know some people. Now's the time to go there."

Ramirez hesitated. The pause itself was rewarding, as far as Jack was concerned. Whoever Ramirez was considering, he was important enough to cause fear and concern. That was just the kind of person Jack wanted to meet.

"All right," Ramirez conceded. "Let's go."

2:39 A.M. PST
CTU Headquarters, Los Angeles

Even when he wasn't around, Jack Bauer dominated the activities at CTU Los Angeles. Tony was up to his elbows in his Jemaah Islamiyah investigation. With Henderson's permission, he'd put two field agents out, wiretaps on every phone they could find for Sungkar's alias and Riduan Bashir's phones as well. Thanks to Seth, Sungkar's e-mails and instant messages were already popping up on Tony's computer as soon as they went out. Sungkar had just received an obscure e-mail, probably in code, but referenced an upcoming visit to Papa Rashad's factory. The e-mail repeated "Papa Rashad's factory" several times, and Tony was sure it was code. He was waiting for data analysis, and his patience was short.

"Jamey!" he yelled into the phone, though his voice carried straight to her. She buzzed him back and said more quietly, "We're on it, Tony, but we're also on this thing with Jack."

"Bauer." The word was not said with any kindness. Even as a fugitive from justice, Jack caused problems inside CTU. The man was a bull in a china shop. "What's going on?"

"Took your advice and spent some time digging into the victim's story. Adrian Tintfass."

"Some kind of small-timer, right? A middleman."

"Yeah, never really on our radar because he'd never done anything big."

"I remember."

Jamey jumped on his words. "But that's just it. He'd never really done anything big because he'd never really done anything. I mean the guy is nonexistent, and then all of a sudden he pops up, gets a label for a few small-scale transactions that might interest local law but wouldn't raise an eyebrow here, and then all of a sudden he's doing this big deal and Jack goes and kills him."

Tony did not see the mystery. "Lots of bad guys do lots of bad things that we don't know about. They get a reputation with other bad guys even if we don't have their whole résumé."

Jamey made a skeptical noise into the phone. "That's where I don't buy this thing with Jack. There wasn't any reason to kill this guy. How many people do you think Jack's killed?"

"A freakin' lot!"

"Right, but do you honestly think he's ever killed anyone he didn't have to?"

Tony paused. "Read his service record, Jamey. It's not that hard to believe—"

"—for somebody who's read the service record. That's why this story stands up to a typical investigation. But I'm talking about us, people who know him. Do you believe it?"

There was another long pause while Tony considered. He put aside his snap judgments and disapproval of Jack's actions. "No," he said at last, "I don't believe it."

Jamey felt a thrill. She'd won a point. "I have a name. It's Adrian Tintfass's widow. Can we send someone to go check her out? No point in me asking Henderson about this, he'll just say no."

"Nina," Tony said. "Get Nina to do it. Now where's my analysis?"

"Got it." Seth Ludonowski was standing at his shoulder, beaming.

Tony hung up. "Go."

Seth didn't bother with any impressive overview of the cryptographics programs, the analysis of semantics, allophones, or any other highly relevant but distracting methodologies used to parse through the intercepted e-mails. He just said, "Papa Rashad's factory is pretty unimaginative encryption for the initials PRF. If you ask me, PRF can also stand for—"

"Pacific Rim Forum," Tony said. "And it starts in about fifteen hours."

2:44 A.M. PST
Boyle Heights, Los Angeles

There ain't nothing like a late night fuck and a late night joint, thought Smiley Lopez. The girl was in the other room, still sleeping off the tequila. She might not remember the ride, he flattered himself, but she'd be sore in the morning. The fatty was in his hand and he took another puff, put his feet up on the little table, and used the remote to flip on the television. HBO, Cinemax (he called it "Skinemax"), Showtime, and still there wasn't a goddamn thing on at three o'clock in the morning. He flipped through channels until he came to ESPN-something-or-other. They were playing reruns of fights, but not boxing. It was that other shit, the fighting where you can hit with your knees and elbows and shit. Smiley liked that sort of fighting. It was more like the street.

His cell phone rang. He was expecting a call from some of his soldiers, but this was a different number. "Yo," he said, knowing who it would be.

"What the fuck's going on?" the angry voice on the line snapped.

Smiley checked the clock on the cable box. "They shoulda finished it right about now, homes. You can ease up."

"No, I can't," the other man said. "Your little homies" —the word was foreign, clumsy, an insult on his lips, and meant to be so— "screwed it up. For the third time!"

Smiley felt a buzz kill coming on and it annoyed him. "Goddamn, *ese*, you the one who told us he'd be tough to pop."

"Well figure out how!" the man demanded. "Or I'll make sure your guys inside burn."

Smiley sat up, his buzz gone in an instant. "Listen to me, *homes*," he said, overpronouncing the word as the other man had. "I ain't Oscar. You get up in my face like that I shove your dick down your throat, I don't care what kinda law you put on me. Got it?" He heard the other man choke back a response. "Besides, you fuckin' want him popped, you do it yourself, fuckin' *maricon*."

"All right," the other man said. "All right. I know he's tough, but you keep after it, or you don't get paid and I will make sure your boys go away." He hung up.

Smiley took another puff.

2:53 A.M. PST
Century Plaza Hotel, Century City, California

Old men don't sleep much. Martin Webb remembered his father telling him that when Martin was a much younger man. Though he was now approaching seventy-three, Martin's mind and memory were as sharp as ever, and he could see the old house in Silver Springs, when he'd bring his kids to visit the old man. He'd stay up late working on the financials for some company or other, long after his dad had gone to bed, only to find his dad waking up and coming down for a glass of warm milk. They'd talk then; those were some of the best talks they'd ever had.

Now Martin was the old man. Even his son Max was in his fifties, and when the family came to visit him in Georgetown and Martin got up for his own glass of warm milk, it was more often his grandson

Jake he'd find up, though of course Jake wasn't doing financials.

At the moment, though, he was alone, and instead of padding downstairs for milk he had called room service.

Old men don't sleep much, he told himself again. But he knew that he had reason to be losing sleep.

The economy. The goddamned economy. It sat there like an engine that ought to start but wouldn't. No, that wasn't the right analogy. Better to say hung there like an airplane whose engine wouldn't start. The plane was losing altitude, gliding on the last of its momentum, and any minute it would plunge.

"That's about right," Martin said out loud to his quiet hotel room.

He was the engineer, the man who was supposed to fix that engine. So far, he had tried every tool in his toolkit: interest rates, of course, which served as his hammer, screwdriver, and wrench. He'd employed the bully pulpit to shame the current administration into fiscal restraint. He'd hedged his bets against overseas markets. All to no good. The Dow looked like a downward staircase. Unemployment was up, and so was inflation, and those two things should not go together. According to last month's index, consumer spending had dipped, and the real estate market was slowing. Consumer confidence—Martin privately called it consumer overconfidence—and the housing bubble were really all that stood between the country and an economic crisis it had not faced in seventy years.

Martin Webb was being humble with himself. Others would say that a third barrier stood between the country and disaster: Martin Webb. Martin was the Chairman of the Federal Reserve. He was not just the grand old man of the economy; in the eyes of many, he *was* the economy. For twenty-seven years he had played nursemaid, steward, lord-protector of the United States economy, and always, always he had managed to make the markets pull themselves up by their bootstraps. He would do it again, at least that's what the *Wall Street Journal* told him. And he was sure the pundits were right. He would do it again.

He just didn't know how.

The warm milk came, and the room service attendant went. Martin sat down and sipped. Right about now was when he needed his son Max or his grandson Jake to stroll in and chat. Lacking Jake, he turned on the television, which bathed him in its hypnotic glow. He flipped channels until his eye was caught by a sports channel. He stopped, and watched two warriors pound each other with tiny gloves on their hands. As the commentator indicated, these were reruns of previous fights, all being broadcast as the prelude to the fights the following night. He'd seen this sort of fighting before—mixed martial arts, they called it—and he admired it. Not so different from the economy, really, with an interesting combination of subtlety and brute strength.

He drank his milk and watched.

. . . .

**THE FOLLOWING TAKES PLACE
BETWEEN THE HOURS OF
3 A.M. AND 4 A.M.
PACIFIC STANDARD TIME**

. . . .

3:00 A.M. PST
CTU Headquarters, Los Angeles

The last fifteen minutes had been Christmas come
early for Tony Almeida. Seth's code cracking had
been brilliant—and it had been followed by quick
work from CTU field agents and techs who'd bugged
Sungkar's house. Thanks to their work, Tony was
now sitting at his own desk listening to a conversation between Sungkar, on his home phone, and an
unknown associate.

". . . and you're sure the other side can deliver?"
Sungkar was asking.

"Their reputation is solid. They want the arms and

in return they can deliver a computer program that will do the job."

"In each country?"

"Yes."

"And the arms, we can get them?" Sungkar queried.

"I have a contact." *Bacharuddin Wahid.* That was the name Seth slipped to Tony as he listened. "I have not worked with him, but I have heard he is reliable."

"We buy the arms, and then trade the arms for the virus," Sungkar summed up. "Let's proceed."

Tony saw the pattern: Riduan Bashir provides the money, Sungkar uses the funds to purchase arms, which he then trades for this computer program, and Jemaah Islamiyah uses this virus to target the Pacific Rim Forum.

The man named Bacharuddin Wahid read an address, which Tony scribbled down. He reminded himself that neither of them had met this arms dealer, and a plan began to form.

3:06 A.M. PST
Mid-Wilshire, Los Angeles

Dan Pascal turned his Crown Vic onto Sweetzer just north of Wilshire Boulevard. His radio chattered with updates as LAPD units rolled into position. Two units were ahead of the target and two were behind. Pascal snatched up his radio mike. "Go," he said.

He stepped on the accelerator and reached Wilshire in a second, just as the blue Maxima passed him. Two cruisers pulled onto the street behind the Maxima, their lights going bright. The other two cruisers pulled out in front of the Maxima, angling themselves to block the street. The blue car hit its brakes and pulled up short. Pascal and the two follow cars pulled up behind, blocking its retreat. Pascal switched his radio mike to PA, threw open his door, and dragged himself out, drawing his Smith & Wesson .45 at the same time. "Stick your hands out of the car window!" he ordered.

Patrol in all four cars had opened their doors and taken cover behind them, weapons leveled. The occupants of the car complied, a set of hands sticking out from each side.

"Open the doors slowly. Get out and lie down on the ground!"

Again the occupants complied, and a moment later two men had climbed out, lying down on the asphalt in the middle of Wilshire Boulevard. As one, the law enforcement officers hurried forward.

Pascal stalked forward, moving suddenly much faster than one might have expected from someone his size. Catching Captain America had been easier than he'd thought. He watched the LAPD officers handcuff the occupants and haul them to their feet. Pascal straightened up to his full height and stared down . . . at two terrified eighteen-year-old kids.

3:11 A.M. PST
InterContinental Hotel, Downtown Los Angeles

Jack and Ramirez parked the just-stolen Nissan pickup truck a block away from the InterContinental Hotel and left it there for someone else to find. They walked into the four-star hotel in downtown Los Angeles. The lobby was quiet except for the Latino man and woman running an industrial-sized scrubber across the tile floor. Ramirez walked over to the house phones mounted over an elegant marble ledge. Picking one up, he punched in 7 plus a room number and waited while it rang.

"No answer?" Jack wondered.

Ramirez shrugged. "He did sound pissed when I called before. Wait—" Now he was talking into the phone. "Yeah, we're here. Okay, Van, we're coming up."

They found a bank of elevators and pressed the button for the twenty-third floor.

"So this was the guy you were working with, the one you murdered for?" Jack asked.

"Sort of. His name's Vanowen. I worked for him, he worked for the guy in charge. I never met that guy. Not sure I want to."

They reached twenty-three and walked down to 2346. It was a good hotel, with wide hallways and thick, soft carpet. Ramirez knocked and the door opened, then closed behind them. The man who'd admitted them was short and round with a thick walrus mustache and close-cropped reddish-brown hair. His arms weren't cut, but they were big, bulging out of his blue polo shirt. He was holding a Glock .40 in his hand.

"It don't figure," he said by way of hello. He motioned for them to sit down on the couch. The hotel room was an L-shaped suite, with a sitting area and, beyond a door, a bedroom. A couch stood near the door, and beyond it was a small counter extending out into the room, creating a divide. Beyond that was the bed.

"It don't figure why you'd break out to come see me."

Jack didn't say anything. He was sure in this case it was better to speak when spoken to.

"It does," Ramirez replied. "We didn't break out to see you. We broke out because someone was trying to kill us. We need a place to hide out."

The man sat down in a chair across from them, the Glock resting casually across his leg. "Rami, you know I owe you and you know why. You need someplace to hide, I'm gonna do it. But I don't know squat about you," he said to Jack.

Jack didn't like seeing the muzzle of the Glock, but at the moment he had no choice. He kept his hands on his knees. "Ask away."

"Tell me a story."

Jack told the story he'd used with Ramirez, the same story Ramirez knew. Like all good lies, it was as close to the truth as possible: he was a former agent for Homeland Security who'd murdered a scumbag and was awaiting trial and decided he didn't want to wait once MS–13 decided to kill him. He told the story of killing Tintfass. The man called Van seemed amused.

"I could check your story," Van said, rubbing his thick mustache. "I got people who could check."

"Knock yourself out," Jack said.

Van figured he would. "Uh-huh. Meantime, why the fuck should I help you?"

"I come in handy, if there's any trouble."

Vanowen waggled the gun. "Why'd there be trouble? I got a legitimate business, ask Rami. No reason for trouble."

"If you say so. I just figured if Rami was going to kill someone, there was something worth killing for and you were okay with it."

"I got people to answer to, people who don't like new faces. I probably oughta kill you right now."

Jack immediately relaxed. He had heard this kind of talk before. It almost always came from someone who had no intention of doing any killing. A man cold-blooded enough to kill him would have done so already, without compunction. Vanowen wanted to appear tough, and he wanted Jack to know that he was capable of killing if need be. But Jack would give him no need.

"I did Ramirez a favor getting him out. He's doing me a favor by getting us a place to lay low. That's all that's going on here. You decide you want some extra help, I've got some skills you might use."

Vanowen did not ease off, but his face shifted. He'd made some decision. "So tell me how you got out of jail."

Jack started to tell the story.

3:28 A.M. PST
Van Nuys, California

There was no such thing as a good way to knock on the door at three-thirty in the morning, so Nina Myers didn't try. Bauer was a fugitive and they needed leads A.S.A.P. She found the little house off Kester Avenue, a square one-room stucco building on a flat square lot. She rang the bell and pounded on a metal door knocker in the likeness of William Shakespeare.

"Who . . . who is it?" called a sleepy, frightened voice on the other side of the door.

"Federal agent, ma'am." Nina held up her ID to the peephole above William Shakespeare's head. "Sorry for the late hour, but I have a couple of urgent questions."

There was a long pause—so long that Nina started to decide whether to sprint around back or try to kick in the door—when the bolt turned and the door opened. The woman standing there was short, with thin black hair, a big nose, and a very unwelcome look on her pale face. She wore slippers and a frayed blue terry-cloth robe that she kept tucking and re-tucking around her body. She opened the door just enough to talk, but kept her body wedged into the open space.

"What questions?" the woman asked grumpily. She had clearly been sleeping.

"You're Marcia Tintfass?" The woman nodded. "Nina Myers. I'm afraid I have a question or two about your husband."

"I figured," the woman snapped. She was waking up, and her sleepiness was turning into indignation at being awakened at such a ridiculous hour. "What kind of question couldn't wait a few more hours until people were awake?"

"The kind that have to do with your husband's murderer, who just escaped from jail."

Marcia Tintfass's eyes popped open. She looked around, as though the killer might jump out from behind Nina. "Come in then."

Nina entered and sat down on the couch in a living room lit only by one standing lamp. Many of the shelves were bare, and Nina noticed two moving boxes in the corner. "You probably know all this, but I gave a big statement to the police already. I really didn't know much about my husband's business."

Nina had reviewed the file on Adrian Tintfass's murder, and learned everything there was to know about Marcia Tintfass, which wasn't much. "I understand. We're really interested in the killer himself—"

"I didn't know him," Marcia said hastily.

"I, yes, I know you didn't know him. We're just trying to figure out why he did it. The man who murdered your husband was an exemplary agent for the federal government."

"Right up until he killed my husband, I guess."

"Are you moving?" Nina asked.

The question caught Marcia off guard. "Oh, yes. You know, now that Adrian's gone, it doesn't, well, you know, it doesn't feel right being here."

Nina nodded but didn't believe a word of it. One

learned a lot from interrogating prisoners, and Nina had interrogated her fair share. Marcia Tintfass's words were totally reasonable, of course, but her delivery had been off. Nina had the distinct impression that, in her sleepiness, the woman had forgotten a line and then picked it up, like an actor recovering in the middle of a scene.

"Are you staying in the city?"

"Well," Marcia said, a little more naturally, "they've asked me to, for the trial and everything. But after that I'm moving to St. Louis."

"Friends there?"

"A fresh start, I guess. It's hard, losing someone. I didn't know how hard it was." Marcia Tintfass had gotten her rhythm now and sounded good.

Nina asked a few more perfunctory questions, questions that might explain the urgency in knocking on the door in the dead of night, but she left as soon as she could. In the car, she called in to CTU and talked with Jamey Farrell. "We need a tap on this phone, and her cell phone, and everything else right away. I guarantee you she's calling someone somewhere right now and she's nervous."

3:42 A.M. PST
Inglewood, California

The CTU strike team moved in with quiet efficiency. This was as close to a routine assault as the real world could provide. They had the layout of the two-story warehouse. Satellite and infrared imagery located the three occupants of the building. City business licenses, auto registrations, and telephone records told them exactly who would be inside.

By the time Tony Almeida got word from every unit in the assault and confirmed that the building was locked down, his people had three men in flex cuffs sitting in chairs in the middle of the warehouse. Two of them were little more than strong backs and mean looks. The man in the middle, according to their intelligence, was Arturo Menifee, although the name he was currently using was Richard Bonaventure. Arturo, born and raised in Florida, was a former procurement officer at Fort Hood, Texas, who decided to keep his skills sharp after his discharge from the Army. The military did a pretty good job of keeping track of its ordinance and weapons systems, but with such a massive operation, especially in wartime, it wasn't all that difficult for a patient man to shave off a rocket-propelled grenade here, an M–60 there. Before you knew it, you could have your own little arsenal for sale.

Tony put his hands on his knees, taking himself down eye level with the seated arms dealer. He didn't say a word, and the prisoner stared back at him, his face alternating nervously between fear and anger as Tony continued to stare. Menifee didn't look much like Tony if they stood together, but a bystander would have described them about the same: medium height, dark curly hair, dark eyes. *I'm better looking, of course,* Tony thought wryly.

"Okay," Tony said at last.

"I ain't telling you shit," Menifee spat.

Tony smiled. "I don't need you to tell me anything. Just talk. I want to hear your accent."

3:47 A.M. PST
InterContinental Hotel

"That's one hell of a story," Vanowen said. He still held the gun, but it was no longer pointed at Jack. Vanowen seemed to have forgotten what it was, and waved it around like a lecturer's pointer stick. "I never met anybody who broke outta prison before."

A knock on the door interrupted them. Vanowen looked perplexed, then went and cracked the door open. A second later he opened it wide, but did not step out of the frame. Jack could not see the other man's face silhouetted by the hallway lights, but whoever he was, he was huge, his bulk filling the entire doorway.

"Mark, you gotta be sleeping now. It's the big day!" Vanowen said.

"Can't sleep," said the big man. "Gotta talk. Let me in."

"I got people."

"Lemme in, Van, come on."

Vanowen hesitated, but then relented. The man who pushed past him looked like a cartoon drawing of a super hero. He was at least six feet, three inches, with shoulders as wide as two men put together, a narrow waist, and muscles that rippled through his American Eagle T-shirt. His face was chiseled out of rock and the bridge of his nose was permanently swollen. Both his ears were grotesquely misshapen. Jack recognized that as "cauliflower ear." Wrestlers get it from bumping their ears against their opponents over and over again.

"Guys, this is Mark Kendall. Mark 'The Mountain' Kendall, former heavyweight champ, and soon to be returning champ."

Jack and Ramirez nodded. Kendall grunted, but clearly had no interest in them.

"That's what I want to talk about," Kendall said. "I gotta know something, Vanny. You've got to promise me that I'll get other fights if I lose this one."

Jack had seen Vanowen slip the gun into his pocket as he answered the door. Now he saw the man slide his hand casually back into that pocket. "Come on, Mark. No promises in this business. You knew the score when you started your comeback." For a man who had just called Kendall the next heavyweight champ, he was suddenly very unsympathetic.

For a man as huge as Kendall, he looked pathetically vulnerable. "I've got fans out there. They want to see me fight."

Vanowen shook his head. "They want to see you come back, Mountain. See if a thirty-six-year-old guy's been out of the cage for four years can still dish it out. You lose, they'll have their answer, and no one's gonna be interested anymore."

Kendall's cauliflower ears turned beet red, but Jack

couldn't tell if it was embarrassment or anger. Not just anger, he decided. Kendall's massive shoulders hung low. He was a beaten man. But Jack was sure the fights hadn't done it. Something else weighed him down. Something he couldn't take care of with muscles.

"Come here, let's talk," Vanowen said. "I got money riding on you today, and your head's not on right. You guys sit tight."

Vanowen led the huge man into the other room. Ramirez stretched himself out on the couch. "Jesus, I didn't realize how tired I was. I'm not used to running around all night like this."

Jack shrugged. He'd done it before. Ramirez turned the television on absentmindedly. Jack watched with him, but his mind was on his next move. His eyes flicked about the room until he spotted a cell phone, undoubtedly Vanowen's, sitting on a chair atop a pile of clothes. Jack got up and stretched. He walked by the chair and palmed the cell phone, then went into the bathroom. Now his movements became much more urgent. He closed, locked the door, and dialed CTU.

3:53 A.M. PST
CTU Headquarters, Los Angeles

Henderson was half asleep at his desk. He wasn't lazy, but it was late and he'd been waiting for updates on the Jack Bauer situation, on Tony Almeida's leads, and on a few other lower-priority cases, and his eyes had started to droop. The ringing phone brought him to attention. The late night operator told him who was calling, and Henderson felt his heart thud against his ribs.

"Jack?" he said incredulously.

"I don't have a lot of time," Jack replied, his voice a hoarse whisper. "How's Chappelle?"

"Turn yourself in, Jack," Henderson said. "You look guilty now. You've got U.S. Marshals all over the city."

"Chappelle?" Bauer asked again.

"No one knows. No explanation for his collapse."

He heard Bauer swear under his breath. "Okay, Chris, I've got to tell you something, but I can't give many details."

"Come in here and tell me, Jack."

"Listen!" Jack commanded, though his voice was still quiet. "None of this is what it seems. I'm working a case. Chappelle knows all about it. There's an FBI unit that knows, too, but I don't have their contact."

Henderson frowned and gave an accompanying skeptical sigh. "Jack, come on. A jailbreak as part of a case?"

"Not that part. I had to do that, but it wasn't part of the plan."

"I'll bet."

"You don't believe me."

"Would you believe it?"

Jack didn't reply, and Henderson heard the low hum of cellular static in the background. Finally

Bauer said, "How much of this is about the Internal Affairs investigation?"

Henderson snorted. He wasn't surprised that Jack had brought up the investigation. Rumors of the inappropriate use of funds had floated around CTU Los Angeles for several months, and the word *embezzlement* had been used. Most of the field agents had been called in, and the word was that Jack had mentioned Henderson's name. "First of all, you and I know that any charge against me is bullshit. Second, I'd never let something like that compromise my integrity."

"I don't care either way, Chris," Jack said. "I'm just on a case and I want—"

"I'm the goddamn Director of Field Operations, Jack," Chris said, "and I have no knowledge of you being on a case. I want you to come in. Or I'll send someone you trust out to get you. How's that?" But the line was dead.

Henderson buzzed his intercom. "Okay, new guy. Did you get that traced?"

"'Course," said Seth Ludonowski. "We aim to please."

Henderson dialed Peter Jiminez.

1 2 3 4 5 6 7 8 **9**
10 11 12 13 14 15 16 17
18 19 20 21 22 23 24

· ·

THE FOLLOWING TAKES PLACE
BETWEEN THE HOURS OF
4 A.M. AND 5 A.M.
PACIFIC STANDARD TIME

· ·

4:00 A.M. PST
Biltmore Hotel

At nineteen, he was still Jorge Rafael Marquez, but
no longer the peasant's son from Chiapas or the
adolescent gangster from Boyle Heights. He went
by Rafael more than Jorge in those days because it
sounded less rural. Rafael, to him sounded cosmo-
politan, a world traveler or, as he fancied himself, an
artist of the new frontier. The new frontier, he had
recognized years earlier, was the Internet. The Internet thrilled him with its offer of freedom: freedom
of information, freedom of discussion, freedom of
purpose.

"*I can't let you do it,*" Amistad Medved had told him, using the phrase Rafael least liked to hear. Rafael had just insisted that they open their operating system to the public.

Medved was his partner, but also his boss. Only twenty-three himself, he was still considered a veteran of the burgeoning world of connectivity. He'd made a small fortune in software design and had used it to began writing his own Web browser. Medved had recognized Rafael's genius immediately and brought him on board, given him a huge number of options, and let him run rampant in the fields of cyberspace. With his gift for patterns, Rafael had written algorithms that shortened the lag time of search engines to nanoseconds. His work had trebled Medved's fortunes and made Rafael himself a rich man.

Then the rumors first started to fly about Internet service providers offering tiered delivery: slower connections for lower-paying customers, faster speed for more money. Rafael blanched. It sounded like the sharecropper scams he'd witnessed back in Chiapas. It reminded him of extortion rackets run by MS–13 back in Boyle Heights. Only this time it was sanctioned by the government.

Rafael had wanted to respond by publishing an algorithm that latched on to high-speed connections regardless of the pay rate. Medved, who had invested heavily in several different ISPs, refused to allow it.

Rafael had walked away, leaving his career behind. He abandoned his name as well, but he was not yet Zapata. He became Zapata a year or two later, *when the Mexican government raided Chiapas and killed his father and his cousin, and he realized once and for all that the Rubik's Cube was a trick, created by leaders to occupy the time and minds of the people. The cube did not need to be solved. It had to be broken.*

Zapata listened carefully as Aguillar told him about the upcoming buy. "I am sending Alliance to meet with the arms dealer. They are providing transportation."

Aguillar saw the flicker of concern cross Zapata's face like a shadow. He waited.

"We used Alliance the last time we were in the United States."

"To transport the Cubans, yes. But you were already using him for his other business, so I assumed—"

"The fight game is different," Zapata said dismissively. "An entirely different sphere. I do not like using the same people too often because it creates a pattern. Patterns can be followed."

"I know, but there was no one else available. Farrigian has disappeared, and the others we have worked with more."

"Okay," Zapata said. "But kill him afterward."

Aguillar nodded. He was done, and should have gone to his own room to get some sleep, but he hesitated. "I'm sorry, Zapata, but I have to ask—"

Zapata smiled. Aguillar had sounded apologetic, but he knew (as did Zapata himself) that Zapata's ego relished these opportunities to play the mentor.

"Why this deal? We could get the equipment we

need from other sources, without trading with the Indonesians."

Zapata nodded. "Two reasons. The first is obvious. These people we trade with will cause their own stir, and that will attract some attention. It's a distraction. But my reason is more . . . aesthetic. I am simply trying to drop the biggest rock I can into the pond."

"I will call Alliance to confirm."

4:09 A.M. PST
InterContinental Hotel

Jack leaned back against the sofa cushions, his feet up on the coffee table and his eyes closed. He wanted to sleep, but would not allow himself the luxury.

Vanowen's phone rang. He popped out of the other room, saying, "You okay now, Mark? Head on straight?"

Mark "The Mountain" Kendall looked far from okay, but he grunted an affirmative, barely looked at Jack and Ramirez, and left. Vanowen talked into his phone a little, mostly listened, and then said, "I'll be there." He snapped the phone shut.

"Okay. Hey, wake up!" Vanowen kicked the feet of Ramirez, who was snoring. Ramirez jumped as if he'd been bitten.

"I have a job this morning," Vanowen said. "Some of the kind of work you were getting involved in, before you went and killed someone, you moron. You want to come?"

Ramirez rubbed his eyes. "Yeah, okay."

"Me, too," Jack said.

Vanowen grinned at him, a big, toothy grin out of his round face. "You I did some checking on while I was in the other room. You fucked somebody up, huh? You're really on the run now."

"Like you wouldn't believe," Jack said.

Vanowen chewed his lip. He seemed to be weighing his innate suspicion against some need. Finally, he said, "Yeah, come. I can use the extra muscle. Besides, ain't nothing you're gonna see Ramirez couldn't have burned me for by now anyway."

4:14 A.M. PST
Inglewood

Tony Almeida had changed out of his old clothes—which looked like clothes that had been worn for days—into a clean shirt and jeans, as though he'd gotten up early instead of staying up all night. Two members of the CTU strike force had changed into civvies as well to pose as his muscle.

They knew Encep Sungkar was coming. When he was still twenty miles away they knew which streets he took, his average speed, and they could have determined his mileage per gallon if they'd wanted to. Tony's team spent the intervening minutes rifling through Menifee's records and the stack of crates under canvas in his warehouse. It wasn't the most impressive stockpile Tony had seen, but it would do some damage. There were four launchers and twelve rocket-propelled grenades, a .50-caliber machine gun that could put rounds right through a brick building, a baker's dozen of M–60s and MP–5s, and other assorted goodies.

Tony's earpiece buzzed as Sungkar's vehicle, followed by a truck, pulled up to his warehouse. He opened the regular-sized door, which was cut into the wall near the huge sliding cargo entrance, as his target approached. He recognized Sungkar from the table in Little Java. Sungkar was small and bespectacled, with a mild manner and a slight smile. But his eyes were intense, and though he walked softly, Tony had the distinct impression of a mongoose ready to spring.

"You Perkasa?" Tony hailed in his best imitation of Menifee's voice, using the alias they'd discovered Sungkar to be using.

"Of course," the Indonesian said, moving past Tony and into the warehouse. His glasses flashed as he looked around. "There is not much here."

"I know how to pack," Tony grunted, following him inside. He borrowed the observation from one of the strike team members, who had noted how efficient Menifee had been at stacking his ordnance. He held out his hand. "Menifee. I like to shake hands with the people I do business with."

Sungkar looked down at Tony's offered hand as though it might contain some disease. Finally he touched it weakly and removed his hand at once. "I have another meeting. Let's proceed."

The buy itself was straightforward: two hundred

and fifty thousand dollars for everything explosive, plus all the assault rifles. Keeping in character, Tony tried to sell them the fifty cal, but Sungkar wasn't buying.

"I'll open the cargo door and your guys can drive in." Tony went over to the huge door, almost the size of the wall, and pressed a button. Hydraulics groaned, and the door rattled up into the ceiling.

There were two men with Sungkar, one of whom had driven the truck. He climbed back in and tried to start it up, but the engine wouldn't turn over. He looked up at Sungkar through the windshield apologetically and tried again. He had no luck, even after fifteen minutes of effort.

While they'd been talking, CTU agents had disabled the vehicle. It wasn't going anywhere.

"I got a truck I can sell you," Tony offered with a friendly grin. Sungkar wasn't amused. While the Indonesians popped the hood and tinkered around, muttering in Malay, Tony said, "Seriously, you need transport to someplace, I can drive you there. No charge. I just want this shit outta my warehouse."

Sungkar considered Tony had seen him check his watch several times, and knew that he had a schedule to keep.

"Just you. Not your men," Sungkar said. "My business associates would not like that."

"No prob," Tony said, although he would have liked to have had a couple of good guns guarding his back. "Let's load her onto my truck."

4:32 A.M. PST
Downtown Los Angeles

Dan Pascal was thinking that Officer Lafayette was a prophet. He really would have preferred to do a manhunt in the bayous.

He was standing with a half dozen other marshals and investigators on the curb of a street in downtown Los Angeles, next to a Nissan Maxima. The same Maxima, in fact, that Jack Bauer had stolen. He was happy to have found the car, but as far as he knew, Bauer had just jacked another one. Or maybe he'd just left the car and gone into one of these fine buildings. Far as Pascal knew, he could be looking down on them right now.

This city was immense. They'd simply vanished into the wilderness of civilization.

Pascal was just thinking how he liked that: "wilderness of civilization." He ought to write that down. But his phone rang and he checked the number flashing. "Pascal. Go ahead, Emerson."

His assistant deputy said, "Marshal, we got a break, looks like."

"Don't hold it in, it ain't healthy."

"A surveillance team downtown picked up some images that might be our man."

"What team? Ours?"

"LAPD. They were on some other case. Some kind of fence named Vanowen."

"I got a link in the car. Send me over the image."

Pascal ambled over to his Crown Vic and punched

up the mini-computer. The image downloaded quickly: a typically grainy black-and-white of a blond-haired man. Pascal always wondered why, in an age when a cop could drive around with a computer in his car and have pictures sent through the ether, security cameras still shot video that looked like the Zapruder footage. But even so, it did look like photos of Bauer. He was with a smaller guy, maybe Latino, and a round guy built like a fireplug.

"That's our guy. Know where he's going?"

"As a matter of fact, we do."

4:38 A.M. PST
Playa del Rey, California

Leave it to Los Angeles to take swampland next to an airport and build million-dollar McMansions over it. Playa del Rey, which had once been little more than the soaking ground for branches of the Los Angeles river during the rainy season, now consisted of long fields of beige and ecru archways and columns, cream-colored walls, and acre upon acre of Spanish tile in burnt umber and sienna.

Of course, all those people in all those mini-mansions gathered all sorts of possessions, and those possessions inevitably outgrew their houses, which meant they had to rent storage. The U-Pack Storage Rental facility did a better-than-break-even business renting storage space to the upper middle class. But the owner made his real money as a depot for the less-savory members of the community who often helped relieve the suburbanites of their excess property.

The U-Pack people also let some of their illegal storage clients use his facility as a meeting ground. It was safe: you needed a pass code to get in, and the upstanding customers almost never visited.

Twenty minutes earlier Jack Bauer had driven with Vanowen and Ramirez to an overnight parking lot near the hotel, dropped off Vanowen's Audi, and climbed into a mid-sized truck with circular logo and the words "Alliance Moving" in blue letters. Two men were waiting, and hopped in the back of the truck.

"You have a lot of businesses," Jack observed.

"Important to diversify." Vanowen nodded, and started the truck's engine.

Downtown to Playa del Rey was an easy drive at that hour, although one could already see early morning commuters easing sleepily onto the 110 Freeway. A police cruiser pulled up alongside for a moment, and Jack, at the passenger window, stared down at it. He wondered what Tony Almeida and Nina Myers were saying about him at CTU. He hoped Henderson had bought his story. If not, Jack wouldn't be safe in Los Angeles much longer. So far he'd managed to stay ahead of the law by remaining unpredictable, but not untraceable. His pursuers would have found the truck, and then the Maxima. His face had undoubtedly been picked up by security cameras at the hotel, but CTU would have to access the data banks in that particular hotel to find him.

The Alliance truck pulled into the driveway of a place called the U-Pack Storage facility. Vanowen hopped out and entered a code into a button panel, and a big iron gate that had blocked the driveway / rattled out of the way.

Vanowen hopped back in and put the truck in gear. "Okay, I took from these guys before. I'm just doing pick up for the guy I do work with" —he threw a knowledgeable look at Ramirez— "and he says there shouldn't be any trouble. Case there is, you're on your own." This was said to Jack.

Vanowen steered the truck up to the largest of three buildings on the lot, next to a big hangar door, then checked his watch with an air of satisfaction. "Quarter till. My dad always said, if you're not ten minutes early, you're late."

"Looks like they're right on time, too," Jack said.

Another truck had rolled in through the iron gate. Vanowen watched it through the truck's big rectangular side view mirror. This truck rumbled past the Alliance vehicle and pulled to a stop in the middle of the driveway. Jack followed Vanowen and Ramirez out of the cab, and one of the two men who'd gotten in back of the truck appeared. The other was nowhere in sight.

The occupants of the other truck appeared as well. There were four of them: three were Indonesian, and Jack's eyes were drawn straight to the smallest—a little man with scholarly glasses and a look of fierce intensity. He was flanked by two more Indonesians, bigger, sporting tough looks, and undoubtedly carrying weapons. Finally, Jack glanced at the fourth man, and found himself looking straight into the eyes of Tony Almeida.

4:46 A.M. PST
Playa del Rey

It took every ounce of self-discipline Tony possessed not to react. That was Jack Bauer. Goddamned-son-of-a-bitch Jack Bauer! What was he doing selling arms to Jemaah Islamiyah? Almeida was one of CTU's best and brightest, and the connection formed in his mind almost immediately. Tintfass had been an arms dealer moving up in the world. Bauer had launched an investigation against him. CTU had decided not to pursue it. Bauer had killed him. What if Bauer was running a little side business of his own? He wouldn't be the first law enforcement agent to take his knowledge over to the dark side. Maybe he'd wanted to take over Tintfass's operation, first using Federal powers to try to destroy him, then taking the more direct approach. Rumors were flying around CTU of misappropriated funds . . . was Bauer at the center of it? Had he been financing his own sales operation?

All these thoughts raced through Tony's mind, but none of them showed on his face. No outside ob-server would have gotten even a hint that Bauer and Almeida knew each other.

"We have your equipment," Sungkar said. "You have our package, of course."

One of the men with Jack, a short bulldog of a

man with a mustache as thick as a shoe brush, nodded. "Right here." He held up two CD jewel cases wrapped in rubber bands. He unwrapped the rubber bands and handed one to Sungkar. "This is most of it. We put the equipment on my truck, and I give you the rest."

Sungkar nodded, having expected this. "Let's get this done." He motioned to his men, one of whom stood off to one side, the cover man, while the other unstrapped a dolly from the back of Tony's truck and began to cart boxes over to the Alliance truck.

Tony didn't know any of the men with Jack. The bulldog was completely unfamiliar. There was another guy with salt-and-pepper hair, but he looked to be no more than hired muscle. The last one wore a thin black mustache. Tony thought he'd seen a picture of him. Was he the other fugitive from jail?

4:50 A.M. PST
Playa del Rey

Jack's heart was pounding, but no one would have known he was nervous. What the hell was Almeida doing here? But Almeida couldn't rat him out. He was obviously on a case of some kind and wouldn't want to blow his cover.

Jack saw Vanowen ease up on Almeida, and his hand went casually to his hip where his Sig was stashed.

"You don't belong here," Vanowen said to Tony.

"Huh?" Tony replied, a little startled, but the bulldog's expression was amused.

"You ain't Chinese or whatever," Vanowen said. "You the token white guy?"

Almeida grinned as if he were amused. "I'm the token whatever, long as I get paid."

The conversation gave Jack the opening he needed. "Amen to that."

Almeida looked at him with those sad-sack eyes. "This'll be a good payday, huh?"

Jack knew that Almeida was fishing. He was about to respond, but his words were cut off by a voice blaring over a loudspeaker. "*This is the police. Put your hands up!*"

Instead everyone went for his gun. Vanowen pulled a .45 from somewhere, as did his bodyguard. Sungkar's two men dropped their packages and did the same. Tony crouched down. Ramirez hit the deck with a shriek. Jack dropped to his knee, his hand going instinctively for his weapon, but he did not draw. The movement cost him. Gunshots sounded, and something fast and hot bit him on the right arm.

Two squad cars had blocked the iron gate, and another one had rolled in from some back entrance, along with a white unmarked car, probably a Crown Victoria. They were surrounded, but neither Vanowen nor the Indonesians were inclined to surrender. Vanown and his henchmen poured fire into the two police cars at the gate, and the cops there ducked for cover. The Indonesians attacked the other way. Someone from the Crown Vic fired a big weapon—.10mm Desert Eagle, had to be—that boomed like a shotgun, and one of the Indonesians went down immediately.

But the others put rounds into the cars, and those officers, too, went for cover.

"What the fuck!" Vanowen said, dropping back near his own truck. He glared at Jack, his most likely suspect.

"You kidding?" Jack yelled back, pointing at his arm now running red with blood.

4:57 A.M. PST
Playa del Rey

Dan Pascal hadn't been in a real firefight since '91. He heard the combined ping-thud of rounds puncturing the door of his car and he smirked. *If it hits me,* he thought, *Lord just let it kill me. I just don't wanna be maimed.*

He raised himself up, just barely over the top of his car, and surveyed the terrain. LAPD was after the arms-selling crew, but Pascal was worried about Jack Bauer. He'd spotted his blond fugitive as they rolled up, but now he'd disappeared. Someone chose his car as a target, and his windshield shattered. He fired a few more rounds from his Desert Eagle, the sound like thunder compared to the little 9-millimeters plinking all around. This wasn't going to last long. They had the bad guys in a cross-fire. He was just reaching for his mic to give more orders through the loudspeaker, when one of the officers in the squad car next to him went down without a word. Then the other one fell, too, and Pascal had a flashback of a little town in southern Iraq, watching three grunts in his platoon drop before someone yelled . . .

"Sniper!" he roared. They were standing next to a friggin' three-story building, which meant that to someone looking down on them they'd be like fish in a barrel. He discharged a few rounds up-angle and slid back into his car as a round chipped at the asphalt he'd just vacated.

4:58 A.M. PST
Playa del Rey

Jack saw Vanowen spin around as a high-caliber round hit him, and something small and shiny flew out of his hand. He needed Vanowen and couldn't let him die. Jack sprinted the short distance between them and caught the other man before he fell, pinning him against the side of the truck.

"We're leaving," he said. He opened the cab and shoved Vanowen inside, following behind. He knew Vanowen's other man, the one who'd disappeared, was on the roof, but he had no problem leaving the sniper behind for the cops to pick up. Jack gunned the engine. Ramirez appeared at the passenger door, threw it open, and scrambled inside.

Jack didn't bother turning around. He jammed the truck's long stick shift into reverse and hit the accelerator. The truck roared and lurched backward, heading straight for the two black-and-whites at the gate. He got a quick image of Tony Almeida glaring at him as he fled.

He knew the cops at the gate were firing at the back of the truck, and he hoped none of them hit the ordinance that had already been stowed. The cop cars came up fast in the side view mirror. Jack gritted his teeth, and a second later he felt his head nearly rattle off his shoulders and the truck plowed into the cars, nearly stopped, then shoved its way between them.

Then he was through. There was no more firing—the cops at the cars were either injured or had taken cover. Jack spared a second to survey the firefight. The Indonesians were firing at the other police cars, and Jack saw flashes of fire from the roof of the storage building. Someone was firing down on the cops. Vanowen's second man. He glanced over at his two companions, both cowering in pain and fear. He switched his SigSauer to his left hand and leaned out the driver's window. It was a ridiculous shot to try—way over fifty meters, with a handgun, firing left-handed. But he saw no reason for cops to get killed. He steadied his left arm and aimed, relaxing. There was a psychological tendency for shooters, aiming at distant targets, to muscle their way into the shot, as though their bodies needed to help the bullet travel. But the opposite was true, of course. The bullet would travel a certain distance, period, and no push from the shooter would help—it would only spoil the aim. Jack relaxed, made his best guess as to windage and the force of gravity, and squeezed.

Then he threw the truck into first and gunned the engine, and they were gone.

1 2 3 4 5 6 7 8 9
10 11 12 13 14 15 16 17
18 19 20 21 22 23 24

• •

THE FOLLOWING TAKES PLACE
BETWEEN THE HOURS OF
5 A.M. AND 6 A.M.
PACIFIC STANDARD TIME

• •

5:00 A.M. PST
Playa del Rey

"Jesus, Jesus," Ramirez whispered with both hands covering his face.

"Goddamn!" Vanowen rasped through clenched teeth, his right hand pressed tightly over his left shoulder.

"It went through," Jack said calmly. There was no pursuit. They had to ditch this truck, though, before the helicopters were in the air. "If no arteries were hit, you might live, but your shoulder's ruined." His own right arm stung, but he'd been lucky. The round had taken off a layer of skin, but hadn't done any real damage.

He saw what he was looking for and made a hard left. There was a long tunnel on Sepulveda Boulevard just south of LAX. He reached it and stopped in the slow lane, then jumped out. The next few moments would be pure luck. He saw headlights approach up the lonely road and enter the tunnel. If it was a cruiser, they were done.

It wasn't. Jack waved at the car, a red Chrysler SUV. The car slowed. Jack jumped in front of it and raised his weapon. "Out, now."

The driver, a forty-ish man in a dress shirt and tie, looked shocked and took a moment to comply.

"The stuff," Vanowen said. "Put as much in as you can."

Jack didn't question. He helped Vanowen into the SUV, then he and Ramirez spent a minute or two tossing the boxes from the truck into the SUV. The delivery was shrinking. They'd loaded only half the equipment into the truck, and only a portion of that would fit in the SUV.

Jack took the SUV driver's wallet, glanced at the name and address, and said, "Okay, Mr. Mullins, I need you to listen." The man was still in shock. Jack tapped him with the Sig to get his attention. "We're stealing your car. You're not going to report it for at least an hour, understand? Get out of here, away from this truck. Call a cab, I don't care. If I learn that the police are looking for this SUV—"

"—if we see a friggin' Amber Alert on the freeway with this license plate number," Vanowen added angrily.

"—well, we know where you live." Jack held up the driver's license as a reminder, then stuck it in his pocket. He didn't wait for a response, and a moment later they were driving away in the SUV.

5:07 A.M. PST
Playa del Rey

Tony was facedown on the asphalt with some huge police officer kneeling on his back. He didn't try to resist, trusting that the whole affair would get sorted out soon enough. The big man cuffed him and sat him up roughly, and Tony found himself looking into a big square face.

"Ya'll want to tell me where Jack Bauer's gone off to?" he drawled in a slow, demanding voice.

Jack Bauer. Tony Almeida rolled his eyes.

5:08 A.M. PST
Playa del Rey

Peter Jiminez rolled up on the scene at U-Pack Storage. He'd heard the radio signals going back and forth, and would have arrived sooner except that he hadn't been aware the surveillance team was specifically hunting Bauer.

He'd gotten the call from Chris Henderson not long before, and Henderson's orders had been crystal clear: Find Jack Bauer, before the police do, if possible.

Jiminez had taken the trace Henderson supplied him and gone directly to the InterContinental Hotel, but he was a step behind. He'd actually intended to go back to Teri Bauer, to start over, when the U-Pack call came through.

The parking lot was clogged with emergency vehicles, and the street outside was blocked by three news vans. Peter parked on the street and slipped under the yellow police line, showing his badge to the uniform there. A moment later he laid eyes on Tony Almeida, sitting on the ground with his hands cuffed behind his back, and a bear of a man hunched over him.

"Excuse me," he said politely, holding up his badge. "Can I help with something?"

The big man stood up, immediately looming over Peter, and studied the badge for a moment. The Counter Terrorist Unit ID seemed to carry some significance for him. "I'm just interviewing a suspect, son. Why don't you wait—"

"That's no suspect," Peter replied. "He's one of us."

Pascal looked from one to the other skeptically. "He was apprehended while committing a felony, and he was seen abetting a wanted fugitive."

Bauer! "Well, I'm sure it's part of a case, Officer—?"

"Deputy Marshal," the big man corrected. "Deputy Marshal Dan Pascal."

Tony looked up at them both. "My name is Tony Almeida. The Indonesians you've arrested, at least one of them is a member of a terrorist organization." He told his story quickly.

Pascal was no stooge. He got on his radio and relayed all their information, and even waited several minutes until he could speak with George Mason, the one CTU agent he'd met before. Finally he was satisfied. He uncuffed Tony and helped him to his feet.

"You CTU people seem to have a talent for getting into trouble," he observed.

"You're leading the Bauer manhunt?" Peter asked.

"That's the job," Pascal replied. "Came pretty damned close, too, but they put up a serious fight. We got wounded, and some of them got away. Woulda been worse, but someone nailed their sharpshooter."

"Sharpshooter?" Tony asked.

"You didn't see? Guy on the roof. Nearly put one through my skull, and he got some of the others. But someone shot him right through the neck. Pretty shot, whoever it was. My guys brought him down a minute ago." He chewed the inside of his cheek for a minute. "So you boys must know him. What's Captain America doing working with these felons when he should be on the run?"

Almeida almost smiled at the Captain America reference. "I don't know. I was on my case and nearly choked when I saw him standing there." But when Pascal turned away to talk to another Deputy Marshal, Almeida pulled Jiminez aside. "I have an idea, though." He repeated his theory about Tintfass.

Jiminez couldn't, or wouldn't, believe it. "I just don't buy it, Tony. Jack's been hunting terrorists since before 9/11. Why would he jump over to the dark side?"

"Money. Or maybe he's tired of it. Or maybe he's running from home." Tony knew that Jack's marriage was a roller coaster.

Jiminez clung to his naïveté. "I still don't think that's Jack."

5:20 A.M. PST
Biltmore Hotel

It really couldn't have worked out better, Jack thought as they pulled into the guest parking area of the Biltmore Hotel.

They'd managed to stop Vanowen's bleeding and put a new shirt on him. Vanowen had said they could not go to the meet—they hadn't picked up a third of the package. He had to go straight to his employer and explain what had happened. Jack, who'd also borrowed a shirt to cover his own bloodstained arm, hid his excitement, but he was eager to meet the man in charge. He followed Vanowen's directions to the Biltmore, which, ironically, was only a few blocks from the InterContinental.

They'd put a jacket over Vanowen to hide the bloodstained shirt, but his face was pale and he needed help to walk. Fortunately there were very few people up and about at five o'clock, and when one of the few, a bellman, looked at them quizzically, Jack just said, "Fun night," and that was it.

They rode the elevator to the eleventh floor and Vanowen guided them to room 1103. The door opened slightly and a face, hidden by the door and the shadows, stared out at them. "What?" the occupant demanded.

"It got fucked up," Vanowen said weakly. "I gotta explain. And get help."

The occupant's eyes studied Vanowen, and then Ramirez, and then lingered for a while on Jack. "Vanowen, Ramirez. Come in. You stay out."

The door opened ever so slightly more, and Ramirez helped Vanowen slip into the room. The door shut firmly.

Jack waited, but not patiently. He'd been through a rough night, as rough as any he'd experienced, but so far the plan was working. Just a few more minutes and it would be over.

Jack pressed his ear against the door. He heard muffled sounds of conversation. The words were lost but the rhythm was calm, typical. Then he heard two muted gunshots, followed by two thuds.

Shit! Jack stepped back, raised his leg, and kicked. The door swelled inward, but the frame held. He kicked again, and the door broke free of its bolt. Jack was inside instantly, SigSauer ready.

Ramirez and Vanowen lay on the floor, each with a small bullet hole in his head. There was an open door leading to the next hotel room—they'd been connected. Jack rushed through in time to see that door swing closed. He burst out into the hallway again and saw a figure running down the hall. "Freeze!" he yelled, planning to shoot anyway. The man turned and fired, missing. Jack dropped to one knee and discharged three rounds at the moving target. His quarry stumbled, but kept running. Jack sprinted forward, the long night forgotten, his heart pounding with the excitement of the hunt.

The man he chased was shorter than he, with dark hair and a Latino look. His quarry ran into the stairwell. Jack followed, with the runner a full flight below him by the time he was through the door. Jack ran down two flights in pursuit, then paused. He leveled the SigSauer and waited. As the man came around the next turn, he fired center mass, and his target dropped.

Jack ran down. The bullet had passed through the hollow of his shoulder and diagonally through his heart. Checking the wound, Jack saw a tattoo on his neck, below the collar line, that read "Emese" in gothic lettering. He hadn't known about the tattoo. It was the same tattoo worn by one of the MS–13 soldiers. Jack was surprised, but he didn't have to worry about it at the moment. He'd brought down Zapata.

Jack heard sirens approaching. He sat down on the stairs next to the body and waited. They could arrest him now.

5:37 A.M. PST
Chatsworth, California

Nina Myers hunched down over the steering wheel, trying to see the street sign. Chatsworth lay on the edge of Los Angeles county, in the northwest corner of the

San Fernando Valley. It wasn't the middle of nowhere, but it was rural enough to be zoned for horses. The streetlights were fewer and farther between, and the street signs were hard to read. It was also far enough out that her GPS map didn't show any roads.

The place she looked for was on a street called Baden, somewhere below the rocky hills that marked the border between Los Angeles and Ventura counties. She was interested in the address because it was associated with a phone number, a number that Marcia Tintfass had called three times immediately after Nina's visit. She was going to find that house and talk to whoever had received those phone calls.

5:40 A.M. PST
Biltmore Hotel

Hotel security had no interest in dealing with a gunman, but Jack heard them moving around up on the floor. They'd surely found the bodies of Ramirez and Vanowen by now. He heard the fire door to the stairwell open twice, then close quickly after a pause. They'd be startled to see Zapata's body lying there, with Jack sitting calmly beside it—startled, and none too interested in dealing with it.

Jack felt his eyelids droop. It had been a long night, and the truth was, he hadn't gotten much sleep in prison for the three previous weeks. He could use a real rest.

When the police finally arrived, they came from

above and below, guns drawn. They proned him out and he didn't resist, letting them cuff him. They led him upstairs to the hallway, now full of emergency personnel, police officers, and one very large man in plain clothes.

"Well, there's Captain America," the big man crowed. "You've had a busy night."

Jack looked at the badge on the man's belt. He was a U.S. Marshal. "I want to talk to Chris Henderson at the Counter Terrorist Unit," Jack said, "or Ryan Chappelle, if he's out of the hospital."

"You can talk all you want once we get you back into jail," the man said.

Jack nodded. There was no need to put up a fight. Even if it took another day, this whole mess would straighten itself out. In jail, they'd put him in isolation, where he'd be safe from MS–13 and their strange vendetta. The biggest mystery for him now was why Zapata had worn an MS–13 tattoo. He'd had no idea of that connection. It was impossible that Zapata had sent MS–13 after him—absolutely impossible. What was the connection?

Jack mulled this over as the big man—Jack heard someone refer to him as Pascal—and another marshal led him downstairs. Pascal didn't engage him in conversation, and when Jack asked two more times to talk to someone at CTU, the big marshal repeated his previous statement. On Jack's third try, Pascal shook his head. "Son, you don't get me. My job ain't to accommodate you in any way. My job is to put you back in your hole."

They reached the hotel's parking lot, and Pascal guided Jack, still handcuffed, over to a beige Crown Victoria. Jack saw bullet holes in the door and guessed it was the same Crown Vic he'd seen at U-Pack. Pascal tucked Jack in the backseat—although unmarked, the car was all cop, with the plastic shield and no door handles on the backseat interior. Then Pascal maneuvered himself into the driver's seat with the other marshal riding shotgun. They drove out of the hotel and turned onto the early morning downtown streets.

The other marshal got on his cell phone for a minute, then turned to Pascal. "The victim was DOA."

Pascal grunted. "Guess you got another one," he called back to Jack. "You keep busy, that's for damned sure. Out less than twelve hours and you steal two automobiles and commit a murder. I don't suppose you're going to tell us what you had against Mister . . . What was his name again?"

"Aguillar," the other marshal said. "Francis Aguillar."

Jack felt the blood freeze in his veins.

5:53 A.M. PST
Biltmore Hotel

Zapata stood in the crowd in the lobby watching the police and paramedics parade in and out. He looked no more or less a part of the crowd than any of the others—an average-sized man with a shaved head, wearing track pants and a zip-up jacket, he passed easily for a guest out for an early morning jog. If anyone asked for his ID, he would have a problem—the Ossipon identity was connected to one of the two rooms. The police would want to know why three men had been killed in or near those rooms, and Zapata had no interest in long conversations with the authorities.

So the Ossipon cover was blown, but Zapata could deal with that. What disturbed him most was how close the authorities had come to him. They had been, literally, within a step or two of catching him. He had not seen the undercover agent himself, but he had known it the minute Vanowen showed up at his door, bloody, with Ramirez, of all people, and saying they had a stranger with them. How obvious. It was a pattern almost too easy to recognize. Did they have so little respect for him that they thought he would not see this pattern? A new element thrown into the middle of his carefully laid plans. Zapata clicked his tongue reproachfully. Would Leonardo fail to notice bird droppings fall on the *Mona Lisa*?

This had been a clumsy effort on the part of the government, he thought, a big blunt instrument. Yes, he had to admit it had almost worked. If Aguillar had not been there to delay the agent . . . Well, the fault was his, in the end. He had fallen into a pattern himself. He should never have allowed Aguillar to use Vanowen again. It had not been enough to cut off Ramirez. He should have removed Vanowen from his list for good.

Well, Zapata thought, slipping on a pair of sun-glasses against the rising sun, lesson learned.

He slipped out of the hotel and went for a jog.

5:59 A.M. PST
Downtown Los Angeles

Francis Aguillar. The name bounced around in Jack's head obsessively. Francis Aguillar. Not Jorge Rafael Marquez? Maybe it was a mistake, or an alias for Zapata. No, not an alias, Jack thought. Aguillar was a known associate of Zapata's who had vanished years earlier. Zapata would never take the alias of an associate.

I got the wrong man, Jack thought. *Jesus, I got the wrong man, and now I'm stuck in here.*

Jack felt the claustrophobic sense he'd experienced in jail when he'd learned that the warden, the cor-rections officer, and Chappelle had all been disabled. The walls that had seemed so unreal suddenly seemed concrete and dangerous. Now, in the backseat of the cruiser, which a moment ago had seemed such a tem-porary thing, he felt hemmed in, trapped.

He was in the middle of that thought when Peter Jiminez rammed the Crown Victoria.

1 2 3 4 5 6 7 8 9
10 **11** 12 13 14 15 16 17
18 19 20 21 22 23 24

· ·

**THE FOLLOWING TAKES PLACE
BETWEEN THE HOURS OF
6 A.M. AND 7 A.M.
PACIFIC STANDARD TIME**

· ·

6:00 A.M. PST
Downtown Los Angeles

Peter's car hit the unmarked police cruiser on the driver's side trunk, spinning it around in the middle of Flower Street, which was still empty at this hour. The force of the crash hurled Jack against the window, where he hit his head with a thud. By the time his vision cleared, someone was opening the driver's door, and Jack had a blurry vision of someone blasting Pascal in the face with pepper spray. The noxious gas only seemed to make the big man angry. He struggled to get himself out of his seat when the assailant punched him in the jaw.

Jack's vision had cleared now, although the scene felt unreal. He saw Peter Jiminez handcuff the marshal's hands to the steering wheel, then rip out the car's radio.

A moment later the back door flew open and Peter was pulling him out, holding up a handcuff key. A moment later his cuffs were off.

Jack didn't bother asking Peter where he'd come from. It didn't matter. He was free, and he still had a job to do. "I need your car," Jack said. "There are police about three blocks from here. We have to clear this scene."

"I'm going with you," Jiminez said.

"Okay," Jack said, and chopped Peter across the jaw with an elbow. Jiminez sagged like a puppet whose strings had been cut. Jack took the handcuffs and locked Peter to the door of the Crown Victoria, took Peter's Para Ordinance .45 and his magazines, his car keys, and his telephone, and jumped into his car.

6:03 A.M. PST
Chatsworth

It turned out Baden was an unmarked street that led up into the rocky hills. This was an alien world, a forest of boulders jutting up from the chaparral. One boulder—Stony Point—was so huge and steep that mountain climbers came up here to practice on weekends. The whole area looked like a movie set dropped into the area by Hollywood producers.

Nina followed it through small winding canyons until she came to a few lonely houses inhabited by recluses seeking the solitude of the wilderness with all the comforts of city life. This was an ideal location—it felt like a whole different state, while being only an hour and a half from downtown.

The house was built ranch-style, one low, single-story building that would be easier to cool in the summer heat. The building was set back from the street, but there were few trees and no shrubbery. The lawn was brown with a few green sprouts fighting to stay alive. This morning's *L.A. Times* lay on the walkway wrapped in blue plastic. They always wrapped the paper in plastic these days, even if it wasn't going to rain.

Nina, her attitude not changed the least since her visit to Marcia Tintfass, pounded on the door. There was no answer. She pounded again. "Federal agent!" she yelled. "I know you're there. You answered Marcia's phone call!"

She didn't know what kind of reaction that would get, but she didn't like being ignored.

The door opened, and a young, well-built man of Japanese descent answered. "Yes?"

Nina showed him her badge. "Agent Nina Myers."

The man frowned, looked behind him uncertainly for a moment, then sighed and said, "That's the second CTU badge I've seen in one day You guys are fucking unbelievable." He reached into his pocket, intoning "ID" when Nina tensed. He pulled out a small wallet of his own and showed her the badge inside.

"Special Agent Jason Fujimora, FBI," Nina read. "Can I come in?"

"Why not," the FBI agent said in disgust. "You're clearly going to blow this whether we help you or not."

Fujimora stepped aside and Nina walked in. There was another man, undoubtedly FBI, sitting on the couch in the living room. And, just stumbling out of his bedroom, sleepily tying his robe around his waist, was Adrian Tintfass.

6:14 A.M. PST
CTU Headquarters, Los Angeles

CTU Headquarters was full of bleary-eyed agents and analysts when Tony walked in. His own eyes stung. It had been a long night with a weird ending. Tony had called ahead to make sure Henderson would still be around. Now he staggered into Henderson's office and sat down heavily in the visitor's chair.

Henderson looked like Tony felt. There were bags under his eyes, which were themselves bloodshot, and his skin was pale.

"Seriously?" Henderson said as though they'd already been talking for several minutes. "He was there?"

"Standing right there, close enough to touch. And of course I was undercover and couldn't do a damned thing—"

"I get it, I get it," Henderson said. "Any idea at all what he was up to?"

"First," Tony said, "I have to ask, Chris. Was Jack undercover? Working on some case that none of us knew about? I won't be pissed. I've been on tight operations, too."

Chris met his gaze steadily. "No way, Tony. Nothing I knew about, and if I don't know about it, my operators aren't doing it."

"Okay, then, if that's true, here's my idea." Tony related his theory: Jack had set up Tintfass for a legal fall so he could take over his business. When that didn't work, he'd killed him. "You and Jack were friends," Tony ended, "so I don't expect you to believe it."

He was surprised to hear Henderson say, "I hate to admit it, but it's not all that far-fetched." He saw Tony's astonishment. "Look, I'm not an idiot. Bauer never plays by the rules. His home life's a mess. He's just the kind of guy to look for an out. Maybe this Tintfass was it."

Tony shrugged. "Well, I can't wait to ask him. I heard they picked him up."

Henderson sighed. "Old news. The new news is that he got away. Some kind of traffic accident. Peter Jiminez was there. Apparently Jack beat him up and took his car."

Nina paced the width of the living room as she mulled over the story Fujimora had told her. "So why wasn't the wife put into witness protection, too?"

The other FBI man, Holmquist, answered. "She will be, but we couldn't come up with a plausible scenario where Bauer killed them both. It's not his style. So the plan is—was, at least—to put him in hiding while she played the weeping widow. Then when the spotlights were off, we'd put them into their new identities."

"Best vacation I ever had," Tintfass commented.

"How many people are in on this operation?" Nina asked. She was surprised Henderson wasn't aware of it.

"I don't think you can even count us," Fujimora said. "This is as much of it as we've got. Tintfass had to go into witness protection anyway. CTU was looking to set up one of its own agents for an undercover job inside the jail. What the mission is, I have no idea."

"Why were you going into witness protection anyway?" Nina wondered. "What was the story?"

Tintfass shrugged and tucked in his bathrobe. "Truth is, it wasn't my idea. A couple months ago I was looking to score off a weapons deal. I'd got my hands on some equipment from a guy I know out of Camp Pendleton. I made a connection with a guy, I don't know much about him. I was supposed to meet his number two, I guess, but I got lost, walked in the wrong door or something, and I think I saw the guy your people want."

Nina saw the rest. "Our people got ahold of the news somehow and caught up with you. They flipped you. Jack Bauer shooting you was the setup that put him in jail so he could hook up with someone."

6:25 A.M. PST
CTU Headquarters, Los Angeles

Peter Jiminez walked tenderly as he returned to CTU. His whole body ached from the impact of his intentional crash, but that was nothing compared to the throbbing in his jaw. He'd never been put to sleep by a punch like that.

Henderson met him practically at the entrance, his voice low but full of frustration. Peter headed off his initial outburst. "I know, sir, I'm sorry. I got him, but I didn't expect—"

"I told you to be ready for anything with Bauer!" Henderson hissed. "You should have taken control of the situation sooner." Jiminez didn't have enough energy to argue. He let Henderson stare him down for a moment. The Operations Director held his anger for a minute, then released it in disgust. "Hell, at least the police don't have him anymore. That's something." He jabbed Jiminez in the chest. "But next time you stay on him and you take care of him no matter what he does."

6:28 A.M. PST
CTU Headquarters, Los Angeles

Tony sat with Jamey Farrell and Seth in the conference room, with Nina patched in on the telephone.

"Unbelievable," Tony said.

"Jack didn't kill anyone." Jamey almost laughed.

Nina piped in. "What I want to know is who knows? Someone's running this operation without telling us. I can handle being treated like a mushroom, but who's watching Jack's back?"

Henderson walked in then. "What's all this about?"

"I want you to tell me," Tony said. "Apparently jailing Jack was a setup. He set himself up to go to jail so he could meet someone on the inside. Is this jailbreak some part of the plan?"

Henderson looked stunned. "What? What are you talking about?"

"You didn't set up this operation?" Nina asked over the line.

Henderson looked at the phone as though it could answer his questions. "What operation?"

"Is the jailbreak part of it?" Tony asked again.

"What the f—!?" Henderson started to swear in frustration. "Stop asking me questions because I have no idea what you're talking about. What operation is Jack on?"

Tony saw that they'd get nowhere asking Henderson anything. "Okay, if none of us know, we need to figure it out. Let's go on the assumption that the prison break was part of the plan, either the original plan or something Jack worked up at the last minute."

"So nothing's an accident," Nina said, following his logic.

"Yes, including the guy he broke out with. Let's get everything we can on him."

6:31 A.M. PST
Mid-Wilshire Area, Los Angeles

He was twenty-one years old, driving on Interstate 5 through the huge San Joaquin Valley between Los Angeles to the Bay Area. He'd left Medved behind two years earlier with more money than he'd ever need, but no sense yet of how to achieve his goals. The world was indeed a puzzle, and he was convinced that it must be broken in order to be rebuilt. But the means had escaped him, even him, brilliant as he was, until now.

The truth was, he had not considered violence until that moment—until the moment word came that his family had been shot in Chiapas while protesting the neglect of the government. He had spent his time in the gang, but that was an alliance born of necessity. He hadn't reveled in those violent acts the way the others did. Still, violence was a tool and, like any tool, in the proper hands it could work.

Rafael was speeding up a lonely stretch of the interstate near the Buttonwillow/McKittrick exit when he committed himself to violent acts. And having

done so, his mind leaped immediately to the conse-
quences, the actions and investigations of the police,
their means and patterns of tracking and trapping
him. Every life, as complicated as it might seem to
the person living it, was a pattern, a set of actions
evolving out of the past and moving into the future
along predictable lines, with predictable connections,
just like the cube. If he was going to remain beyond
their reach, he would have to break those patterns.
Now.

Rafael stopped the car, right there on that empty
stretch of road. He left the keys in the ignition, his
cell phone on the seat, and his wallet in the glove
compartment. Wearing only the clothes on his back,
he walked up into the hills, and Jorge Rafael Mar-
quez was never seen again.

Zapata ended his jog in the Larchmont area, a fortress of affluence just west of downtown, besieged on
all sides by the lower classes. On the way, Zapata had
dropped his Ossipon identification, credit cards, and
cell phone in various trash bins. He was now naked
before the informational world, but he'd been there
before, and it did not bother him. Besides, he had
other contacts and different associates. Zapata cooled
down from his jog by walking. When he came to a
pay phone outside a 7–Eleven, he stopped.

"Emil Ramirez," Jamey Farrell read aloud. "Arrested on Federal charges of embezzlement and murder. What would Jack want with him?"

Tony studied the data sheet on Ramirez. "Alliance," he muttered, reading a list of known business contacts for Ramirez. The shootout at U-Pack came back to him. "There was a truck with the word *Alliance* on the side. What was the name of the guy?"

"Vanowen," Seth said. "He's the other corpse in the hotel room. He's not going to be answering any questions."

Tony snapped at him. "Follow the connections. Jack hooks up with this Ramirez and busts him out of jail. Jack turns up with Ramirez at an arms trade with Vanowen. I doubt it's a coincidence. Jack was climbing the ladder. Ramirez to Vanowen. Vanowen to . . . who?"

"Whoever shot him, you can get on that," said Nina, now back in the office.

Chris Henderson had sat at the table, practically sulking. Finally he said, "Why don't we have more information on these guys?"

"I don't know," Jamey said.

"Right. So how was Jack conducting some kind of operation without any intel at all? It seems like we're filling in huge blanks with big assumptions about Jack."

Nina said, "You still think Jack has just gone to the dark side? He didn't kill Tintfass!"

Henderson shrugged. "Tony's theory. I just think it might be possible. You and I both know that Jack has always had one foot on the dark side anyway."

Nina fixed her eyes, catlike, on the Director of Operations. "You're pretty quick to go to the worst-case scenario on this. Is it something personal?"

Henderson's ears turned pink. "What do you mean, personal?"

"I just wonder if the rumors are true. Jack dropped your name to Internal Affairs over some misappropriation—"

"Go to hell!" Henderson exploded, slapping his open palm on the table. He was halfway out of his seat as though he was going to lunge at her. "I don't give a damn about any rumors. I'm doing my job with a clear head. You're the one who's thinking of Jack as a goddamned hero without a shred of evidence."

He looked at the others, challenging them one by one. No one said anything about the rumors. But after a pause, Tony said, "I'm not willing to assume Jack's just turned rogue. There's a reason for all this. So, assuming you don't mind that we continue, I'm going to find it."

6:42 A.M. PST
UCLA Medical Center

It does not take much to make a disguise. Thick-rimmed glasses, so the eyes focus on the glasses rather than the face. A hat, but not pulled down to hide the eyes, just sitting atop the head to change its shape and hide the hair. Celebrities whose faces appeared daily on televison and in tabloids got away with it. Jack Bauer, whose name was known to few and whose face had not been broadcast by the news during the escape, certainly managed it.

He abandoned Peter's car in a public parking structure in Westwood and walked a mile to the medical center. He strode right through the lobby, past the security guard, and up to the information desk.

"Ryan Chappelle, please? He was admitted last night."

"Five-thirty-four," said the plump Asian nurse at the desk. "But you'll need to check in before seeing him. Visits are restricted."

Jack nodded and went to the elevators. A short ride brought him to the fifth floor, where the elevator doors opened onto a circular desk and a sleepy attendant. "Morning," he said, smiling as she yawned.

"Ah, morning, sorry," she replied.

"I'd like to visit room 534," he said innocently. "They told me I had to check in?"

"With the guard." The nurse nodded, pointing down the hall.

Jack was happy to see that 534 was out of view. He walked down the corridor, turned a corner, and then went straight up to the uniformed guard sitting by room 534. The man was sleepy, but the purposefulness of Jack's stride brought him to attention and he stood up, grabbing a clipboard.

"Help you?" he asked.

Jack nodded. "I hope so, they told me I had to see you."

He glanced at the clipboard, which made the guard look down, too. Jack popped him in the throat with the webbing between his thumb and index finger, gagging him. Then he kneed the man in the groin, doubling him over. Jack wrapped an arm around the guard's throat and squeezed until he went limp. Jack glanced down the hall. No one came. No one had heard.

He pulled the unconscious guard into the room and used his own cuffs to shackle the man to the sink in the bathroom, then closed the door.

Ryan Chappelle looked like a naked mole rat on life support. His skin was pale in the fluorescent hospital light, and he seemed smaller than usual lying in the railed bed. "You picked a goddamned terrible time to get sick," Jack muttered.

Jack wasn't sure of his next move. His knowledge of medicine was rudimentary, and if the medical team here couldn't bring Chappelle out of his coma, he couldn't imagine how he could do it. But then the medical team wasn't as desperate as he was, and in his experience desperation counted for something.

A doctor walked into the room, a woman with a tired, heavy look on her face. "Oh," she said in surprise. "Have you seen the guard?"

"He's around," Jack said, glancing at her name tag. "Are you his doctor?"

"Czikowlis." She nodded. "Who are you?"

"I work with him," Jack said evasively. "And I need him to wake up right now."

The doctor smirked. "Yes, that would be nice. I wish that worked on all our patients."

"It has to work on this one," Jack insisted. "What's wrong with him?"

"Coma," Dr. Czikowlis responded. Maybe it was her long night, but she took an instant dislike to this visitor, coming so early in the morning and asking so many insistent questions. "It came on suddenly. I'd . . . you work with him?"

Jack read her tone and guessed that she had some vague awareness that Chappelle worked for the government. He played on it. "Yes, ma'am. I hope you understand that I can't show you any kind of ID. But we work in the same unit." He lent a vague, clandestine-sounding mystery to his words.

Dr. Czikowlis nodded. "I guess. To be honest, I'm not sure what to do. Apparently it came on suddenly. It's got all the indications of a barbiturate overdose, but the tests came back negative."

Overdose. That sounded right. Jack could not believe it had been a coincidence that Chappelle and Cox and the warden had all gone down at the same time. Someone had taken them down.

"If it were an overdose, how would you treat it?"

"Well, the simplest way would be to lower the level of barbiturate. You can do that with a gastric lavage and time."

Jack shook his head. "I don't have time. What if it were an emergency?"

The doctor looked at him as though he were an idiot. "It's not an emergency. He's on life support, he's stable."

Jack had no more time for subtlety. He pulled Peter's gun from under his shirt and said, "Imagine it's an emergency because I'm pointing a gun at you, Doctor. Now what would you do?"

Dr. Czikowlis gasped and looked around as though the security guard might suddenly appear.

"Stay calm," Jack said soothingly. "I don't want to hurt you or him. I just need to ask him a question. I think someone poisoned him. Get him awake. Now."

Dr. Czikowlis hesitated. She was not particularly heroic, but she was responsible for this patient, and she did not like demands being made on her. Still, her mind went instantly to the treatment. Massive amphetamine injection. Prep nitropresside to prevent cardiac arrest. She might be able to wake him up without causing much damage to him.

"Now," he repeated, a little more threateningly.

The doctor weighed the risk versus the reward and then went to the cabinet.

1 2 3 4 5 6 7 8 9
10 11 **12** 13 14 15 16 17
18 19 20 21 22 23 24

· ·

THE FOLLOWING TAKES PLACE
BETWEEN THE HOURS OF
7 A.M. AND 8 A.M.
PACIFIC STANDARD TIME

· ·

7:00 A.M. PST
Marriott Hotel, Downtown Los Angeles

The phone rang shrilly, jolting Mark Kendall out of his sleep. He sat up, his huge heart pounding in his chest. He looked around, befuddled by the confusion of deep sleep. His sense of himself and his place came back to him as the phone continued incessantly. *Hotel. Saturday. Fight day.*

"Hello?" he said in a rough morning voice.

"Hey." That soft voice, that understanding voice. He loved that voice.

"Hiya, babe," he said, rubbing his eyes. "How are you ladies doing?" His eyes focused and he checked the clock. It'd be about ten in the morning back home.

"Oh, you know," she said breezily, "up all night at the clubs, breakfast at the Waffle House, then appointments at the hair salon. It's a full life."

He laughed. She always made him laugh. But then he heard crying in the background, crying that pierced him and dug into his gut. "How's she doing?"

"The same," his wife said, suddenly weary. "She can't stop crying, poor thing. I took her back to Dr. Krasnoff, but he says we can't use any more pain medication. We might have to put her back in the hospital."

Mark grumbled, "They don't help her there, either."

He heard his baby wail even louder in the background, as his wife said, "She needs that operation."

"I know. She'll get it," he vowed.

"Markie, I just wanted to call and say I hope you know, you're my, my champion, either way. I hope you know that."

He smiled, big and boyish in that way only she could make him feel. "I love you. And I'm going to get her what she needs. I promise."

"I'm going to watch tonight."

"You are?" She had never come to his fights, never even watched them on pay-per-view.

"It's your big comeback. I figured it's time I worked up the guts. You're going to do great."

He looked at the envelope the bald little man had given him. He hadn't opened it. But he hadn't thrown it away, either.

"Like I said, I promise. I'm getting her what she needs. No matter what."

7:16 A.M. PST
UCLA Medical Center

Before Dr. Czikowlis could slide the syringe out of the IV shunt, Ryan Chappelle's chest heaved and his heart rate soared, turning the monitors into panic buttons. His eyes popped open and he gasped like a man coming up for air.

"Jesus, it worked," the doctor said. "You know what this means?"

"Yeah, I can talk to him," Jack said.

"It doesn't make sense. The tests came back negative. No barbiturates in his system. This shouldn't work."

Jack leaned over Chapelle, but said to the doctor, "Someone poisoned him. That same person could have switched the test results. Chappelle!" He tapped Chappelle's thin, pale cheek. "Chappelle, it's Bauer!"

Chappelle turned toward Jack, but his eyes were unfixed. "Chappelle!" Jack called out again.

"Bauer," Chappelle whispered, his voice barely audible. "Should be . . . jail."

"Yeah, I know. I need help. I need you. I need your Zapata resource!"

Chappelle breathed a long but shallow, rattling breath.

"Your Zapata resource. I need her now."

Chappelle blinked several times before saying breathlessly, "Gerwehr. Talia Ger . . . wehr . . . RAND."

"Gerwehr," Jack said, his shoulders releasing enormous amounts of tension. "Thanks. Thanks, Chappelle."

7:24 A.M. PST
Beverly Wilshire Hotel

Martin Webb woke up without the alarm, but feeling heavy. Old men didn't sleep, but they needed to. It was after ten o'clock on the East Coast. That's what he got for staying up till all hours watching sports on television. He sat up and put his feet down, slowly turning his feet in circles the way his physical therapist had told him to, trying to get the circulation going in his feet. His steel-trap mind recalled clearly training camp from his college football days, but to his feet they were a distant memory.

Martin put his glasses on and checked the clock. "Oh, damn it, old man," he said aloud, "all you've got left is your brain and it's turning to mush. That call is right now."

Martin dialed the front desk and had them put a call through to the Secretary of the Treasury at his home.

"Lou, it's Marty. Is now still good?"

Across the country, Lou Friedman sat in the leisure

chair in his den, but he was anything but leisurely. As Treasury Secretary, he was ostensibly responsible for the country's coffers, and those coffers were dangerously low, while the debt to other nations was alarmingly high.

"No time like the present," he replied glibly. He'd known Marty Webb since college. A good man, maybe the best man to lead them out of this mess. "So what do you think of the President's stimulus package?"

"Malarkey," Webb said. "More like a favor to big business than a goose to the economy. I'd rather see more effort put into lowering the value of the dollar overseas."

He and Marty had gone through this debate before. "You know that's going to mean less revenue for businessmen here."

"It'll mean more volume," Webb replied, as weary of the debate on his side as Friedman was. "We're not talking about benefiting a few of your political friends. We're talking about real stimulus. More volume means more revenue overall, including shipping, packaging, lower prices for imported goods."

Friedman sighed. "Marty. You and I both know that a word from you is going to do more to relax Wall Street and the consumers than anything else. The plan isn't all that important. Your endorsement is everything. "

Webb caught the whiff of politics. It was unavoidable, of course. But Martin had become the Fed Chairman because he saw it as a way to serve the public good without prostituting himself too badly.

Of course, his distaste for politics didn't mean he was politically inept. He knew that Lou was giving him an opening.

"I know the papers will print what I say," he said coyly.

Lou chuckled. "I was hoping you'd go on the Sunday shows. We could get you on *Meet the Press*, anything else you were willing to do."

"And say what?" Webb asked, getting to the point.

"And say you think the President's stimulus package will be just the thing to return us to the robust economy we all expect, especially the tax incentives . . ."

"Hmm."

". . . and the devaluation of the dollar to stimulate overseas trade."

Martin hesitated, letting thin white noise fill the void between them. This price was a bit higher than he wanted to pay, but he wasn't sure the country could wait much longer. The economy needed a plan and, more importantly, it needed the confidence of the citizenry to keep the consumer engines churning. And Martin Webb knew, without ego, that his word would go a long way toward bolstering that confidence.

"The devaluation process first, Lou," he said finally.

Lou let out an audible sigh of relief. "Deal. You're going to save us, Marty. I know it."

7:39 A.M. PST
West Los Angeles

Jack jogged back to the parking lot where he'd dumped Peter's car. His feet hurt—he'd been on the run for hours. The sun was fully up now, which re-invigorated him a little, but he hadn't been this exhausted in quite some time. He was going to steal his third car since breaking out of jail; he was getting good at it. This one was a green Chrysler Sebring. He chose it from the monthly parking area, hot-wired it, and drove it out, paying the full days' fare because he didn't have the ticket.

Talia Gerwehr's address was listed and not far away. He headed for Beverly Glen.

7:46 A.M. PST
Larchmont Area

Zapata sat at a small, circular café table outside the Starbucks on Larchmont Avenue, nursing a caramel machiatto. He had a decadent habit of patronizing Starbucks. He pretended to himself that he was getting to know his enemy, but the truth was, he simply enjoyed it. He doubted it would survive his vision of anarchy, and he wanted to savor the elegant process that created elegant coffee on an assembly line before it disappeared for good.

And of course he liked to watch the people. At this moment in time, this Starbucks was the center of a ripple reaching out, touching all their lives. Coffee or not, he would have loved to have blown up that coffee shop, just to watch the disruption in the pattern of their existence.

He gave some thought to his larger plan. The ability of the Federal authorities to get so close was still disturbing, but he could see the reasons clearly, and that comforted him because it meant he could fix the problem.

Losing Aguillar was a setback, but a minor one. The real question was whether his goal could still be accomplished. After due consideration, he did not see why it could not succeed. The authorities could know nothing. Vanowen knew nothing of his real plan, and Ramirez knew less than nothing. Aguillar's knowledge had died with him. Besides, his plan had already been set in motion. There was no reason to stop it, even if Zapata wanted to leave town.

But he was not ready to leave. He wanted to see the ripples.

As he finished the last sip of coffee, a gold Lexus pulled up to a metered space near the Starbucks. A blond man got out and began searching. Casually, Zapata stood and walked over to him, holding out a latte he had been saving. "Kyle," he said.

The blond man looked at him uncertainly at first, then recognized him. "That's a good look on you," he said with a laugh.

"So I've been told. Do you mind if I spend the day at your house?"

They got in the Lexus and Kyle said, "As long as you promise me the kind of chaos I can profit from, you can stay there all week."

. . . .

**THE FOLLOWING TAKES PLACE
BETWEEN THE HOURS OF
8 A.M. AND 9 A.M.
PACIFIC STANDARD TIME**

. . . .

8:00 A.M. PST
UCLA Medical Center

Nina reached the elevator at the same time as a John Wayne look-alike. "Ma'am," he said, motioning her to enter first. She did and then turned, watching his enormous shoulders fill the elevator doors, which closed behind him. She checked the elevator's weight capacity.

He grinned. "They grow 'em big down in the Gulf. But I just think light and the elevator does the rest."

He reached for the fifth floor button and saw that she'd already pushed it. He smiled at her again, but this time his look showed that he was assessing her.

Finally, he stuck out his beefy hand. "Dan Pascal, U.S. Marshal." With his left hand he brushed back his brown jacket, showing the badge now attached to his belt.

"Nina Myers, Counter Terrorist Unit," she replied. "I guess we're headed the same way."

Pascal chuckled. The sound was a low rumble in his chest. "Truth to tell, ma'am, I don't know which way I'm headed, your boy's got me turned around every which way."

"He does that to everybody."

The elevator opened on the fifth floor and they walked together to Ryan Chappelle's room. Several uniforms were already there, including the one who'd been handcuffed to the sink. There was also a woman in a doctor's coat—Nina had been told her name was "Chick-ow-liss" but you wouldn't have known it by looking at her name tag. And there was Chappelle, lying unconscious on the hospital bed. Nina decided that he looked more lifelike than she'd ever seen him.

Nina let the U.S. Marshal introduce himself. He had a down-home quality that put people at ease, and he clearly used it to his advantage.

"I know you've already given your statement to these fellas," Pascal said, "but could you run through it again, just 'cause I'm slow."

Dr. Czikowlis looked bent, but not broken, as she told her story. The fact of having a gun pointed at her had clearly unnerved her, but there was no fear in her voice when she described Jack himself. She seemed to regard him with a certain amount of respect for having done what he'd done. Nina thought begrudgingly, *He does that to everybody, too.*

Aloud, she said, "So Chappelle was awake?"

Dr. Czikowlis nodded. "He'll wake up again. Now he's just asleep, unconscious. Not a coma, though. That man was right. He was a victim of barbiturate poisoning. But the test came back negative, so—"

"There was a mistake on the tests?" Nina asked.

Pascal shifted back onto his heels, clearly content to let her take the lead and ask the aggressive questions.

"Well, they were wrong. The man with the gun said he thought the test had been switched, but I don't know anything about that."

"Tell me again what Mr. Chappelle said when he was awake."

"He wasn't awake for long. The man asked him about his Zapata resource. He seemed really desperate to get it."

Nina's eyes flickered, the only outward sign of her complete inward shock. "What was that he asked again?" she said casually.

"Zapata," Czikowlis replied certainly. "He said 'Zapata resource.' Mr. Chappelle whispered a name, and then he collapsed. The man with the gun locked me in the bathroom and left."

"What was the name Mr. Chappelle whispered?"

The doctor shook her head. "He was barely conscious. It was Taylor Gerber, Talia Gerber, something like that."

Nina nodded. "I see. Hard to hear. Is Mr. Chappelle going to recover?"

"Oh yes, now he will. He'll sleep for a few more hours, though."

Nina nodded again and walked out, aware that Pascal was following her.

"Ms. Myers, I'm hoping you're going to share the information you've got," he said over her shoulder.

Nina stopped at the elevators. "You just got all the information I did."

Pascal smiled a smile big as the delta. "The information she gave. But not the information in your head."

Nina hesitated. There was a lot she could tell Pascal, if she'd wanted to. Tintfass was alive. Jack was not a murderer. But she didn't know the whole story yet, and if there's one thing she did know, it was that you didn't show your cards until your hand was complete. She stepped into the elevator, but not far enough to let him on. "I wish I could help you, Marshal."

"Deputy Marshal," he corrected as the doors closed, "and I'll find out one way or the other."

8:13 A.M. PST
Beverly Glen

Beverly Glen was a small West L.A. neighborhood of pretty houses bordered by upscale Brentwood on the west and the 405 Freeway on the east, one of the few enclaves of affordable (by L.A. standards) housing on the West Side.

Jack parked the stolen Pathfinder on Church Street

and walked around the block to the street that paralleled Talia Gerwehr's east-west street, but one block north. He'd driven through the neighborhood twice already, looking for anything suspicious, but if the house was being watched, the watchers were good and he couldn't find them. To make their job harder, he walked to the house just north of the Gerwehr place, so that the two backyards abutted. Casually, Jack walked up the driveway to that house, then turned to the side gate and walked down the side yard. He passed several windows without looking in. He strode purposefully across the backyard—a small open space with a red oak hot tub that had been fashionable in the early eighties—reached the fence, and hopped over.

Talia Gerwehr's backyard was small and landscaped with curving lines of brick and recently laid sod, dominated by a grand old oak tree. The elegant yard communicated with the house through a set of richly varnished French doors. Jack saw movement within the house, guessed that whatever alarm there was had been turned off, and popped a hand through one of the French doors' glass frames. He reached in and had the door opened before the sound of tinkling glass faded.

Talia Gerwehr came around the corner with a cordless phone in her hand and a quizzical look on her face. When she saw the gun in Jack's hand, her look changed to shock.

At the same moment, her phone rang. "Hello?" she said, trying to take it all in at once. "Yes, this is Talia Gerwehr. What, um, what can I do for you, Marshal?" She looked at Jack Bauer, and then at the gun again, as she listened to the caller. "Um, no, I understand. I don't know why that would be. But everything's fine here. I was just leaving for my office, though, would you, would you rather send someone there? All right, fine." She hung up the phone and then said, "So you must be Jack Bauer."

8:27 A.M. PST
CTU Headquarters, Los Angeles

They were waiting for Nina when she rushed into the conference room, having broken innumerable traffic laws to get back to headquarters. Tony was there, and Henderson and a number of other field agents, along with half the analytical staff.

"Jiminez coming?" she asked quickly.

"Jiminez is in some hot water," Henderson explained. "It looks like he tried to free Jack from custody."

"That may have been a good thing," Nina replied.

Henderson shrugged. "We'll see. Go ahead."

"Okay, here's what we know," she summed up for all involved. "Jack didn't kill Tintfass. We know that because Tintfass is alive and being handled by the FBI. Jack broke out of jail with a guy named Emil Ramirez. We assume it wasn't a coincidence that they broke out together. Jack seemed to be following some kind of trail, which deadended when Ramirez and another business associate got shot, along with one Francis Aguillar. When that trail ends, Jack goes to Chappelle, pumps him full of uppers to kick him out of a coma, and asks about . . ." She paused to make sure they were all listening, "Zapata."

Murmurs rippled around the room, but it was Tony who spoke up. "Zapata? The anarchist? Is that who Jack's after?" His question was directed at Chris Henderson.

The Field Operations Director rubbed his hands in an act of ablution. "I've got no part in this. If I did, I'd be filling you all in right now."

"Well, Chappelle did, because he had some resource on Zapata. It looks like they were making a run for him."

Another murmur filled the room, and this time it contained an undercurrent of admiration. Every analyst and operator in the room had heard of Zapata. He was unique in the world of international terrorism because he was not, strictly speaking, a terrorist, at least not according to the most current definition. If he could be called a terrorist at all, Zapata was a throwback to the Weathermen and the Red Brigade of the seventies, not fighting for any particular cause or homeland, simply looking to destablize the status quo. But even the Red Brigade had wrapped themselves in the flag of socialism. Zapata was a pure anarchist: he endorsed no cause, he took no side.

"He isn't an Islamic fundamentalist. He's not a fascist or a communist," Nina was saying, rounding out a picture of Zapata for anyone who needed it. "We think he helped the Basques bomb a train station. But then he gave the Spanish government information that helped them arrest a couple of ETA members. He blew up polling places during the last Venezuelan elections, and that helped the new leftists there gain power. But then he bombed power stations of the leftist government in Venezuela.

"He's famous," she continued, "for having no patterns. Impossible to trace. Makes lots of associates and then drops them. They say he spent a year helping the Chechens fight the Russians, but just because it helped destabilize the Russian government. Then all of a sudden he stopped. We think it was because he realized the Chechnya crisis was actually helping the Kremlin solidify power. If it's true, he saw that coming a year before anyone else did."

"Which brings us to the last thing," Tony Almeida said, taking over for Nina at her signal. While she'd raced over, he'd gathered more information on Zapata. "We should all start with the idea that Zapata is a genius. He started out life as Jorge Rafael Marquez."

Seth Ludonowski, who'd been slumped in his seat, sat up with a start. "Oh shit," he gasped.

8:34 A.M. PST
Talia Gerwehr's House

Jack sat in one of Talia's living room chairs and drank the coffee she made for him, but he didn't let himself relax. According to Talia, the Marshal had said he'd contact her later, at her office, but he wouldn't put it past them to send units to her house anyway. The Marshal running the manhunt was clearly squared away, since he'd pounced on the arms trade so quickly.

"Chappelle told me about you, but I didn't know what to expect," she said.

Jack laughed. "You're not exactly seeing me at my best." Sitting in her clean house, drinking coffee, he was now painfully aware that he stank of dirt and sweat and the sulfur smell of firearms. He hadn't even managed his shower the night before, when all this had started.

Talia Gerwehr, on the other hand, was immaculate. If she worked at a think tank, Jack knew what thoughts the men there were thinking. She was in her mid-thirties, with flawless olive skin and smooth dark hair swept away from her face. Her appearance was very much like the appearance of her yard and her house: plainly but elegantly designed, simple but rich.

"I saw the news. They didn't give your name, but they gave Ramirez's, so I assumed—well, I assumed it was all part of the plan."

Jack sipped his coffee. As the hot liquid went down, he realized how empty his stomach was. "It is now. I had to get out quickly, and everyone who knew why I was in was out of action. It was either you or the FBI guys who had Tintfass, but I figured you'd be easier to get to."

Talia nodded. "I'm just glad Chappelle told me

about you. He didn't give much more information."

"This operation has a tight lid," Jack agreed, "which is making all kinds of trouble."

"The truth is, that was my idea, not Chappelle's. You're not going to catch Zapata any other way."

"I'll manage," he said.

Talia Gerwehr studied him for a moment. She found herself instantly fascinated by Jack Bauer, suddenly standing there in her house, strong and certain and utterly physical. He was action to her thought. If she was the electrical pulse firing between synapses, he was the muscle that flexed.

Because Talia Gerwehr, despite her good looks, was a creature of the mind. A member of Mensa, captain of the debate team, wannabe poet with a few scribblings in the *Hudson Review* and the *Atlantic Monthly*, she had a Ph.D. in mathematics from MIT, where she had published extensively on chaos theory. She'd assumed she'd gain tenure at some university somewhere, but a trick of fate introduced her to the RAND Corporation, a think tank in Santa Monica, California. Soon after that, she'd begun to learn about a particular terrorist—anarchist, really—called Zapata, and she had made him the focus of her studies.

8:36 A.M. PST
CTU Headquarters, Los Angeles

"No, no," Seth Ludonowski repeated. "I don't know anything about Zapata. I don't even know what an anarchist is. But I sure as hell have heard of Jorge Rafael Marquez. Every computer geek this side of 1995 knows him."

Tony scanned through his Zapata notes. "He made a fortune in computers."

"He raked in huge dollars!" Seth said admiringly. "And he deserved it. He wrote algorithms that were pure genius. Half the systems we run in here use software built on his ideas. I had no idea that Jorge Rafael Marquez had become a terrorist."

8:38 A.M. PST
Talia Gerwehr's House

"Of course," Talia continued, "knowing his original name means nothing. Sometime in the late 1990s he managed to disappear, and I mean completely. The fortune in his bank accounts vanished. They found his car and identification on the side of the road in Central California. No one has ever heard from Marquez again."

"How do we know it's the same person?" Jack asked.

"Truth is, we don't," she admitted. "But again, it doesn't matter. The Marquez identity is a dead end anyway."

8:39 A.M. PST
CTU Headquarters, Los Angeles

Tony continued, "No one's come close to catching him. He never follows any patterns, and he isn't attached to any cause. Totally unpredictable. Conventional wisdom says that the usual policing techniques won't work."

8:40 A.M. PST
Talia Gerwehr's House

". . . so they recruited you to apply chaos theory to tracking him," Jack finished for her. "It's an interesting idea. And it almost worked. I was one room away, but he escaped."

"He's smart," Talia said. "Maybe one of the most brilliant minds on the planet, at least in his field. If his computer work is any indication—and pretty much it's all we have—he has an incredible aptitude for deduction; he takes small bits of data and extrapolates them, reaching fairly huge conclusions that are usually right. At least, we assume they're right because he keeps succeeding in his plots, and no one catches him. That's what his computer programs did, you know. He wrote them for Internet search engines. You type in one or two words and, based on those hints, the search engines find what you need. The same technique feeds right into voice recognition systems, deep space exploration satellites, and pretty much, if we ever develop real artificial intelligence, some of his work is going to be at the foundation of it."

"You sound like you like him," Jack said. "He blows people up."

Talia had clearly heard this criticism before. "My job has been to get to know him. There's no sense letting my ethics get in the way of that, because he doesn't. I don't approve of him at all. But if you ignore his intelligence, you'll never catch him."

"So where does chaos theory come in?" Jack asked.

Talia smiled, and her skin actually seemed to glow. "Ah, now that's the interesting part. The working theory on Zapata is that he uses his ability to recognize patterns in order to avoid them himself. If there are no patterns, any leads you get don't matter, because there's no path to follow. It's all random."

"Anarchy," Jack said. "Chaos."

Talia held up her finger. "That's just it. There's no such thing as chaos."

It occurred to Jack that Talia Gerwehr had never stood in the middle of a rioting mob, but he let it slide. She continued. "Anarchy is not chaos. Anarchy literally means 'without leaders.' That's definitely what Zapata is after. He seems intent on breaking down structures, all structures of any kind. But chaos, well, chaos doesn't exist."

"So what's chaos theory?"

"A cool-sounding name for exactly its opposite," Talia said. "To make a long story short, chaos theory says that events that seem chaotic are really the result of a huge series of small events that, happening one after another, make the outcome seem like chaos. The popular example is this: a butterfly flaps its wings in Beijing and you get a storm in Los Angeles. The butterfly makes a tiny puff of air, which contributes to another tiny event, et cetera, et cetera, and then you have a big event."

Jack may not have been a Mensa member, but he could follow this. "You're suggesting that there's a pattern somewhere in Zapata."

"Somewhere," she agreed. "It's just too complex for us to find it yet. Nature does not abide chaos, Agent Bauer. All things fall into some sense of order. Frankly, he does have one obvious pattern: he follows no patterns."

Jack said, "Well, I've got one lead to follow, whether it fits into your theory or not. I need you to help me get information on a gang tattoo. Zapata's guy had one, and it's the second one that I've seen since last night. Can you access confidential records?"

Talia said, "Yeah, but not here. My office computer can."

"Let's go."

8:55 A.M. PST
CTU Headquarters, Los Angeles

Henderson, for some reason, was the lone holdout in the room, and since he was Director of Field Operations, his opinion held sway. "I get all this interest in

Zapata," he was saying. "But there's still no direct evidence that this Ramirez was involved with him. None of the victims at the Biltmore have any connections to him. For all we know, it was an arms deal gone bad, and that's that."

"Then why would Jack go to the hospital to get information from Chappelle?" Nina replied, her neck turning red.

Tony agreed. "We need to put the word out that Jack isn't a suspect. He didn't kill anyone, so there's no crime. We need to reel him in so we can help him."

"Absolutely not!" rasped a thin, wraithlike voice.

They all turned to see Ryan Chappelle standing in the doorway looking like a harbinger of death. He slumped against the wall weakly, but his eyes stared defiantly out of his bloodless face. "No one contacts Bauer. No one!"

· ·

**THE FOLLOWING TAKES PLACE
BETWEEN THE HOURS OF
9 A.M. AND 10 A.M.
PACIFIC STANDARD TIME**

· ·

9:00 A.M. PST
CTU Headquarters, Los Angeles

Chappelle limped forward, and someone vacated a seat so he could sit. It was a measure of his popularity that, although they would move out of his way, no one offered to help him sit down. He slumped back in the chair, gasping for breath. He did not speak.

Finally Tony couldn't wait any longer. "Chappelle, we have to get him in. The police are hunting him. He's got no resources. He's—"

Chappelle nodded. "Right. That's it. That's what we need."

"What? What are you talking about?" Surprised questions popped up from several agents.

Chappelle gathered his breath again and they waited like so many impatient children attending an old man. "He needs to be . . . outside the system. It's the only way we'll catch Zapata. If we work with the usual methods, we'll get made. It's happened every time."

"It happened this time, too," Henderson pointed out.

Chappelle managed a weak smile. "Close. Arm's reach, what I heard."

Henderson was caving at last, but he looked unhappy about it. "I still don't get it. You hate Bauer. Why were the two of you running this and not any of us?"

Chappelle's chest jumped up and down slightly. He was laughing, but didn't have enough breath to make noise. Finally the tremors subsided. "Hate Bauer. Yes. Goddamned loose cannon. Doesn't follow orders. Rules. Right guy for this job."

And they all saw the logic of it without further explanation. If Zapata was a genius for seeing patterns and predicting the actions of his opponents, who better to send after him than Jack Bauer, who infuriated his superiors with his habit of playing outside the lines?

"How'd you know that this Ramirez was working with Zapata?" Tony asked.

Chappelle heaved a huge sigh. The deep breath seemed to lend him more strength. "Didn't. Not really. Some minor intelligence that Ramirez had worked with a middleman named Vanowen. We had hints that Vanowen had done a job for Zapata, planning something here in the U.S. Water, please."

Someone opened a bottle of water. Chappelle wet his lips and continued. "Truth is, Zapata never seems to work with the same people for long. We figured Ramirez and Vanowen would be out of the loop by the time we got to them. I figured the case would dead end, but the worst-case scenario was that Jack Bauer spends a few weeks in jail, and that was all right with me, too."

A few people chuckled at that.

"And the jailbreak?" Nina asked.

Chappelle threw up his hands feebly. "That's all Bauer. Only that guy would take an undercover investigation and turn the city upside down."

9:17 A.M. PST
RAND Corporation

The name RAND was simply a contraction of "Research and Development." RAND itself was a massive nonprofit project dedicated to improving public policy through research. RAND had its hands in every aspect of government consultation, from environmental issues to broad-based discussions of the "new" military to endorsements or criticisms of specific pieces of hardware.

RAND had several restricted areas, but the office space required little more than an employee badge and a guest signature. The security guard gave Talia a familiar wave and asked Jack to enter his name on a sign-in sheet. Bauer made up a name and scribbled "A. Predolin" on the sheet in sloppy writing, then they were through.

Talia's office was on the second floor of a quiet building where Jack imagined dozens of brilliant minds behind closed doors, brooding and contemplating.

"That's what it's like," Talia quipped. "Lots of us just sitting around thinking brilliant thoughts."

"Where I work, too," Jack added.

Talia laughed. "Actually, there are a lot of meetings. Informational meetings given to us by intelligence agencies; we give presentations to them. There's a lot of dialogue. Here."

They reached her office, a small but functional space with a desk set against a wall, a computer screen, and shelves full of books. Jack recognized *The Elegant Universe* by Brian Greene and *The Dancing Wu-Li Masters* by Gary Zukav, neither of which he'd read. The rest of the books were way over his head. There was a Rubik's Cube on the desk next to her mouse.

"I don't have access to LAPD information," Talia said, sitting down at her computer, "but if it's in a Federal database, I should be able to find it." She spoke succinctly, but without enthusiasm.

"You don't think this is going to work," Jack said.

"I hope it will," she corrected, putting a positive spin on his comment. "It just doesn't fit Zapata. I can't imagine anyone he worked with having a tattoo that could lead back to him."

"He wasn't expecting the guy to get shot twenty yards from his hotel room," Jack pointed out. "And remember, this was all right when we got close to him."

She accepted his point with a small shrug. A few quick strokes and two different passwords later, she was inside an enormous government registry. At Jack's direction, she did a search for "Emese." Nothing came up.

"Try getting information on MS–13," Jack requested.

Talia didn't type anything.

"MS–13," Jack repeated. "The letters 'M' and 'S,' and—"

"I know what it is," she said at last. "Zapata was part of that gang."

"No kidding." Jack felt a tiny knot form just below his lungs; it was a good feeling, an exciting tension, the feeling the hound gets just before the start of the hunt.

"If Zapata was Marquez, yes, I think Marquez was part of MS–13 in its early days. Not for long. And I don't know why he left, but . . ." Her voice trailed off as she began typing. A moment later, her computer screen altered and they were looking at an image of the tattoo Jack had seen twice before: "Emese" was a conjunction of the Spanish letters "eme" and "ese." This one had a tiny "WB" connected to the bottom right part of the number three, which a caption explained stood for "West Baltimore," but otherwise it was identical to the tattoos Jack had seen on Oscar and Aguillar.

"You said the inmates who attacked you had the same tattoo?" Talia asked incredulously.

"Yes."

"Do you think Zapata is on to you? He tried to kill you in prison?"

Jack shook his head. "Maybe, but it doesn't make sense. If he knew something was wrong then, he never would have let Ramirez get that close to him. And I have no idea how he could have known what I was up to in the jail. If he knows that, he's not a genius, he's a psychic."

"Zapata has evaded CTU, the CIA, the FBI, the Russian GRU, the Cubans, the Israelis, everyone. I wouldn't put it past him."

"I'll be sure and ask him in person. Can you get me a name and address for the top of the food chain with MS–13 in Los Angeles?"

Someone knocked on Talia's door. She was so engrossed in her research that she simply said, "Come in."

Jack turned as the door opened and he found himself staring up at the big U.S. Marshal who'd arrested him earlier.

He was fast for a big man, and smart. He didn't go for his gun. Instead he jabbed Jack in the face with a short left, or tried to. Jack slipped inside it and threw a punch to the big man's liver. He missed, hitting solid muscle. Pascal was big, but he wasn't flabby. He grabbed Jack by the hair with his left and punched him in the face with a right fist the size of a soccer ball. Jack heard a ringing in his ears and knew he couldn't take another one of those. Plus they were making a racket; he didn't know how much noise they were making which meant they were making too much. He blocked the second punch, then slammed his own hands down on top of the hand holding his hair. Unexpectedly, he took a bow, dropping his shoulders to the ground. Pascal grunted, the leverage on his trapped wrist dropping him down to one knee. Jack kicked, connecting to the Marshal's groin. Then he kicked him in the face, and Pascal went limp and quiet.

Jack closed the door and listened. No noise, no movement. Maybe no one had noticed.

He turned to check on Talia. Her face was white and her eyes were wide, watching Jack as though he were a wild animal that had stalked into her office.

"I could use that address as soon as possible," he said.

9:41 A.M. PST
Pacific Coast Highway, Malibu

The Reel Inn was one of those beach dives that looked terrible, smelled terrible, and served great food. It consisted of a weather-stained wooden shack—once painted blue but now faded to a stormy gray—and a neon sign that worked at least half the time.

This early on a Saturday morning it was deserted, except for three men who sat on one of the outdoor benches staring across Pacific Coast Highway toward one hundred yards of sandy beach and then nothing but ocean.

Kyle Risdow, the blond man who had picked up Zapata earlier, lay flat on his back on one of the benches, yawning. This meeting had little to do with him directly, so he spent the time dozing and trying to think of unique concepts for online porn websites.

Next to him, Zapata sat upright, but he was otherwise equally relaxed. He had a new identity now, thanks to the third member of their little group. If anyone asked, he was now Bernard de la Plaz.

The third member of their group was a Ukrainian named Franko. Although it was Saturday morning on the beach, he still wore dark jeans and a black leather jacket. He was fingering a piece of paper with an address.

"I only have one question," Franko said in precise but heavily accented English.

"A man without a question is a man without a brain," Zapata said.

Franko held up the piece of paper. "You want to get rid of this person because they worked for you. But now I work for you. Will you want to get rid of me, too?"

Zapata smiled. The sun was growing stronger. It felt good on his bald head. "Lots of people who've worked for me are still alive."

"Hmm," the Ukrainian pondered. "That is no answer."

"I like this man, Kyle!" Zapata said. "You're sharp, sir. But don't worry, I have no intention of killing everyone. Just do this job, get paid, and have a good life."

Franko nodded, picked up a brown paper bag full of cash, and walked away.

"He'll do it, right?" Kyle said.

"You're not seriously asking."

Kyle laughed, amused and, more likely, impressed by Zapata's confidence. "Have you ever been wrong?"

Zapata stared out across the beach. It was a fair question, an important question that merited a thoughtful answer. He considered his major decisions since the day he'd walked up into the hills and away from his identity. The tasks he had set for himself in the last few years, from Venezuela to Eastern Europe and the Middle East, appeared in his memory like so many bits of a Rubik's Cube. One by one they had spun into place and yes, now and then he had encountered some difficulty—the Mossad agents who'd sniffed around his activities in Jordan, the national policeman who'd caught on to his alias in Buenos Aires—but always he'd foreseen it several moves ahead and simply shifted the puzzle in a new direction.

At last he said, "No."

Such a significant statement to be summed up in one small word, Zapata thought without ego—and that was part of his genius, part of his success—that he had no ego. He had never been the victim of any government investigation in part because he'd never been the victim of his own pride. A good plan was a reflection of the realities on the ground, not a reflection of the planner's genius. Zapata had always succeeded because he was brilliant, but also because he was clear-sighted.

All of this was lost on Kyle. Kyle Risdow was not a terrorist, nor was he an anarchist, and he lacked utterly the perspective and intelligence to appreciate Zapata's genius. He was a much more common type of villain: a profiteer and opportunist. He had been making money from instability since Hurricane Andrew in Florida back in 1992, when his little grocery store had miraculously survived and he'd jacked his prices up one hundred percent.

"Good," Risdow said smugly. "Then after today I should be even richer."

9:51 A.M. PST
Staples Center

Mark Kendall jogged around the Staples Center. The huge digital display on the side of the complex read "Professional Reality Fighting Championships Tonight!"

He had hours still before his real warmup began, but he was full of nervous energy. He felt more like a kid in his first fight than a veteran in what the odds said was his last. He wasn't afraid of his opponent, but he was afraid of failure. He was afraid to hear his baby girl crying in the background on the next telephone call. He was afraid to hear the sadness in his wife's voice, the pure, undiluted sorrow of a mother who cannot help her child. He couldn't bear that. He didn't care about the fight, but he couldn't bear to let his family down.

And what if he did? What if he failed them?

Kendall put a big hand on the pocket of his track suit. The envelope was in there.

Was the little man serious? And could he kill someone?

The answer to the second question came easily. Yes, he could. For his daughter he could do anything. And he would do it if he had to, for his baby. He'd known that the minute she was born, when he held that tiny creature that had come through him and out of his wife's body, and finally understood what all his size and strength were built for. They were built to protect that baby. And that's what he would do now, no matter what the cost.

Slowly Kendall removed the envelope. He opened it. The writing inside was very direct, the same way the bald man had spoken. It told him about the bank account that would be activated in his wife's name the same day he completed his task. It told him that the account would be closed if the authorities ever found out. And it told him who to kill.

Kendall read the name. He hadn't heard it before, or at least he didn't remember it. But it sounded important.

He felt fear—more fear than a man his size ought to feel. But then he thought of his baby girl, and he steeled himself to act.

9:58 A.M. PST
Boyle Heights

Jack parked Talia Gerwehr's car on Seventeenth Street, looking for the address Talia had plucked from her computer. The houses here were large, but run-down. This was a de-gentrified neighborhood that forty years ago had been an upper-class enclave overlooking downtown. But three generations of gang warfare had made the houses forget their past. They were old, sagging hulks now, occupied by a mixture of hardworking families who kept to themselves and gang members with too much time on their hands.

Jack found the house. According to the Federal anti-gang task force, it was the home of Ruben "Smiley" Lopez, suspected leader of the main L.A. branch of MS–13. It was a large, two-story Colonial-style house perched at the top of a long red brick staircase. The tumbled slope below the porch had once been landscaped, but now was nothing more than dirt and weeds. The house itself was dirty white, with several windows covered over in cardboard and tape.

Jack climbed the stairs, not sure how to approach, when he heard a scream and a soft puff—the sound of bullets being fired through a silencer.

1 2 3 4 5 6 7 8 9
10 11 12 13 14 **15** 16 17
18 19 20 21 22 23 24

. . . .

THE FOLLOWING TAKES PLACE
BETWEEN THE HOURS OF
10 A.M. AND 11 A.M.
PACIFIC STANDARD TIME

. . . .

10:00 A.M. PST
Boyle Heights

Jack pulled his weapon—the Para Ordinance .45 he'd
taken from Peter Jiminez—out of his waistband and
sprinted up the last few steps. He kicked the door
hard, but the door held and electric shocks forked up
his leg. As run-down as the house looked, the door
was reinforced. Jack kicked again, hard, and this time
the frame surrendered and the door swung inward.

Jack bobbed his head inside and then out again just
as he heard the soft *pfft! pfft!* again and two bullets
thudded against the door where his head had been.
He knew his kicks had alerted the gunman, whoever
he was. In a different situation, Jack would have

stuck his weapon around the corner and emptied a magazine into the room, but he had no idea who was there, or if Lopez was the gunman or the victim, and he needed Lopez alive. Through the open door he saw a couch in the middle of the room. He dropped low and dived forward, rolling as he hit the floor and finding cover. He felt something tug his pants leg as he rolled, but he didn't think he'd been hit.

The living room was big and opened up to the right of the front door, so most of its space was now behind him. To the left of the front door, now in front of him, the house opened onto what looked like a dining room. In between, and set farther into the house, was a staircase that climbed to the second floor. A hallway led to the back of the house and probably the kitchen. Jack glanced behind him to make sure his back was secure—there was nothing but another couch, a few chairs, and a fireplace. There were empty beer cans scattered on the furniture and floor, and the distinct smell of cannabis.

He stayed low, peeking around the side of the couch, across the parlor, and into the dining room. He saw nothing, but he heard a girl's sob. Then the girl squealed, and two people appeared in the doorway. In front was a frightened Latina wearing a short cotton nightgown, sobbing and staring at Jack in terror. Behind her, using her as a shield, was a hard-looking man in a black leather jacket, most of his white face hidden by the girl's shoulder. He had his left hand in her hair and his right hand on a mean-looking Smith & Wesson.

"Back off!" the man ordered in a thick Slavic accent. He moved himself and the girl toward Jack and the door.

Jack had no idea who he was, but the man clearly mistook Jack for someone who would hesitate in that situation. Jack raised up to one knee, steadied his weapon, and fired a hair's breadth above the girl's shoulder. The round was meant to go right between the taker's eyes, but it had been a long night for Jack. The bullet grazed the man's temple, drawing an angry red line from the corner of his eye to the back of his ear.

He was tough, whoever he was. He flinched at the bullet, then immediately shoved the girl toward Jack. Even if Jack had shot her, her momentum would have carried her into him. Jack leaned out of the way, trying to fire, but a red-hot bullet bit him on the right shoulder and he felt his gun arm go numb. His right arm again! He stumbled to the floor and lost his weapon. He saw the black-jacketed man slow and steady himself for a finishing shot.

At that moment someone else roared and surged out of the dining room, slamming into the assassin from behind. The newcomer was a big Latino man wearing a wife-beater. But his hands were tied behind his back. He used his shoulder and momentum to ram the Slavic gunman, who stumbled forward into the couch. He spun with an elbow, catching the bound man in the temple.

Endorphins masked the pain in Jack's right arm, but he couldn't move it, so he jumped up onto the couch and landed heavily on the gunman's shoulders. He wrapped his left arm around the Slavic man's neck and grabbed the barrel of his gun. Jack couldn't seal a proper choke this way, but then the gunman couldn't reverse his weapon and shoot Jack, either. At the same moment, the Latino man rose unsteadily to his feet. He kicked the man once in the stomach.

The Slavic man clearly had had enough. He let go of his weapon, leaving it in Jack's hand, elbowed Jack in the stomach, and dropped out of his hold. He bulled past the Latino and sprinted out the door.

Jack paused a moment, gasping for breath. His right arm hung heavily at his side. The bullet seemed to have plowed a furrow along the width of his forearm, glancing off the bone. He forced himself to flex his fingers. He could move them, but it was going to hurt like hell in a minute. He looked up at the other man. The Latino was in his mid-twenties, red-faced and angry, still staring out the front door as if he wanted to chase down the other man.

"Smiley Lopez?" Jack said.

"Yeah," the other man said. "Who the fuck are you?"

"I think I'm the guy who just saved your ass." Jack dropped the gun he still held, stepped off the couch and behind Lopez. His hands were tied together with flexcuffs. "You have any wire cutters?"

Lopez said something to the girl in Spanish, and she replied. "The kitchen," Lopez said. "The drawer by the back door."

Jack went into the kitchen, found the right drawer,

and came back with a pair of red-handled cutters. He snipped the plastic cuffs off and gave them to Lopez, who freed his girlfriend.

"Who was that?" Jack asked.

"Don't know," Lopez said, "but when I find out, I'm gonna pay some people a visit." Lopez casually picked up the weapon Jack had dropped and pointed it at him. "So who the fuck are you?"

Jack ignored the threat of the weapon. His right arm was more mobile now, but it was also on fire. "I came here for information. There's a guy I'm after, and I think you know how I can find him."

Lopez gave the girl an order and she scurried off to the kitchen while Lopez sat down in a chair. "Fuckin' cop. I'm not giving you shit."

Jack sat down, too. "He's not one of yours. In fact, he's a guy who left MS–13."

"Nobody leaves."

"He did. Tell me where to find him, and I'll make sure your guys at the Federal Holding Facility get out."

Jack wasn't prepared for the effect this had on Lopez. The gang leader laughed, showing big white teeth and huge dimples. When he smiled, his face changed from a sneer into something oddly jolly. "You guys must be desperate. You're the second *cabron* in two days to offer me a deal. What the fuck, my homies in the jail giving you too much trouble? You want to get rid of them?"

"I want Zapata."

This statement had a totally different effect on Lopez. He went suddenly cold and serious. "You aren't a cop. Not a regular cop."

"You're right. But I do want Zapata. So give him up, and your boys go free."

Smiley Lopez studied this stranger. If he'd been raised in a different neighborhood, he might have grown up to be a lawyer or a businessman. As it was, he was a shrewd entrepreneur, but he dealt in drugs and muscle. This blond man struck him as someone to bargain with. "Maybe I could do it," he said at last. "But not just for my homeboys. I want to get back at those *pendejos*."

"This guy who tried to kill you."

"Fucking Russians or Ukrainians or whatever. We're in a war with them."

"You want me to go after him?"

But this still wasn't enough for Lopez. "More than that, *ese*. I know these pieces of shit are moving a whole lot of crystal meth. How about you go take it from them and bring it to me."

"I don't have the time to find them—"

"Make the time, *ese*. That's the deal."

"I take down these Russians and bring you the crystal meth, and you'll tell me where to find Zapata?"

"You got it."

"Why should you trust me?"

Lopez grinned. "What trust? I get the tina or I don't. You come back, we'll talk about Zapata."

Jack considered, but he had little time and less of a choice. "Deal."

The Biltmore Hotel was unusual because the front of the hotel had become the back. Modern traffic needs had forced the owners to create a modern entrance in what had been the rear of the hotel. The tragedy was that the original front doors had opened onto a grand lobby with a beautiful double marble staircase leading up to a mezzanine. So that this glamorous room would not go to waste, the management had turned it into an opulent dining room.

Martin Webb was having breakfast in that dining room with his grandson. Jake was a bigger, stronger version of Martin as a young man. In his early twenties, Jake was over six feet and solid, but not so muscular that it slowed him down. He was a good-looking kid, too, and he turned lots of heads as they walked through the lobby to the restaurant. There was a minor scuffle among the waitresses arguing over who would serve his table. Jake took it all in stride.

Martin ordered eggs and pancakes—even in his seventies, he had a healthy appetite—while Jake ordered egg whites and fruit.

"For a man's man, you eat like a girl," Martin joked.

"One more day, Grandpa," Jake said. "Tomorrow I'm going to stuff my face. But I can't feel heavy today."

"Then you're going to quit this stuff and go into finance like your grandpa and your dad, right?" Martin said lightly.

Jake laughed. It was a long-running joke between them. They both knew well that Jake had neither the brain nor the temperament for financial matters. He had inherited all of his grandfather's athletic genes and none of his financial ones. He was ready to let the joke pass, as it usually did, but his grandfather turned suddenly serious.

"Actually, Jakey, I have to say at this moment I'm jealous of you. This life you're leading right now, it's a good life. Stick with it for a while. I can't say that having a lot of responsibility is all that fun."

Though not a CPA, Jake was no idiot. He understood the responsibility on his grandfather's shoulders. "You'll find a way out of it, Grandpa. You're the Wise Old Man of the Fed, right?"

"Old," Martin agreed. "And I'm what's left of a man. But wise?" He sighed. "Well, I have to go on the TV tomorrow and sound like it, anyway. I lost sleep last night, thinking of it. Oh, hey," he said, brightening. "I saw you. ESPN was doing some late night preview of the fighters for the Professional Reality Fighting matches tonight. They did a big story on you."

Jake smiled. "They like pumping up the young guys sometimes."

"The ones with a future," Martin said. "I know how business works. They think they can market you."

"If I win tonight," Jake agreed. "Are you going to watch on TV?"

Martin sighed. "You know, my boy, I'm going to do one better. I'm going to come to the fights."

"Great! I mean, don't feel like you have to, Grandpa, I know what's going on—"

Martin held up a hand to stop him. "I already made some calls. I canceled my dinner, and I got a ticket. As for tomorrow" —now he waved his hand dismissively— "I've been saying what I say for years. No one's going to surprise me with a question. Tonight, I'm coming to watch my grandson."

Jake was genuinely excited. He loved being a professional fighter, but he had always felt a twinge of guilt that he could not follow the family path. His grandfather's endorsement meant a lot to him. "I'm excited now. I'm definitely going to win this one for you. And you can come to the back after the fights, and meet some of the other big names."

"I'd be honored," Martin said. "So who is your opponent? Does he know what he's gotten himself into?"

Jake laughed. "He's a tough guy, but he's older. A former champ named Mark Kendall."

· ·

THE FOLLOWING TAKES PLACE
BETWEEN THE HOURS OF
11 A.M. AND 12 A.M.
PACIFIC STANDARD TIME

· ·

11:00 A.M. PST
CTU Headquarters, Los Angeles

Dan Pascal walked into CTU Headquarters like a bull
slotting up for his rodeo rider—all calm and still, but
tense and ready to buck. He made and received the
obligatory introductions with various personnel there:
George Mason, whom he recognized from last night;
Chris Henderson, who looked like a no-nonsense
fellow; Ryan Chappelle, who looked like a walking
corpse; Tony Almeida, a good-looking fellow who
stared at him out of sleepy eyes, and some others.
Pascal heard himself make short, charming quips at
them in his usual Louisiana style, but inside, he was

seething. He was pretty goddamned tired of chasing this Jack Bauer around, and the fact that Bauer had beaten him up had not improved his mood. Once he'd recovered, Pascal had grilled Talia Gerwehr, but gotten nothing from her except the fact that her work was top secret. He had no choice but to accept her story that she thought she was helping a Federal agent. At that point, Pascal had gotten tired of playing games and gone right to the source.

"Enough with the how-do-you-do's," Pascal said, sitting down on the edge of a table that creaked under his weight. "I've got local law enforcement and U.S. Marshals running around all over this city looking for Jack Bauer. I've had that sumbitch kick me in the testicles and I've had one of your own people smash my nice government-issue car. I need someone here to tell me what the hell's going on, and I need it right now!"

Pascal hadn't actually raised his voice much, but the angry rumble from his chest, combined with his size, made him intimidating.

Unfortunately, he was in a room full of people who did not intimidate easily. "I'm not sure we can tell you, Marshal," Henderson said calmly. "But we are working on a case of a sensitive nature."

"Jack Bauer is out in the field," Chappelle added. He'd been recovering slowly but steadily. "We expect him to be out for some time, under deep cover. He may not be able . . . to . . . contact us . . . for . . ."

Chappelle's voice trailed off in astonishment, because Jack Bauer had just walked through the door.

11:07 A.M. PST
CTU Headquarters, Los Angeles

Jack walked into CTU Headquarters tired, hungry, and wounded. He'd been shot twice in the same arm, and on top of that he'd been punched, kicked, and smashed by a car. He was ready for a little more down time.

So he could be forgiven for feeling a moment's dread when he walked past the astounded faces of analysts at CTU and into the conference room to find Marshal Pascal waiting for him. The big man jumped up from the table where he sat and lumbered toward Jack like an avalanche.

Jack pulled his gun from his belt and pointed at Pascal's barrel chest. "Stop," he said calmly.

All two 270 pounds of U.S. Marshal froze.

"I'm not guilty," Jack said simply. "And I'm sorry I kicked you. But I'm also in a bad mood, so if you take one more step I'm going to shoot you."

Pascal didn't back down, but he didn't advance, either. Finally it was George Mason who stepped between them. "Easy, boys. You were both doing your jobs. Let's leave it at that."

Chappelle didn't seem to care about the tension between the two men. He was glaring at Jack, so angry that some of the color actually returned to his face. "Bauer, what the hell are you doing back in?"

Jack expected that. He didn't even mind Chappelle's irritating tone. "It was time. I need to find someone now."

As quickly as he could, Jack summarized the events of the last fifteen hours. It was a long story, but Jack had been called before enough special committees to know how to summarize his actions, and after four or five minutes the CTU team had a clear picture of what was going on.

"It almost worked," Chappelle said. "You came close."

"One room away," Jack agreed. "I'll still get him."

Tony Almeida had listened closely to Jack's story. A few details still bothered him. "There are still holes, though. Why was MS–13 after you in prison? Was Zapata after you even then? Was it coincidence?"

"Didn't MS–13 have a grudge against you from before?" Henderson suggested.

Jack nodded his head. "Yeah, I just don't know why they'd come after me this hard. Could be just coincidence. If that's the case, then I just lucked out with the tattoo. Whatever is going on, right now they're my only link to Zapata. Ramirez didn't know much, but he knew something was going on tonight. I'm going to get Lopez what he needs."

Dan Pascal had listened to Bauer's story with growing incredulity. He was a man's man and a tough cop, but what Bauer had been through sounded beyond belief. But this last statement wasn't just astonishing, it was criminal. "Hold on there, Captain America," he drawled. "You ain't really going to steal crystal meth from one gang and give to another?"

"Yes, I am," Jack said.

"Don't you think that's criminal?"

Jack nodded. "What do you expect from a guy who just broke out of jail?"

"There are still a whole lot of questions," Tony said stubbornly. "Only three people had direct knowledge of Jack's innocence: Chappelle, the warden, and the corrections guard. All three of them were attacked or put out of commission when Jack was attacked. Who did that? Zapata?"

"Not Zapata," Jack said. "If he was on to us then, we'd never have gotten as close as we did."

Henderson jumped in. "Besides, there's something more urgent to focus on. We don't know what Zapata is targeting."

This observation triggered an eruption of voices all talking at once. Several theories bubbled to the surface, the most immediate of which was espoused by Tony Almeida. Tony had a calm, steady voice, but somehow he made it cut through the din.

"It's got to be something to do with the Pacific Rim Forum," he insisted. "The Jemaah Islamiyah guys were for real. They were using a code that we" —he nodded toward Seth— "that repeated the letters PRF. We think it stood for Pacific Rim Forum."

"Do we even know if those e-mails were going to Zapata?" George Mason said skeptically.

"Gmail accounts bouncing off ISPs in public networks in libraries," Jamey replied. "We couldn't trace them."

Jack considered this. "Well, we were both working with middlemen, and that's definitely Zapata's style."

"But Zapata also walks away when there's trouble," Nina pointed out. "Maybe our job's already done."

Chappelle was unsatisfied. "We don't know that for sure. There could have been trouble on every one of his other bombings or attacks, we just didn't know about it. Besides, he might think he's closed the door on us by killing those two middlemen. We need to work on the assumption that Zapata is still moving toward his goal. Any suggestions besides the Southeast Asian forum? Any other targets?" A cacophony of voices erupted. "One at a time!"

Jamey Farrell declared over a few other raised voices, "The Chairman of the Fed is in town. I'm not sure he's much of a target . . ."

Pascal snorted. "Right now he is!" Everyone looked at him, and he shrugged. "Ain't any of you that buy stocks? My 401(k)'s goin' down the tubes. Right now, I had a choice between savin' my mama and savin' Webb, I'd have to give it some thought."

Jamey thought of herself as a thorough analyst and didn't appreciate this slow-talking newcomer on her turf. "He's been on our list since the beginning," she sniffed. "But he's not a visible target. Four-fifths of the population couldn't even name the Chairman of the Fed."

"The rest listen to every word he says," Pascal replied.

Tony took Jamey's side. "But there's nothing about the Chairman or his schedule that matches the PRF code. "

"I ran it twice," Seth confirmed.

"Besides," Tony pointed out, "it seems like Zapata has been trying to get ordnance. I doubt he'd need that much armament to go after the Fed Chairman."

"But," Nina said, "you're saying Jemaah Islamiyah, but they weren't after explosives, they wanted some computer virus."

"What's the status of Jemaah Islamiyah?" Chappelle asked.

Tony said, a little unhappily, "Down but not out. We caught or killed two men in the gun battle, but Encep Sungkar got away."

"That was our fault," Pascal confessed. "My people jumped in to get Bauer. We didn't know there was an operation in progress."

Jack had been silent for a moment, listening. The analysis was bouncing all over the place. Explosives, Jemaah Islamiyah, the Pacific Rim Forum, computer viruses, MS–13. It was . . . chaos. "A butterfly flaps its wings in China," he muttered.

"Huh?" Nina said, overhearing him. The others stopped talking, too.

"Just something this analyst at RAND said," Jack explained. "Chaos theory. When a system is so complicated that it looks like chaos, but there's some order hidden in the middle of it. That's what Zapata does. That's why he's hard to track. He's got us chasing our tails."

Tony frowned. "Are you suggesting we ignore JI?"

Jack nodded. "I think we should ignore anything Zapata lets us get close to. He didn't care about Ramirez or Vanowen and walked away from the weapons we brought him at the hotel. If PRF was that easy to crack—"

"Gee, thanks," Seth interjected.

Jack ignored him. "—then we should throw it out because Zapata didn't think it was important. The only thing I think that has knocked him off balance was when I got near him at the hotel and killed Aguillar. We know from phone records and card key files that he was in the next room right before then. Killing Aguillar was the closest we've come to him, and Aguillar led us to MS–13. I want to stay on that trail."

"Then do it," Chappelle said. "Get what you need and get back in the field. Tony and Nina, you support him. Everyone," he said, standing up to gather their attention. "I know you aren't used to hearing this from me, but don't think inside the lines on this one. Zapata will spot us like he's spotted everyone else. Now go."

The next fifteen minutes were filled with the less glamorous but vital work of the data analysts. Jack needed as much information as he could get on a Russian or Ukrainian gang operating in West Los Angeles. CTU tapped into the computers of LAPD, Santa Monica PD, the Federal anti-gang task force, Immigration, and Customs. Getting the general information was easy—LAPD had formed a joint task force with the FBI to investigate a gang of Ukrainian immigrants suspected of criminal activity. The man Jack needed to get to was Sergei Petrenko, head of the Ukrainian outfit. Thanks to the Patriot Act, the NAP Act, and its successors, CTU tapped into Petrenko's cell phone and e-mails immediately. Inside of ten minutes, Jamey Farrell and her crew were analyzing his phone records, his e-mails, every shred of electronic communication that Mr. Sergei Petrenko had used recently.

"He's a careful one," Jamey told Jack as the analysts continued their review. "He doesn't say much or write much. But he has been talking to someone a lot." She checked her notes. "Felix Studhalter. Looks like he's a buyer and distributor."

"Have they ever met?" Jack asked.

"Phone records wouldn't show that, of course, but I don't think so. It looks like we have a different kind of break. The FBI's joint task force has been on these guys for a while. It looks like they have someone undercover in the group. Code name Ivan of all things. Looks like Ivan's been feeding them bits of information. Felix is new business for them, and the buy is supposed to go down today. I guess that's what your gang-banger friend heard about."

Jack formed a plan immediately. First, they would track down Felix Studhalter and detain him. Jack would go to the buy in his place, steal the drugs, and get them to MS–13.

He checked his watch. It was almost noon. If Ramirez was right, then whatever Zapata was planning would happen sometime today. And, Jack realized with a pang of frustration, Zapata still had him running around in circles.

He walked down the hall to clean his wounds and found himself side by side with Chris Henderson.

"Thanks for all the help last night," Jack said sarcastically.

"You have no idea how much I've helped you," Henderson spat back.

Jack stopped. "What kind of help did you give me last night when I called you at four o'clock in the morning!"

"I had no idea you were on an operation—"

"But you know me," Jack retorted. "And you still left me out in the cold. I never thought you'd want so badly to get even."

Henderson squared up on Jack. The two agents faced each other like boxers just before the fight. "This has nothing to do with that Internal Affairs thing. I don't give a damn who you dropped my name to. I'm not guilty of anything."

Jack's eyes drilled into him. "When I mentioned your name I was doing my job. If I find out you're try-ing to screw me, this will get really, really personal."

· ·

**THE FOLLOWING TAKES PLACE
BETWEEN THE HOURS OF
12 P.M. AND 1 P.M.
PACIFIC STANDARD TIME**

· ·

*12:00 P.M. PST
CTU Headquarters, Los Angeles*

For the first time in a long time, Jack climbed into a car that he hadn't stolen. He'd taken a minute just before the hour to clean himself up and dress his wounds—the second bullet wound on his right forearm stung like hell and would require attention eventually, but his arm functioned—then found a change of clothes. Jamey had downloaded a picture of Felix Studhalter, and Jack compared himself to it in the mirror. They looked nothing alike, but Studhalter's hair was light brown, not so far off from blond, and according to information from a prior arrest, Studhalter was roughly the same height. If Sergei knew his buyer only from description, the sting might work.

Now he started the engine of a borrowed black Chevy Tahoe and started the engine. It was at that moment that another car pulled into the secure parking area at CTU. Jack saw Peter Jiminez behind the wheel with an enormous purple bruise on the left side of his swollen face.

Their two cars, facing opposite directions, pulled up to one another. Peter's eyes flashed as he saw Jack, and the parts of his face that weren't purple turned an angry red.

"Peter," Jack said out the window of his car.

"Jack," the younger agent grunted through a nearly immobile jaw.

"It wasn't personal," Jack explained. "It was part of the job. Chappelle or Henderson will catch you up."

"We've all got jobs to do," Jiminez said coldly.

As Jack drove out, Henderson parked and entered CTU. He received two types of looks as he walked toward Henderson's office: surprise and sympathy from those who hadn't heard about his encounter with Jack; and amusement and sympathy from those who knew how he felt. He walked up the stairs to Henderson's office and entered without knocking, then closed the door.

"Where the hell have you been?" Henderson asked, looking up from the files on his desk. He was digging through all the information he could get on MS–13.

"Planning ways to burn Jack Bauer," Jiminez muttered.

12:05 P.M. PST
Temescal Canyon Road

Kyle Risdow had a nice split-level house in Temescal Canyon, an upscale neighborhood overlooking the ocean between Santa Monica and Malibu. He'd paid cash for it back in 1994, right after the Northridge earthquake rocked Los Angeles. He'd bought a bunch of damaged homes at rock-bottom prices, slapped new drywall and paint on them, and sold them "as is."

Risdow was examining proformas on a business proposition, but he kept one eye on Zapata. He wasn't suspicious; he was fascinated. He did not consider himself Zapata's friend—if he gave the matter any thought at all, he'd have guessed that Zapata had no real friends. Friends were connections, and connections caused patterns, and Risdow knew enough to know that Zapata abhorred them. In fact, he was sure that this was the last time he would see the anarchist. They had had a peripheral connection on a previous event, when the middlemen Zapata was using had brought Risdow in to finance the operation. Something about Risdow had attracted Zapata—Kyle suspected it was his complete lack of compunction—and the anarchist had shown up at his door two years later, planning to crash an oil tanker in the Gulf of Mexico and allowing Kyle to profit from the cleanup effort. Now there was this. To be honest, Kyle wasn't even sure why Zapata had brought him in this time. But he did know that Zapata abandoned his colleagues soon after the job, and he expected the mysterious anarchist to vanish forever.

At the moment, though, Zapata was answering his cell phone and then listening with consternation. A moment later he hung up and stood perfectly still, staring at the wall.

"Something?" Kyle asked.

"Franko didn't finish the job," Zapata said simply. "He was interrupted by another gunman."

"A gunman? Or a cop?"

"That is what I was considering."

Zapata continued to stare at the wall, but what he saw was a complex network of nodes and lines, each connected to each. "Not a cop," he said at last. "Franko said he never identified himself and just came in shooting. The police don't behave that way."

"Maybe it was nothing to do with you."

"Maybe." But Zapata felt a tug in his chest, a little twinge of anxiety. He considered abandoning his current project and leaving the country. But he saw no way in which the authorities could follow a path to his intentions. Even if, by the slimmest of chances, Smiley Lopez could point to him in some way, the MS–13 leader had no reason to cooperate with the authorities.

"Still, fortune favors the prepared mind," he murmured, quoting Louis Pasteur. He had created an escape plan during his last adventure in Los Angeles (a riot; his involvement had gone totally unnoticed by the authorities) but had not needed to use it. He thought, with a quick update, the same plan would work perfectly well. "Kyle, I need a map of the city streets."

12:14 P.M. PST
Los Feliz

Felix Studhalter wasn't a permanent resident of Los Angeles. He'd rented a house in Los Feliz, but only for a month or two while he conducted business. According to CTU's intelligence, he mostly moved heroin but had recently pursued the crystal meth craze. He'd been convicted once and served a few years in state prison, but had been paroled. Now he was back in business, if the LAPD was to be believed. They were simply waiting for him to make his next move.

Nina and Tony weren't going to give him the opportunity.

Nina knocked on the door of the rented bungalow and smiled when Studhalter answered. He was about forty, with puffy cheeks and a little too much skin around his neck. "Mr. Studhalter?" she asked pleasantly.

"Who are you?" he asked casually.

She stepped into the room, and he immediately tried to slam the door on her. She shouldered it back open and charged in. Studhalter was no fighter. He turned and ran through the half-empty, rented living room and into the kitchen, where he met Jack Bauer, who'd just kicked in the back door.

The drug dealer stopped and raised his hands. "Arrest me, what the fuck. I haven't done anything."

Jack motioned him back into the living room where both Nina and Tony waited.

"Back so soon?" Nina asked.

"What's this about?" Studhalter demanded. "You guys can't be cops."

"Sit down." Jack pointed at the couch, and Studhalter obeyed. He was nervous, but not panicked. He was an ex-con, and prison held no unknowns for him. He was also smart enough to know his place in the world. "This ain't about me," he said. "No way this is about me."

Jack nodded.

As Jack interrogated Felix Studhalter, another car drove up in front of the house, and Nina saw Peter Jiminez exit. She met him on the walkway. "Isn't this overkill?"

Peter worked his swollen jaw. "Henderson wants me to take this guy back to CTU. He thinks there might be more we can get out of him once Jack's done"

"You've heard of the phone," Nina said.

"You two are supposed to check out the Pacific Rim Forum site. He says he wants someone with more experience." Jiminez looked miserable. "I've got years doing protective services with Diplomatic Security and he thinks I don't have the experience. So I get stuck with prisoner transport."

Jack walked out a moment later. "He's all yours," he said to Nina. "He's cooperative enough. And this can work. He's never met the Ukrainians before, and he's supposed to arrange a meet with them. I'm playing him and making the call now."

"Change of plans," Nina said, pointing at Peter.

"I'm taking him in," the young agent explained.

"Okay," Jack said. He didn't spare more than a quick glance at Peter. He had liked Jiminez well enough, and he was aware that he'd become a kind of father-figure to the younger man, but he had time for neither hero worship nor shattered expectations at the moment.

Nina had no desire to get in the middle of the dispute, so she went back inside.

"Jack," Jiminez started. "Look, I was pissed before, you could tell. I even went in to Henderson to bitch about you. He set me straight. I'm sorry, man, I just—you know, I have a lot of respect for you, and to take a shot like that right after I'd, I mean, smashing the car and everything—"

Jiminez was stumbling over his words. Jack choked back his frustration. The kid was saying something nice, and if several sessions of marriage counseling had taught him anything, it was to listen when the other person said something nice. "Thanks, Peter. Thanks for getting me out of that police car." He shook Peter's hand.

Jack went to his car and got in. He had Studhalter's mobile phone with him, and he dialed the number the drug dealer had given him.

"Yeah?" said a rough, accented voice on the other side.

"Hey, this is Studhalter," Jack said. "Give me Sergei."

"When do you want to meet?" said the other man, obviously Sergei.

"Now. I want to move the stuff now, too."

Pause. "You're in a hurry now, all of a sudden?"

Jack let his answer come naturally, not rushed and defensive. "I have some buyers in Okahoma City. The sooner I get to them, the more money I make."

"Okay. Come to me. If the feelings are good, we'll go for a ride."

Sergei gave him an address in Santa Monica, and Jack hit the road.

He hadn't driven for more than a few minutes when he realized there was another call he needed to make. Probably it was a call he should have made hours earlier, but he had forgotten. The conciliatory conversation with Jiminez had reminded him. He dialed.

"Hello?" Teri's voice was inquisitorial. This was a number she did not recognize.

"Ter, it's me."

"Jack." He couldn't tell if that sound in her voice was anger or relief. Maybe it was both. "What's—?"

"I'm good. It's all good now. Thank you. Thank you for everything."

And suddenly she was crying on the other end of the line. He did not interrupt her. A moment later her sobs subsided, and she said amid her tears, "God, I was so scared last night, I've been so scared, and all the time keeping this secret—"

"I know, I'm sorry, I really am," he said, meaning it. It hadn't been fair to expose her to danger. He'd already asked too much of her by just going undercover in prison. He'd told her, of course, but then he'd insisted that she maintain the secret. That hadn't been hard—Jack's work wasn't well known to their friends and neighbors, and he traveled enough that a three-week absence, while unusual, wasn't suspicious. But she'd slept every night with images of him in prison. "But that part's over. The police know that I was undercover."

"So you're coming home?" she asked hopefully. "Kim hasn't seen you in—"

"Today, later. But I can't yet. I still have work to do."

Even before she spoke, he sensed the change in tone. It was as though the word *work* had opened a huge chasm between them that no cell phone could reach across. "Okay," was all she said.

"Ter, you know, what I'm wor— when I'm involved in something like this, I—"

"I know, Jack. It's important. I'll see you when you get home."

1 2 3 4 5 6 7 8 9
10 11 12 13 14 15 16 17
18 19 20 21 22 23 24

• •

THE FOLLOWING TAKES PLACE
BETWEEN THE HOURS OF
1 P.M. AND 2 P.M.
PACIFIC STANDARD TIME

• •

1:00 P.M. PST
CTU Headquarters, Los Angeles

Ryan Chappelle was feeling more like himself. That is to say, he was feeling peevish and unhappy. Of course, at this particular moment he had two reasons to be unhappy. The first was that someone had given him a barbiturate overdose. The second was that Jack Bauer, of all people, had saved him.

It did not occur to Chappelle to admire Bauer for the sacrifices he'd made in the last few weeks. Not a day went by without some field agent somewhere surrendering his blood or his family time for the sake of his country. The possibility that Bauer might give more than others was, in Chappelle's opinion, over-shadowed by the man's willingness (he would say eagerness) to flout policy and procedure.

As for the fact that Bauer had been instrumental in getting close to Zapata, well, as far as Chappelle was concerned, that proved his own good use of resources.

Chappelle considered Zapata his personal nemesis. Chappelle despised terrorists. He considered them evil and immoral, villains willing to kill and maim the innocent to achieve their ends. But at least they had an end goal, abhorrent as it was. Zapata was not immoral, he was amoral. He had no end in mind; he simply worked toward the deconstruction of the world as it was. Anarchy. Without leaders. Preposterous. The man had to be destroyed.

"You wanted to see me?"

Chris Henderson entered the office where Chappelle had made himself comfortable.

Chappelle motioned for him to sit down. When Henderson had settled in, he said, "This Internal Affairs investigation is heating up."

A look of disgust crossed Henderson's face. "It's all anyone's talking about."

"From what I've read, it looks like Jack Bauer's the one who's been doing the talking. About you."

The scowl on Henderson's face deepened, his frown lines becoming sinkholes. "I assume Jack said what he thought, even though he's wrong."

Chappelle nodded. "Being wrong never occurs to him. The man's a hard-headed smart ass. Frankly, I'd love to see him brought down a notch or two."

Henderson hesitated. "Is this what you called me in to talk about?"

The Regional Director seemed not to have heard him. "Between you and me, I've been tempted to pack his parachute myself, if you know what I mean, then let him jump out of the plane and just see what happens. But something always holds me back. Maybe it's my own sense of right and wrong, but no, now that I think of it, it's not that."

"I'll bite. What is it?" Henderson asked.

Chappelle leaned forward. "It's that as much as he's a rule-breaking pain in the ass, Bauer does what he does to get the job done. He doesn't do things to stop the job from getting done."

"Is there a point here?"

"Yes," Chappelle said. "You know how much I dislike Bauer, and that's even though I admit he tries to help the mission. Do you have any idea how miserable I'd make someone who was actually trying to stop the mission?"

Henderson's mouth went dry. He tried to smile. "Pretty miserable, I'll bet."

"Pretty goddamned miserable," Chappelle agreed. His eyes did not waver from Henderson's face. Like a snake, he did not blink. "If I found out that someone tried to sabotage the Zapata mission just to save their own skin from the Internal Affairs investigation, especially if they did something to me as part of their sabotage, I'm going to personally see to it that person is crucified."

"What the hell are you implying with—"

"That's all," Chappelle said.

1:11 P.M. PST
Santa Monica

Sergei's address was easy enough to find—a small Craftsman just north of Main Street, on the border between Santa Monica and Venice. The neighborhood was straight middle class, and except for the brown, untended grass, the Ukrainian's house blended in perfectly well.

Jack climbed the three steps to the porch and pushed the old metal doorbell. There was a slightly rusty screen door that opened outward, but he left it closed and waited. After a moment, the inner door was opened by a small man who barely reached Jack's shoulder. He studied Jack with bright, aggressive eyes, and Jack had that same, cautionary feeling one gets while being sniffed by a guard dog.

"Malenkiy, let him in!" someone ordered from inside.

Jack pulled open the metal screen door as Malenkiy stepped back. Jack walked into a house that looked like it had been decorated by a couple of college boys, with haphazard furniture and cheap prints on the walls. The hardwood floor was badly scratched in places.

Sergei was sitting on a brown faux leather couch. He had the same sharp eyes as Malenkiy, and they wore the same hawklike nose and thin brown hair, but Sergei was much bigger, taller and broader than Jack. He was reading the newspaper. Jack noticed that Malenkiy remained behind him and off-angle, ready for trouble.

The drug dealer folded the paper and stood up. "Mr. Felix Studhalter," he said in a gentle accent, offering his hand. Jack shook it firmly. "We do not know each other. I must search you."

"I'm carrying," Jack said. "I'm sure your guy is, too."

Sergei nodded. "I am not concerned about guns."

Jack understood. He'd re-equipped himself with a SigSauer, which he carried in a pancake holster at his hip. He popped it out and laid it on the edge of the couch, then slipped off his jacket and pulled up the long-sleeved T-shirt until his chest was visible. He turned around slowly. He was not wearing a wire.

"Good," Sergei said pleasantly. "Now we can do business. Why, again, have you hurried up our deal? Something about St. Louis?"

"Oklahoma City," Jack corrected. "Like I said, the sooner the deal is done, the more I make."

"Who is in Oklahoma?" Sergei asked.

Jack shook his head. "I make money because I know them and you don't."

Sergei sighed. "We are all middlemen. So, this is how it works. You and me and Malenkiy are going to our little warehouse. We are going alone, and you are bringing cash. For cash, you get crystal meth and the truck it comes in—"

"Do I know the truck is clean?"

"Your grandmother could sell it to a policeman," Sergei assured him.

"And what makes you think that, all by myself, I'm going to go somewhere with the two of you with a bag full of cash?"

Sergei grinned. "Because it is the only way you will get the deal."

Jack made a show of hesitating, assessing Sergei and his miniature. The truth, of course, was that this arrangement was fine with him. Tucked into the compartment under the back area of his SUV was a briefcase full of cash courtesy of CTU. Jack was perfectly content to hand it over and drive away with the meth, which he'd deliver to Smiley Lopez in return for information. LAPD and the FBI could sort out the gang-bangers and the drug dealers. He had a global anarchist to catch.

1:22 P.M. PST
Don't-Shoot-the-Messengers
Carson, California

Gabriel "Pan" Panatello hung up the phone, having just received the most unusual phone call of his life. He was the owner of Don't-Shoot-the-Messengers, a messenger company (and a name) he'd inherited from his jerk brother-in-law a few years back. He'd taken it partly because his wife nagged him to do it, and partly because the messenger service was a convenient front for his small-time drug deals and transportation business. The thievery wasn't much more profitable than the actual delivery, but at least it wasn't boring pencil-neck work. Pan got to keep his hand in the pot even though, as far as his wife, Tapia, knew, he'd gone legit. Plus, it allowed him to give work to some of his pals from Folsom, and that made him feel like a hero.

This call, now. This call was way out of the ordinary. Ironically, as crazy as the job was, the first thing Pan did was very pencil-neckish. He called his insurance company to make sure the insurance was up to date on all six of his cars. 'Course, he realized right away that that was stupid—he couldn't use all his own cars for this. Maybe one, but the rest had to come from somewhere else. So next he made the first of several calls to some of the guys from the cell block.

"Hey, Doogie, it's Pan. Yeah, listen, man, you still looking for work? Naw, man, not exactly. You still got a car? Yeah, I got my own, but I can't—just listen. You're gonna need your own car, and it might not run too good afterward, but I'll give you a legit loaner. Okay, here's what you gotta do . . ."

1:25 P.M. PST
Santa Monica

A few minutes after they left Sergei Petrenko's house in the drug dealer's big black Mercedes, Jack and his two new acquaintances pulled up in front of a building that was neither a warehouse nor little. They were parked in front of a large condominium complex. Sergei had activated his phone and muttered something in Russian or Ukrainian, which brought a man in a black leather coat and black cap out of the complex's security gate. The man sauntered across a short strip of lawn, jerked open the back door of the Mercedes, and dropped himself heavily into the backseat next to Malenkiy and behind Jack.

Jack's heart had started to pound in his chest, trying to crack his ribs from the inside, the minute the man in black had appeared. He knew this man. It was the assassin he'd run into at Smiley Lopez's house.

Sergei spoke to the newcomer in Russian, and Jack picked up the name Franko. Franko replied in terse, unhappy sentences. Sergei responded sympathetically, but Malenkiy laughed. Franko thumped him in the chest, and the two began to squabble.

"You'll have to forgive my friends," Sergei said to Jack. "This one has had a bad day."

Jack stuck to the things that would concern Studhalter. "Now there are three of you and one of me."

Sergei nodded agreeably. "Your math is excellent. I will not try to trick you when we count kilos."

They dropped down onto Pacific Coast Highway, headed for the beach.

Ryan Chappelle was on the phone with Tony Almeida, discussing the Pacific Rim Forum site down at the Ritz-Carlton in Marina del Rey.

"If we're going to cover this by tonight," Tony was saying from the freeway, "we need to scramble several full teams."

"Who's on security already?" Chappelle asked. "Somebody's got to—"

"Wong is liaison," Tony said, referring to a junior field agent assigned to coordinate information between CTU and the other agencies (including LAPD, the FBI, and security personnel for each country involved in the conference). "But we're talking about eleven countries."

Chappelle outlined a strategy: rank the countries by order of importance and impact from Jemaah Islamiyah's perspective, starting with Indonesia; analyze the schedule of each country and look for anomalies that might create openings; examine the protocol written for installation security at the Ritz-Carlton . . . The list was extensive.

"Hold on," Chappelle said. "I'm getting buzzed that Peter Jiminez is on the line. Some kind of emergency." Chappelle put Tony on hold and took Jiminez's line off hold. "What is it, Peter?"

"He surprised me, sir," Peter said. "I'm sorry, Almeida and Myers said he was compliant. I let my guard down. I'm sorry—"

The hair on the back of Chappelle's thin neck stood on end. "Talk sense, Agent Jiminez. What are you talking about?"

"Felix Studhalter," Peter explained. "He escaped."

Chappelle swore. He dialed the number of the cell phone Jack Bauer was carrying, but all he got was an out-of-service signal.

1:38 P.M. PST
Topanga Canyon

The weather wasn't hot enough to attract a huge beach crowd, so Pacific Coast Highway was open. Sergei Petrenko's Mercedes cruised up the coast, reaching Topanga Canyon in no time, and turned up the winding highway into the Santa Monica Mountains that separated L.A.'s inland valley from the ocean. East of Santa Monica, where the mountains looked down on Beverly Hills, Hollywood, and downtown, the hills were stacked with expensive "Hollywood Hills" homes. Out here, though, on the fringe of Los Angeles county, the mountains looked and felt rural thanks to distance and no-growth laws. Long before it was a highway, Topanga Canyon had been a footpath for Native Americans and the winding, double-ess curves of the road memorialized the ancient trail.

Jack couldn't have known it, but to reach Topanga he had passed Temescal Canyon, where Zapata was held up, and if he had traveled on Topanga Canyon up into the heart of the San Fernando Valley, he would

have arrived at the safe house where Adrian Tintfass
was having lunch.

But he couldn't have known, of course. Besides,
his mind was thoroughly preoccupied with Franko
sitting right behind him. After several anxious minutes, Jack decided that Franko either wasn't going to
look closely at him, or hadn't seen him well enough
to identify him. He therefore settled into a watchful
quiet as the three Ukrainians spoke to one another in
Russian.

The Mercedes climbed up the steep road into Topanga Canyon. For several miles there were no buildings at all, just the bare beauty of the chapparal.
Jack pulled his cell phone—actually, Studhalter's cell
phone—out of his pocket and checked it: no bars.

"No service up here," Sergei pointed out.

As the road leveled out at the top of the pass, they
drove through the tiny hamlet of Topanga. Several
unmarked lanes branched out from the main highway, and Sergei took one that was almost invisible
under two huge oak trees.

This lane was paved for a hundred yards, then
turned to uneven dirt. As the Mercedes bounced
along, Sergei spat a curse in Russian.

Franko, from the back, answered in English.
"You're an old woman, complaining about your blad-
der. We have to pave the road or you got to get yourself a fucking truck."

Sergei scoffed. "I didn't come to America to be
driving a truck."

Several jarring minutes brought them to a shack

that must have been someone's mountain cabin or hunting lodge, once upon a time. Although more rustic and a bit more run-down than the house in Santa Monica, it impressed Jack with the same quality: not so run-down as to attract attention, not so well-kept that it prevented the owners from worthier pursuits.

There were already two cars parked in a wide dirt patch in front of the shack: an old seventies Dodge truck that looked like it belonged, and a BMW 560i that didn't. Sergei parked next to the BMW. All four men got out and walked up the dirt patch to the house.

Now or never, Jack thought. He turned to look around, staring squarely into Franko's face. Franko stared back, his eyes vaguely threatening. There was no sign of recognition in his eyes.

They walked into the building, which was neither a mountain cabin nor a hunting lodge. It was a crystal meth lab. Crystal meth. Methamphetamine. Tina, a corruption of sixteen, from one-sixteenth of an ounce. Providing a cheap, powerful high, crystal meth was rapidly replacing cocaine and heroin as the suburban drug of choice.

"You will excuse if we don't go inside," Sergei said. Jack understood. Meth labs were notoriously dangerous places because the chemicals, including ephedrine, being boiled down were notoriously unstable. Meth labs didn't just catch on fire; they were immediately engulfed in flames. "This place blows," Jack observed, "you're going to burn down the whole mountain."

Sergei shrugged. "This place blows, either I am safe in my house or I am inside there. Either way, is not my problem. Inside here, we produce half a million hits every two days. That's a whole lot of tina for five dollars a hit."

Jack made use of the information Studhalter had given him. "I never said five dollars."

"Relax, we are friends here, relax," Sergei laughed. "Five dollars for the user. For you, two dollars."

Jack nodded satisfactorily.

The door opened and two more people came out. One was another hard-looking Slavic man, although this one lacked the bright, intelligent eyes of the two Petrenkos. The other was an anachronism—a beautiful woman with long blond hair, tied into a thick Viking braid down her back. She hopped off the porch and threw her arms around Sergei, who buried his face in her neck and hair, growling pleasurably at her in Russian.

Malenkiy chuckled and whispered something to Franko, who laughed and nudged Jack. "Our combination scientist and cock tease. Sergei pays her double because he's trying to get up her skirt. He'll give half the money in that briefcase to get his piston greased."

"Is that my truck?" Jack asked, pointing at the Dodge.

Sergei heard him and dislodged himself from the blond. "Yeah. Give us a few minutes to load the shit and count your cash, and we'll be done." He barked an order to Malenkiy and the slow-moving Slav, who both went into the shack and came out with bundles wrapped in plastic.

"I've seen you around."

Jack's heart popped up into his throat. Franko was staring sidelong at him. "Or you look like someone I know."

Problems were best faced squarely, so Jack turned straight to the Russian. "I doubt you've seen me. I haven't been in town that long."

Franko chewed his lip for a minute, then shrugged. Jack turned away, but felt the other man's eyes linger on him.

"Okay," Sergei said, apparently resigned to the fact that he wasn't getting any more action from the blond. "Let's see the money."

Jack held up the briefcase, but before Sergei could take it, a phone in his pocket rang.

"Cell service?" Jack said curiously.

Sergei tapped his own temple. "Satellite phone. For the man who has everything."

He pulled the phone—a bit larger than the average cell phone—out of his jacket and answered in Russian. "Oh, sure," he said, nodding politely at Jack and excusing himself with a gesture. He stepped away and said, "I don't think so, no. Well, if you say so. I'll talk to you later." He hung up and turned back to Jack. "I'm sorry. It's rude, but business. You know. Now, the money?"

Jack held the briefcase flat and popped it open, revealing the top layer of twenties and fifties. When he looked up from the case, he was staring at the black hole of a handgun. He frowned. "Do you want a check instead?"

Sergei spoke in Russian, and Franko drew his own gun. The blond watched curiously. Malenkiy, just coming out of the house with another load, set it down and produced his gun. The fourth Slav stopped, still holding his parcel.

"I get some funny calls on my satellite phone," Sergei said. "That one was from Felix Studhalter."

1 2 3 4 5 6 7 8 9
10 11 12 13 14 15 16 17
18 **19** 20 21 22 23 24

· ·

THE FOLLOWING TAKES PLACE
BETWEEN THE HOURS OF
2 P.M. AND 3 P.M.
PACIFIC STANDARD TIME

· ·

2:00 P.M. PST
Topanga Canyon

Without hesitation, Jack tossed the briefcase at Sergei and lunged toward Franko. But the Russian had been tough enough when he was outnumbered. Now he was even more difficult. The muzzle of his gun clipped Jack across the temple, spinning him around. Jack allowed the spin to carry him full-circle and he swung his fist against the Russian's head. But Sergei dropped low, hugging Jack's legs and shouldering him to the ground. Jack sat up, grabbing Sergei by the hair to peel him off, but Malenkiy had reached them by then and Jack caught his booted foot squarely in the face.

The little Russian put his knee on Jack's chest and jabbed a gun against his cheek.

"Don't," Sergei ordered. "Too close to the house. And too close to the road for the sound."

Jack's head was spinning from the kick, but he felt their hands paw him, taking his gun. He had no idea what sort of screw-up had given Studhalter the opportunity to call, but if he survived this, someone was going to catch hell.

"I don't know who you are. I don't care, either. I'm taking your money and my tina," Sergei said.

Jack gambled. "I'll tell you who I am. I work for the government, but I'm not here to sting you. I'm here to buy your crystal meth and use it as a trade for another case. Wait!" At the word *government*, the little man had cocked back the hammer on his weapon. "Wait! I don't give a shit about your meth lab or your drug dealing. That's not my job. I have another case and I need the meth for a trade. That's all. Take the money, give me the meth, and it'll be just like you sold to Studhalter."

"Except you work for the government," Sergei observed. He barked in Russian. Jack heard Malenkiy's name, but understood nothing else. Malenkiy kept his knee on Jack's chest and the gun in his face, and Jack was sure the little man would use it despite Sergei's orders, if Jack gave him a reason, so he kept still for the moment, staring past the gun and Malenkiy's eager eyes and up into the blue sky. It wasn't often Jack looked up at the sky. It was clear today, and peaceful.

Sergei and Franko seemed to be finishing the transfer of crystal meth from the lab to the truck. A moment later, Jack felt hands haul him roughly to his feet. Sergei, Malenkiy, Franko, and the slow one all had weapons trained on him. Sergei barked at Malenkiy, who nodded, while he and Franko backed away and then hurried over to the truck.

Malenkiy snapped at Jack in Russian and pointed up the hill past the little shack.

"That way," the other Russian said. His forehead sloped and his lower jaw was slack. He eyed Jack curiously.

Jack saw no opportunity to attack, so he acquiesced, walking up the hill with the two Russian men on either side of him and the girl behind. Uphill from the house was a trail winding its way through the brown grass. He followed it, always with the men flanking him and their guns steady. The trail climbed to the top of a small rise. There it made a sharp turn, running along the edge of a ridge overlooking a steep barranca. The trail continued into the mountains, but the Russians stopped at the edge of the precipice.

Jack had to make his move now. He tensed his muscles, but before he could do anything, Malenkiy gurgled. Jack glanced at him. His body was stiff and trembling, his eyes wide as choking sounds came from his throat. Taser wires protruded from his body, reaching backward. Jack just had time to realize that the blond girl held the taser when she kicked the slow-witted Russian in the chest, sending him backward over the cliff, tumbling down the hill.

With superhuman effort, the vicious little Russian tore the taser barbs out of his body. He tried to raise his gun, but Jack pushed it aside and punched Malenkiy in the face. The little man followed his comrade down the hill.

Jack turned to the blond girl, who had rearmed her taser. Her face was cool and calm as an iceberg. "Ivan?" he asked.

She spoke in perfect English. "Who the hell are you?"

"Jack Bauer, Counter Terrorist Unit," he explained. "And thanks."

"Thanks? Jesus!" she said, anger melting her icy facade. "Do you have any idea how badly you screwed this?"

"Tell me later!" Jack said. He ran down the hill. He had to get that crystal meth.

The undercover FBI agent, "Ivan," followed him. By the time he reached the shack again, he saw that the truck and the Mercedes were gone. He jumped into the BMW.

Ivan threw open the passenger door. "You don't have the keys!"

"I've had a lot of practice." He tore the panel out from under the dash and hot-wired the car in a few seconds. By this time Ivan was in the car with him. She scolded him as he kicked up dust on his way down the lane.

"Four months! Four months of that gorilla's paws on my ass! And you come along and blow the whole operation!"

He reached the paved part of the lane and sped up, reaching the main highway in seconds. Dust drifting on the highway suggested that Sergei had turned right, inland, so he followed.

"What gives you the right to—aggh!" He burned rubber onto Topanga Canyon, throwing her almost into the driver's seat.

"Seatbelt," he cautioned. "I can't explain even if I had time. I need that supply of crystal meth. I'm happy to bring down Sergei, but it's not that important to me. My case is bigger."

"Bigger! Bigger than four months of my—"

"Yeah," he said, and focused on the road. The speedometer was up in the eighties already. The BMW's tires squeaked warningly as they tried to grip the asphalt on the sharp turns. One curve came up faster than Jack realized, and the BMW rubbed against the metal guard rail. The blond shut up for a minute, her face losing all its color.

"Shit, you're going to kill us."

On a rare straight piece of road, Jack saw the Mercedes and the truck down below. He accelerated.

"Okay," the woman said, her voice changing tone. "Okay, okay, we, um, got off on the wrong foot. I'm Sue. Agent Sue Mishler, FBI. Jesus!" At the next turn, the BMW lifted off its two left wheels for a second.

"Call for backup," she said. "Why not call for backup!"

"No signal," Jack grunted. But that wasn't the reason. He couldn't call for police backup. They would confiscate the meth, or at least tie it up with paperwork until he could extricate it, and he had no time.

Reckless driving closed the distance between them, and on the next straightaway Jack pulled up close behind the Mercedes. He used the driver's console to lower the passenger side window, letting in the roar of the wind.

The silhouette looked more like Sergei. Jack saw him look into the rearview mirror and then look down without changing his demeanor. He must have glanced backward, seen a man and a woman in the BMW, and assumed all was going according to plan.

"Do you have a gun?" he asked over the noise.

Sue put her hand into her pocket, then hesitated. She engaged on a brief internal struggle, then produced a Glock .40.

"Get ready to shoot him."

Jack gunned the engine and swerved into the opposite lane, pulling up next to the Mercedes. Sergei glanced over at them and the grin collapsed on his face. "Shoot him," Jack advised.

"I can't! He hasn't done anythi—"

The first two shots shattered the passenger window behind them.

Sue flinched, then swiveled her upper body like a turret and brought the Glock to bear. Jack kept his eyes on the road, but at the corner of his vision he saw her calmly squeeze off three rounds. The Mercedes veered away, clipping the back of the Dodge pickup and then disappearing from sight.

"Nice," Jack said. "Now don't shoot." He needed the truck intact. The Dodge fishtailed a little, then straightened itself out. Jack pulled up even enough to see Franko appear startled, then recover and glance over at them. "Trade places!" Jack commanded. He slid over until he was practically on top of the FBI agent. She had no choice but to take his place at the wheel. She planned to pull over the moment she was at the wheel, but somehow during the switch Jack had plucked the gun from her hand.

"Son of a bitch!" she yelled.

"Stay with him!" Jack warned, seeing the BMW drop a little behind. But Sue Mishler was no trained driver. Jack saw that she was losing ground, the BMW's nose now halfway down the side of the Dodge. Jack hauled himself up out of the window. The two vehicles rounded another hard curve, and Jack nearly flew off. He clutched at the windshield wiper and scrambled on to the hood. Gathering himself, he leaped across the space between the BMW and Dodge and landed heavily on the edge of the cargo bed, his face planted in the plastic wrap that covered kilos of meth.

Jack threw himself over the side and into the cargo bed. He tried to stand up, but the Dodge swerved violently as Franko tried to throw him off. Jack half crawled up to the outside of the cab and dropped low when he saw Franko raise an arm. He heard the shots only as short, sharp claps, all but drowned out by the roar of wind and engine. Blindly, Jack raised the Glock, so close it almost touched the glass, and poured six rounds into the cab as glass shrieked and shattered. In response, the engine roared but the truck swerved. Risking a look, Jack saw Franko slumped against the steering wheel like a rag doll. But they weren't slowing down, so his dead weight had to be resting on the accelerator.

Through the front windshield, Jack saw the Dodge heading for the edge of a precipice.

He scrambled up and jack-knifed his body, nearly upside down, into the cab, grabbing onto the steering wheel and swerving away from the abyss. He couldn't reach the brake, so he steered the truck as best he could as he wormed his way inside, pushing Franko's blood-soaked corpse out of the driver's seat. The Russian's dead foot came off the gas pedal and the truck began to slow. Jack shoved Franko over to the passenger side and settled in. The truck belonged to him now.

Suddenly the dark shape of the BMW flew past him, swerved back into his lane, and started to slow down. She was a determined agent. She knew her duty. Jack liked her.

But that wasn't going to stop him.

He reduced his speed for a moment, waiting until they'd cleared the precipice and were driving through a cut in the mountain with sheer walls on either side. Then he gunned his engine, lurching forward. The Dodge struck the back of the BMW to the sound of tortured metal.

Jack caught a glimpse of Sue Mishler's surprised, frightened face as he ran her into the side of the mountain.

1 2 3 4 5 6 7 8 9
10 11 12 13 14 15 16 17
18 19 **20** 21 22 23 24

· ·

THE FOLLOWING TAKES PLACE
BETWEEN THE HOURS OF
3 P.M. AND 4 P.M.
PACIFIC STANDARD TIME

· ·

3:00 P.M. PST
Temescal Canyon

"No offense, but you seem a little overconfident to me," Kyle Risdow said.

He and Zapata were sitting beside his backyard pool, enjoying the afternoon sunshine. Kyle was drinking a mojito and Zapata was nursing a Pacifico.

"Because I'm relaxing here?" Zapata said, closing his eyes and lifting his face up to the sun. His shaved head exposed more skin to the sun's UV rays, and he found that he liked it. "It's just about planning."

"Not just that. Your plan itself. How do you know it's going to work?"

"Oh," Zapata said, a little wearily. "It's not complex. Have you ever done Rubik's Cube?"

"That puzzle thing? Can't stand puzzles."

Zapata wasn't surprised. Kyle was not a creature of intellect or, really, of ambition. He was simply a creature of money. "Let me educate you. In the cube you create corners that are like anchors. Preserve them and you finish the puzzle. Break them up, and you fail. A few sections support the whole. Remove the small piece and the whole thing falls apart."

"But that's just a game," Kyle said lazily. "Life is more dynamic, more flexible."

"Not really." He drank his beer. Seeing that Kyle was unsatisfied, he continued. "This idea is not original to me. The U.S. Army, for instance. Their strategies involve understanding what they call 'centers of gravity.' They try to understand what is most important in a battle, in an occupation. When they fail, it is because they do not identify the right center of gravity."

"And you think you've found one that will do that will help throw this country into chaos."

Zapata nodded.

3:05 P.M. PST
Topanga Canyon

Sue Mishler was unconscious, but not badly hurt. She hadn't been wearing her seatbelt during the pursuit. The BMW's airbag had deployed when she hit the wall and the force of it had thrown her back against the driver's seat, knocking her out. She might have a miserable case of whiplash, but her neck was fine.

Jack jumped back into the Dodge truck and drove off with the crystal meth. He had to get to Lopez.

3:07 P.M. PST
Marina del Rey, California

Tony Almeida stood in the center of the wide, high-ceilinged lobby of the Ritz-Carlton Hotel in Marina del Rey. The hotel was, at the moment, the most beautiful fortress Tony had ever seen.

"Tight as a drum," Nina said, voicing his thoughts. "If Jemaah Islamiyah is doing anything here, I don't see how they're going to succeed."

Tony had to agree. A combination of local law enforcement, the FBI, and security units from the visiting nations had established a standard three-layer security system with a wide perimeter, including emergency response vehicles, a middle field of screens and checkpoints, and a final layer at the entrances and around the individual dignitaries. All meeting and public areas had been swept several times for bombs, and every guest not registered with the Pacific Rim Forum had been (unbeknownst to them) subjected to a background check. Even if he was right, and this was the terrorist target, the conference was as guarded as it could be.

"Why is that son of a bitch always right?" Tony muttered.

"Who? Jack?" Nina said.

"Yeah. Every goddamned time."

"No, he's not!" Nina laughed. "Are you insane? Not even close."

"You don't think—"

"The thing about Jack isn't that he's always right. The thing is that he's always eventually right. He just keeps fighting until he gets it right." She shook her head and spoke with grudging admiration. "No, I always figured that Jack's secret isn't that he's always right. It's that he isn't afraid to be wrong."

3:14 P.M. PST
Temescal Canyon

"Mao understood it," Zapata was saying. Kyle was drowsy from the sun and alcohol, and he was nodding. Zapata noticed, but didn't care. He was not without ego, and now and then he enjoyed fleshing out his theories. "Centers of gravity. That's how he defeated the Nationalists in China. He understood that the goal wasn't to win a certain piece of territory, it was to wear the enemy down. He fought and ran, fought and ran, making the enemy stretch his supply lines thin. The center of gravity wasn't a line of battle, it was a method of fighting. Modern terrorists understand it. The center of gravity isn't to be moral. It's to terrify the enemy into changing his way of life. It is utterly effective.

"The system, as it is currently run, simply doesn't work. There is no effort at equality. There will never be equality, of course. There never has been. But there is supposed to be a movement toward it. Things should get a little better. But they don't. Seven hundred years ago an Aztec peasant was brutalized by his priest-kings. Five hundred years ago he was massacred by the Spaniards. And ten years ago he was oppressed by the aristocrats. No, it's not working. It's a puzzle without a solution. I'm going to break it. This country is the key. And the key to this country is its economy."

3:20 P.M. PST
Boyle Heights

Jack parked the truck in front of Smiley Lopez's house. He'd crossed the east-west access of Los Angeles on Mulholland Drive, riding the spine of the Santa Monica Mountains to avoid as much traffic as possible. The Dodge's bullet-ridden back window—not to mention the dead body crammed in the leg area of the cab—were bound to attract the attention of any policemen who saw it.

Smiley Lopez was sauntering out of his house by the time Jack exited the truck. The gang leader wore a plaid shirt over his wife-beater now. His thumbs were stuck in his pockets and he walked belly first, nodding his head admiringly.

"No shit," he said. "You got the stuff."

Jack nodded. "And I brought you a present." He opened the passenger door. Franko's dead face stared out at them.

"No shit," Lopez said again. "You gotta come work for me full-time, homes."

Jack shook his head. "Zapata."

Lopez clicked his tongue. "Come inside."

He turned and walked up the steps with Jack close behind.

"You know, that *pendejo* was one of us back in the early days. Shit, he was even one of the ones that got us thinking of going big, organizing and shit. But he didn't stick around. He still comes around once in a while."

"You guys do him favors?" Jack asked.

"We don't do favors for nobody," Lopez retorted. He opened the front door. "He pays."

They walked inside. Jack saw another gang-banger standing by the couch. It took him a moment to realize it was Oscar, and that Oscar was holding a gun.

"Hey, *ese*."

3:26 P.M. PST
CTU Headquarters, Los Angeles

"How could you let that happen!" Ryan Chappelle fumed.

Peter Jiminez blushed. "I blew it."

"No!" the Regional Director said sarcastically.

"He sandbagged me. He gave up so easy, I didn't expect any trouble—"

Chappelle sneered. "You fell asleep and put this whole mission in jeopardy."

"Not to mention one of our agents," added Christopher Henderson, hovering nearby.

"Is . . . is there any word?" Jiminez asked timidly.

"No," Henderson replied. "We can only hope for the best."

3:27 P.M. PST
Boyle Heights

Jack felt the pressure of the gun tucked in his waistband, but he knew he couldn't get to it in time. Lopez was standing to his right. He'd have to go for the gang leader and hope Oscar was afraid to shoot his boss.

"I got out, too," Oscar said. "But no one seemed to care much about me."

"Funny thing, though," Lopez added, "somebody wants you dead, and they pay for it. So I figure now that we have the tina, we just—"

Jack lunged to his right. Oscar squeezed off one round and then, as Jack expected, he stopped as the line of fire swept across Lopez. Jack wrapped his left arm around Lopez's neck and ducked behind him as he drew the Glock.

"Go back to jail, Oscar," Jack said. "I'm through just beating you up."

Oscar's eyes widened and he shouted something in Spanish. Lopez replied angrily in the same language until Jack choked off the reply. "I'm counting to three," Jack warned Oscar, who continued to point the gun at him.

"One . . ." He fired. Oscar's head snapped back and he fell. Before he hit the ground, Jack punched the muzzle of the Glock into Lopez's temple and shoved him forward. The Salvatrucha stumbled and turned around to face Jack and the gun.

"I'm done playing with you," Jack stated. "I want Zapata."

"I'm not telling you sh—"

Jack shot him in the foot. Lopez screamed and kicked his foot back in pain, falling onto his side and clutching his foot, pouring a stream of Spanish obscenities. Jack moved forward and put his knee on the Salvatrucha's chest, pressing the gun against his cheek. "Last chance."

"Risdow!" Lopez said with the pistol jammed into his face. "Kyle Risdow."

Jack kept his knee down but eased the pressure off the gun. "Who is he?"

"No fucking idea!" Lopez practically sobbed. The bullet had shattered his foot. "Zapata doesn't tell me shit. I just heard the name once."

Jack smacked Lopez's forehead. "Who hired Oscar to kill me?"

But Lopez was too busy crying in pain. Jack patted him down to make sure he had no weapons, although the gang-banger looked too far gone to be a threat. He pulled his cell phone out.

3:41 P.M. PST
CTU Headquarters, Los Angeles

Ryan Chappelle took Bauer's call. "What have you got?"

"Kyle Risdow," Jack said. "Run that name and tell me where to go. Also, send someone over here. I've got someone here who knows who's trying to kill me."

Chappelle paused. Almeida and Myers were still in Marina del Rey, along with most of Henderson's field agents. He didn't have many choices. He put the phone back to his ear. "I'm sending Peter Jiminez."

A few minutes later, Jamey Farrell was watching her screen fill up with information on Kyle Risdow. There were six of them in the Los Angeles area, but Jamey began to weed them out quickly. Two of them were grandfathers. One was mentally disabled. Two others were incarcerated in Folsom and Chico, respectively. The last one lived in Temescal Canyon.

3:46 P.M. PST
Boyle Heights

Jack couldn't wait for Peter to arrive. He pulled Oscar's belt off his corpse and used it to strap Lopez's hands behind his back. He didn't worry about the feet.

He found two sets of keys on the coffee table next

to a wide flat ashtray. He took both sets out back where two cars were parked—a 70s Cadillac and a silver Mercedes 560SL. Jack took the Mercedes and raced toward Temescal Canyon.

3:48 P.M. *PST*
Staples Center

Mark Kendall moved in front of the mirror in his basement warmup room, 238 pounds of muscle bobbing and weaving, dropping down into a sprawl as an imaginary opponent rushed him. To the amateur observer, he moved like a huge, muscled cat, explosive and slick. But Mark wasn't an amateur. He saw himself as he was: an older version of himself, a half step slower, a half thought behind.

Kendall popped back up and pivoted, working on his footwork. As he did, the door opened and a young man walked in, then froze.

"Oh, damn, wrong room," the man said. Their eyes locked. It was Jake Webb, his opponent. They'd met face to face at the weigh-in yesterday, but today was different. Today was fight day.

Webb bowed out without another word. Kendall watched him back up, and all he could think of was how young and strong the other fighter looked. He turned back to the mirror and stared at his face, with its bent nose and rough edges. He wanted to say that his skin sagged from too many punches, but he knew it wasn't the fight he saw. It was age.

The envelope. The money. His daughter. These were the things he saw as he continued to punch at the mirror.

3:54 P.M. PST
Temescal Canyon

Twice black-and-whites had rolled up behind Jack, sirens blaring, but both times they'd been waved off by calls from CTU. Breaking every law that got in his way, Jack reached Temescal Canyon in record time. He was out of the car practically before it stopped rolling. Without hesitation he walked up to the house, then swung around to the side gate, which was unlocked. He swung around and passed by the pool until he came to a set of French doors. Those doors, too, were unlocked, so Jack walked in. At just the same moment a bald man walked out of the kitchen and stared at him in surprise.

Jack raised his gun. "Federal agent! You're under arrest."

1 2 3 4 5 6 7 8 9
10 11 12 13 14 15 16 17
18 19 20 **21** 22 23 24

. . . .

THE FOLLOWING TAKES PLACE
BETWEEN THE HOURS OF
4 P.M. AND 5 P.M.
PACIFIC STANDARD TIME

. . . .

4:00 P.M. PST
CTU Headquarters, Los Angeles

Seth Ludonowski didn't like what he saw. While
Jamey had been running down information on Kyle
Risdow, he had been digging up data on Encep Sungkar for Tony Almeida. There was no doubt he was
a bad guy, and no doubt that, given the chance, he
would love to disrupt an event as important as the Pacific Rim Forum. But Jack's cautionary comment—to
suspect any information that Zapata allowed them to
get—had stuck with him.

He had pursued the connection between Sungkar
and Zapata—Sungkar had gotten hold of weapons,
which he then traded to Zapata for a computer virus.

It occurred to him that they'd assumed Sungkar had contacted Zapata. But since tracking Sungkar, they'd gathered a whole portfolio of data on him.

"Jamey, am I crazy?" he asked.

"To work here," she muttered from her terminal.

"No, I mean it. Will you look at this?"

She sighed and stood up, then leaned over to his terminal. For a moment the rows of phone numbers, date lines, and names meant nothing to her. Then, as she assessed the information, her face took on the same confused look that Seth wore.

"Well, there must be communication sources we missed. A cell phone number, a pay phone . . ."

Seth shrugged. "Okay, but we have all these sources, all used several times. You think he was careful the first time and then not again?"

"All we can do is guess," Jamey admitted. "But if this is right, then Sungkar didn't get in touch with Zapata. Zapata's people were the ones who started negotiations with Sungkar."

4:02 P.M. PST
Temescal Canyon

"Name!" Jack said, grabbing the man by the shirt and pushing him to the ground. The man didn't struggle at all, but spread his hands out in compliance.

"R-Risdow!" he said in a quavering voice. "Kyle!"

Jack yelled him down, scanning with his eyes and his gun. "Who else is here?"

"No one," the man whispered.

Jack waited another moment, listening. His breath came short, too short for so little exertion. He hadn't slept in longer than he could remember. Fatigue was starting to get to him. It occurred to him that he should have had the area sealed off, called for backup. Was exhaustion clouding his judgment? But no, police backup might have made too much noise. CTU didn't have any other agents to send. He'd done the right thing.

"Get up," he said, hauling the man to his feet.

Risdow was short, with a shaved head and green eyes. "Who are you?"

"Federal agent," Jack said again impatiently. "Where's Zapata?"

"Who?"

Jack glared at him. "The last guy who made me ask twice, I shot him in the foot."

Risdow believed him. Jack could see it in his eyes. He watched the familiar internal struggle of the prisoner about to break. There was no question that he would break. He just had to put up a fight for a moment longer so he felt better about himself.

"Gone," Risdow gasped as though he'd been holding his breath. "He said he had something important to do."

Jack put the gun to Risdow's head. "I'm in no mood for games."

"Okay, okay!" Risdow squealed. His eyes went nearly crossed trying to see the gun touching his forehead.

"I know you know Zapata. I know you know what he's up to," Jack said, although in truth he wasn't sure. All he really had was the word of an MS–13 gang leader. But he didn't have much time left, so he had to push. "Tell me what his target is."

"I don't know what you mean," Risdow pleaded. Jack studied his face, listening carefully to his voice. There was a tension in the voice and posture of the innocent, a particular desperation caused by the fear of being misunderstood. Jack saw it in the stress on Risdow's face and heard it in his trembling voice.

"Yes, you do," he said anyway, leveraging the man's fear. "You've worked with him before. He's told you something."

"Nothing!"

"Something," Jack snapped back. "A place, a name."

"Well . . ." That was it. Risdow hesitated, but he was already broken. Interrogation subjects often hesitated right before they gave up their secrets. It made them feel better afterward. "He said something about the Pacific Rim Forum. That's all I know!" he added when Jack started to press further.

The conference, Jack thought. *Tony was right.* "Is he on his way there?"

"I guess," the man said. "I swear I don't know."

He kept his eyes on Risdow while he reached for his phone.

"Look, can you let me go?" Risdow asked. "I'm not involved in this, I swear. I'm a businessman. I don't do violence."

Jack was about to ask him if he'd heard of conspiracy or aiding and abetting, then tell Risdow to go to hell, but he hesitated. He was on Zapata's trail now, and it was very possible that Zapata didn't know it. The anarchist had no reason to think MS–13 would have helped him, and in fact Smiley had tried to betray him even after Jack had gone way outside the lines to strike a deal. The last thing Jack needed now was to scare him off.

4:16 P.M. PST
Boyle Heights

Peter Jiminez stood in Smiley Lopez's living room and called headquarters. "Henderson? It's me. Yes, I'm here. The guy's dead."

4:17 P.M. PST
Temescal Canyon

Jack hurtled down Temescal Canyon, then swerved onto PCH, determined to get to Marina del Rey as soon as possible. If there was an attack there, Tony would need all the help he could get. The ocean was to Jack's right, the sun just starting to drop down behind his right shoulder. He glanced in the rearview mirror. His eyes stung from dryness and fatigue. *Forget it*, he told himself. *You've been here before.* Energy was an act of will. Victory was an act of will. He would not be tired.

His phone rang. "Bauer."

He heard Ludonowski's voice. "It's Seth—"

"The Forum," Jack interrupted. "It's the Pacific Rim Forum."

Jack heard white noise, then: "It can't be."

Bauer snapped, "I just told you it is. I got it from—"

"Jack, it's Jamey on the line, too. The forum isn't right. We tracked the communications between Zapata and Jemaah Islamiyah. They're pretty one-way. It was Zapata who initiated the conversations. He's the one who put the idea out there. The e-mail that mentioned 'Papa Rashad's factory' came from an IP address at a Starbucks a block from the Biltmore where Zapata was staying. Another came from a café in Pacific Palisades, less than a mile from Risdow's address."

Jack absorbed this information quickly. "You're talking about what I was talking about. Zapata making us chase our own tails."

"Giving us a pattern to follow," Seth observed.

"Then he lied to Risdow, too," Jack said, accelerating through a yellow light. "He seemed sure it was the forum."

"How do you know?" Seth asked.

"We can ask him when he gets in," Jamey said.

"I'm not bringing him in," Jack replied.

"I know," Jamey replied, sounding a bit confused. "The police are."

Her bewilderment was contagious. Jack felt it creep through the phone into his chest. "What are you talking about?"

"The police. They collared Risdow. We put an APB out automatically, even though you were headed for his house. Santa Monica PD picked him up on Lincoln."

Jack swerved out of his lane and onto the sidewalk, standing up on the brakes and bringing the borrowed Mercedes to a halt inches from the fence of a public parking area.

"Are you saying Kyle Risdow was on Lincoln Avenue five minutes ago?"

Jamey was now impatient as well as confused. "Well, yeah."

"I just came from his house. I was talking to him five minutes—"

Pressure welled up in Jack's chest, threatening to burst like a capped volcano. It couldn't be. He couldn't have made such an amateurish—

"Bring up a photo of Risdow. Tell me what he looks like."

Seth answered. "Hold on. Driver's license photo from a couple of years ago. Caucasian, pretty typical WASP-y type. Blond hair, blue eyes. Six-foot-one according to this—"

"Damn it!" Jack yelled. Stupid. Bush league. Weak. Letting fatigue make him so sloppy.

"Jack, what's wrong?"

He was too angry at himself to be embarrassed. "I think I just let Zapata go."

4:24 P.M. PST
Sunset Boulevard, Pacific Palisades

That had been interesting.

Zapata was driving a rented Ford Mustang down Sunset Boulevard, careful to accelerate to the speed of the traffic around him. His heart was still beating rapidly, though with excitement or fear, he wasn't sure. Maybe they were the same.

He was forced to acknowledge the presence of luck. As a general rule, he did not believe in it. Luck was the name given by the uneducated to unaccounted-for variables that happened to unfold in their favor. He, Zapata, had always believed that all variables could be calculated if one were meticulous.

This particular event, however, could only be fortune smiling down on him. He had not in his wildest dreams expected any government agent to make the connection between Kyle Risdow and himself. There was, quite literally, no connection that anyone could follow. For the first time in his adult life, Zapata had been utterly and completely shocked by the appearance of the blond man (his ID had said "Bauer") at the back of the house, and because he believed in coincidences even less than he believed in luck, he knew for certain this was the same man who had killed Aguillar, the same blond man described by Franko, who . . . Ah.

That was it.

Synapses fired across his brain, bridging the gaps in the story. The blond man who "hadn't acted like a cop" had saved Lopez. He was a government agent with some sort of special license. Maverick behavior. Zapata understood the premise without needing to know the details. They had sent a maverick after him, someone who did not follow the normal patterns of law enforcement behavior. Zapata saw all the events laid out before him like a storyboard. The agent was thrown in jail, befriended Ramirez, gotten close— literally, a door away. But Zapata had seen that coming. The minute Ramirez broke out of jail with a "friend," Zapata had ordered Aguillar to kill him and Vanowen. But Aguillar had died, too, and Aguillar had an MS–13 tattoo. Bauer had tracked it to Lopez, and managed (again, luck!) to reach him before Franko could do his work.

Zapata could not see how or why Lopez would have cooperated. Lopez could not have known that he had contracted Franko to kill him. As far as he knew, Lopez hadn't even known about Risdow. But then, Zapata thought, Smiley was sharper than he showed and he kept his ears open. He could have heard Kyle's name mentioned, and hoarded the information like a pack rat. But even if Lopez had information, why would he give it to a Federal agent? That part, Zapata could not fathom. There were not enough data.

Briefly, very briefly, he considered abandoning his plan. He'd done so before. No particular scheme held any special place in his heart. His goal was anarchical, not political, and he had always adhered to the maxim that discretion was the better part of valor. There would be other targets.

Yet, he had to admit, he was feeling something else; something new. Pride. That was it. His ego was now involved. No one had ever come close to laying a hand on him, and here this Agent Bauer had come within arm's reach of him twice in less than twenty-four hours. He was proving to be a formidable opponent.

4:37 P.M. *PST*
Century Plaza Hotel

"Gentlemen, we have to wrap up," said Martin Webb, rising from the conference table.

The three other men at the table also stood up. The nearest, Frank Nye, from the Board of Directors of Dow Jones, looked aghast. Martin had never seen him in anything but a three-piece pin-striped suit done for him in Bond Street in London. Today he was wearing khaki slacks and a polo shirt. "Marty, you can't be serious."

"Why not?" the Fed Chairman asked.

"Well, well," Nye huffed, "the problem's still in front of us."

Martin nodded seriously. "And it won't be solved on a Saturday night."

One of the other men, Marion Zimmer, staggered forward. Old enough to have been born when Marion was still a man's name, his body creaked but his mind was still sharp. "Come Monday, if the markets crash, the country will go with it. You're the one with your finger in the dike, Webb, and you want to go? We were scheduled for another hour. I flew all the way from—"

"I think we've covered everything," Martin said. He wanted to see his grandson's fight, although, truth be told, they really had covered everything. They were four old men who wielded great power, but because they were so old, and had wielded power for so long, they'd forgotten that power had its limits. At a certain point, the markets had to be left to chance. "I know what to say tomorrow in the news. I'll put a brave face on for Monday's bell, and the rest will take care of itself."

He left them behind, their faces frozen like old, wrinkled stone, and headed down to a car waiting to drive him to Staples Center.

4:41 P.M. PST
405 Freeway, Sepulveda Pass, Los Angeles

Pan needed the money, so he'd taken one part of the Zapata job himself. That way he could keep his overall cut, plus one-sixth of the share for the drivers.

Besides, this was the weirdest thing he'd ever heard of, and he wanted to see it up close.

He was driving northbound on the 405 Freeway, one of the main arteries that carried traffic into and out of Los Angeles, and even on a Saturday, it was packed. However, because it wasn't a work day, there was just enough space to gather speed, which was what Pan did as he moved toward the top of the pass.

Zapata had given explicit instructions as to where he should do the job—at least a hundred yards below the Mulholland Avenue exit. So just as he drove underneath the sign that said MULHOLLAND EXIT ¼ MILE, Pan did his job: he gunned the engine and swerved hard into traffic, shutting his eyes tight. He heard the shrill squeal of tires, felt the jarring impact of another car before he heard the horn sound, and then his world went white as the airbag exploded outward. Vaguely he heard crash after crash after crash as the Saturday drivers on their way out of the city smashed into one another.

At almost exactly the same time over on the 101 Freeway, Pan's friend Doogie did almost exactly the same thing.

This happened six times, on two other major freeways, and on two main surface streets in West Los Angeles. At the moment, as far as anyone knew, they were just six separate accidents on the Los Angeles freeways.

4:49 P.M. PST
CTU Headquarters, Los Angeles

If there was anything Jack hated worse than Chappelle's tirades, it was Chappelle being right when he went on one.

"All this goddamned work for nothing!" the Regional Director fumed. "You let him walk out the front door."

Jack had learned long ago to face his mistakes, not to garner sympathy but in order to move beyond them toward a solution. "I'll fix it."

"How?"

"Still working on it."

Jack pushed past Chappelle and into the main part of the headquarters. "Jamey! Seth!" But he had already reached them by the time they jumped to their feet.

"He's here, he's after something," Jack said without a hello. "I need to know what it is. Now."

Jamey said, "We've already run down our list of possible targets. The Pacific Rim Forum fit all the criteria."

"We're missing something," Jack said. His mind was racing. There was a pattern here, the kind of pattern Zapata would have seen. He was missing it, and that made him angry. "We have to find it."

"Uh . . ." It was Seth. "Can I go?"

Jack was startled. "What? No!"

Seth glanced from Jack to Jamey, hoping she'd be more sympathetic. She was his direct superior, but this Jack Bauer seemed to take charge of whatever situation he was in. "Um, I want to go. I've been here since yesterday." Jack and Jamey continued to stare at him. "Yesterday being a whole day ago. I haven't seen the sun."

"We've got a job to do, Seth," Jamey said.

"I've been doing it," the young man replied. "I have plans tonight."

Jack curled his lip. "Tell her you can go out tomorrow night."

"It's not that. I'm going to the fights tonight. Silva versus Harmon, baby!" he said excitedly, but he saw that they didn't understand what he was talking about. He pleaded to Jack. "Oh, come on, you must watch mixed martial arts fights."

Jack shook his head.

"Well, there are huge fights tonight, and I have tickets. It's the Professional Reality Fighting championships. I really don't want to miss it."

"You've got to be kidding," Jack said.

"No, I'm not. Those tickets cost me two hundred bucks."

Jack shook his head. "Not that. The name. Did you say Professional Reality Fighting?"

• •

THE FOLLOWING TAKES PLACE
BETWEEN THE HOURS OF
5 P.M. AND 6 P.M.
PACIFIC STANDARD TIME

• •

5:00 P.M. PST
Staples Center

Mark Kendall was sitting on the floor of the room
that served as his waiting room and training room
as his corner, Max Kominsky, wrapped his hands.
Kominsky wasn't big on pep talks, so he kept quiet
while Mark brooded. He wanted to call home again,
but Kominsky had drawn the line at three calls. Fight
time approached.

Someone knocked on the door and then opened it.
A black face with an infectious toothy grin popped in
and spoke in Portuguese. Mark recognized him immediately: Salvatore Silva, the current heavyweight

champion. An older face appeared beside him, square-jawed and missing several teeth. Ramon Machado, the trainer they called the kingmaker.

"He says good luck," Machado translated.

Kendall nodded, not standing up so that Kominsky could finish his work. "Tell him I said thanks."

More Portuguese. The big black man's dark, gleaming eyes studied Mark over his toothy grin. "The champion says he hopes you will win . . ."

"Thanks again," Mark said.

". . . because he'd rather fight you than Jake Webb!" Salvatore Silva roared with laughter and disappeared.

Mark heaved a huge sigh. "They're all against us, Maxie," he said.

Kominsky shrugged. "Me, I get nervous around company anyway."

5:04 P.M. PST
Staples Center

Martin Webb reached downtown Los Angeles just ahead of what looked like unbelievably bad traffic. His driver, Johan, said there were bad accidents all over the freeways, and that the traffic was snarled all across the city. They parked across the street from the Staples Center and walked to "will call," where Jake had left tickets for them.

The big black lady behind the counter took his name and plucked the tickets out of a file box. She eyeballed Martin as she put the tickets in his hand. "You're Martin Webb, the Fed guy."

Martin nodded with a wink and a confidential smile. "Tonight I'm just a grandfather."

She bobbed her head at him. "Well, you better come back as the Chairman come Monday mornin', 'cause I'm countin' on my stocks to help me climb outta here." She motioned to the four beige walls of the tiny ticket office.

Martin smiled. "Ma'am, I don't really control the stock market—"

"Oh, I know you do." The big lady laughed, ignoring customers that were coming up behind them. "You wave your magic wand and make it all better. Enjoy the fights, ya'll."

The Fed Chairman nodded at her and went inside, accompanied by Johan. Jake had reserved great seats for them. They weren't floor seats because, according to Jake, you really couldn't see the raised cage from down there. They sat in the first row of the raised seats, with an eye-line view of the fenced cage where the fighters would meet.

"Do you ever watch these fights, Johan?" Martin asked.

Johan, who acted as the Fed Chairman's bodyguard and driver, nodded. "Machado is going to take him apart in the first minute, I think."

"Excuse me, excuse me!" someone said, pushing past the Fed Chairman. A man with a shaved head slipped past them and sat down a few seats away. "Oh, I'm glad I made it," he said with a grin at Martin. "The traffic's terrible!"

5:14 P.M. PST
CTU Headquarters, Los Angeles

Chris Henderson was sitting in his office when the call he'd been dreading came in. "Agent Henderson, this is Anthony Becker, Internal Affairs."

Henderson's heart sank, but he was a professional. His voice was steady. "Internal Affairs? Don't they give you guys weekends off?"

"We need to interview you, Agent Henderson," Becker returned. "I think you know what it's about."

Henderson squeezed the handset next to his ear until his knuckles turned white. *Damn, damn, damn.* "Well, okay. First thing Monday. Do you want me to come to you?"

"Actually, tomorrow is better. Better to get it over with, you know?" Agent Becker said smoothly. "Then you have the whole week ahead of you once you're cleared."

"Right," Henderson said. "Sunday it is."

He hung up, then used the intercom. A moment later Peter Jiminez marched up the stairs to Henderson's office.

"Close the door," Henderson ordered. Peter did so. Once they were alone, Henderson's normally stoic features bunched up into a violent bundle of knots and veins and muscles. "Why the hell is Jack Bauer still alive!"

5:17 P.M. PST
CTU Headquarters, Los Angeles

Jack hung up the phone. "Get this. Webb had no definite plans to see the fights until today. That's why the visit wasn't on our schedule."

"But," Seth asked, "if even the target didn't know he was going to be there, how would Zapata know?"

"Because that's what he does," Chappelle interjected. "Get down there, Bauer."

5:18 P.M. PST
CTU Headquarters, Los Angeles

Peter Jiminez glared back at Chris Henderson. "What do you think I've been trying to do!"

Henderson stood up from his seat, pacing the width of his small office. "Jesus, this is bad. Internal Affairs wants to interview me tomorrow. They're not coming in on a Sunday to run a Bible study with me. Damn it!"

Christopher Henderson's plan had almost worked. It had come so close to working so many times in the last few hours.

He'd been behind it from the beginning, of course. Bauer's testimony would seal his fate once Internal Affairs started chasing the misappropriated funds. Jack had to die. Henderson had known it for weeks. The only question was how to do it without being blamed.

Chappelle had kept his little Zapata scheme close to the vest, but Henderson was no idiot. There was no mission being run out of his field office that he didn't catch wind of, even one as tight as this. In fact, the confidential nature of the scheme was what inspired Henderson to hatch his own plot. Only a few people had known that Jack Bauer was innocent, and that his presence in the Federal Holding Facility was a setup to get him close to Zapata. Henderson had planned carefully to have them removed, so that Bauer would have no avenues of escape. Chappelle had been the easiest of the three—a large dose of barbiturates had put him down almost immediately. Henderson had known the hospital would conduct blood tests, of course, but he was a clandestine operative. Slipping into a hospital lab and switching the test results had been child's play.

Bargaining with the MS–13 gang-bangers had proved relatively easy as well. Smiley Lopez had been eager to hire his men out as killers, especially when Henderson offered reduced or commuted sentences as a prize (the fact that he could not actually have had any sentences reduced did not bother him at all). That Jack had embarrassed some of their soldiers once before gave the Salvatruchas additional motivation.

It should have been easy. It should have been over hours ago. Isolate Jack in the jail. Have the Salvatruchas kill him. Over, done, end of story.

But it hadn't happened that way. Jack Bauer had fought off the assassins not once but twice. In fact, the bastard had somehow used the fights to get even closer to his quarry Ramirez, and once he realized he was isolated, he'd somehow organized a prison riot to cover his escape.

From that moment on, Henderson's plan had gone downhill. He'd put Jiminez on Jack's trail, first watching the Bauer house. That lead had turned hot almost immediately when Bauer contacted his wife and asked her to make a delivery for him. Henderson, trying to keep himself and Jiminez at arm's length, had sent MS–13 again, but they'd proved just as inept out of prison as in.

"You had him," Henderson swore under his breath. "You had him in your hands and you let him get away."

Jiminez knew exactly what he was talking about. He'd gone downtown to find Jack and deal with him, but the U.S. Marshals had picked him up first. Even Henderson had to admit that the younger agent had taken a bold step: ramming Pascal's car and freeing Jack. Jiminez's intention had been to help Jack escape, kill him, and dump him somewhere. But he hadn't expected Jack to overpower him.

They had one more crack at Bauer when he assumed Studhalter's identity. Jiminez had let him escape, hoping he'd contact his Ukrainian suppliers, which he'd done. But once again Bauer had fought out of his predicament. The man was a goddamned prodigy.

The only thing that had gone right was when Jiminez got to Smiley Lopez first. Jack had left him alive, of course, but Lopez might have identified Henderson as the man who'd plotted to have Jack murdered, so Jiminez had put him out of his misery.

"So what now?" Jiminez said. "We giving up?"

"Give up?" Henderson said in a voice heavy with sarcasm. "Follow the nice men to the prison? No. You need to kill Jack Bauer."

"What, right now, in the middle of CTU? I'm not going to prison for you."

"We both took a piece of that money," Henderson retorted. "You're going to prison anyway, unless you kill him."

Jiminez knew he was right. There was no way he was going to spend the rest of his life in Leavenworth over a few hundred thousand dollars that no one should have missed anyway. And if Jack Bauer had to die to make sure Peter Jiminez didn't end up fighting off bull queers in prison every day, then so be it.

Henderson's phone rang. He answered and listened for a minute, then nodded. "Good, keep me informed." He hung up and smiled at Peter. Now's your chance. Jack just left for the Staples Center."

5:25 P.M. PST
Staples Center

Zapata sat a few seats from the Chairman of the Fed, glancing his way once in a while but mostly observing the crowd slowly filling up the huge sports arena. The fights were sold out, with most spectators there to watch the much-anticipated title fight between

Salvatore Silva and Ben Harmon. The Kendall-Webb fight was on the undercard, and was scheduled as the second fight of the night.

Several giant monitors hung from the high ceiling. Later, they would show the fight to the spectators in the cheap seats, but for now, they showed promotional video with interviews of the fighters, their past records, and highlights from earlier fights. The more he watched, the more certain Zapata became that Kendall would lose his fight. Young Webb was peaking, and Kendall was washed up. And the moment he lost, his chances of earning any big money from the fight game were reduced to zero, and he would take the offer.

5:32 P.M. PST
101 Freeway, Los Angeles

Jack's car sat in the middle of the worst traffic he'd ever seen in Los Angeles. The freeway was a parking lot, and according to the news, every other freeway looked exactly like this one.

"It's unbelievable," he said to Tony Almeida over the phone. "Can you get to the Staples Center?"

"I can't even get *to* the freeway!" Almeida yelled in general frustration.

Jack hung up and dialed CTU, getting Chappelle. "We've already alerted security at the Staples Center," the Regional Director said before Jack could even ask. "They can't roll any more units downtown.

The whole city's paralyzed. But they have three or four black-and-whites there for every event. I'm having those uniforms go inside and stay close to the Chairman."

"Good," Jack said. "I'm on the 101 near Cahuenga. Can you send a helicopter for me?"

Chappelle paused. "Are you serious?"

"I guarantee you Zapata is there. I need to be there now. I've seen his face."

Chapelle said, "We should evacuate. Or lock down."

"No," Jack replied sharply. "He'll find a way out. I don't want to warn him."

He hung up before Chappelle could object. He glared at the endless stream of cars before him, gleaming in the last rays of sunlight like a river of steel. "What the hell's going on!" he yelled.

5:35 P.M. PST
Los Angeles Department of Transportation

Darren Spitz had worked for the Department of Transportation for the better part of two decades, and he'd never seen anything like what was going on that afternoon. Los Angeles traffic was always bad, but at least it flowed. If anyone understood that, he did. He was employed by the city planner's office, and he specialized in traffic flow patterns. The end result of his job was pretty mundane—he helped determine how long the traffic lights stayed red or green, and how those changes related to the timing of other traffic lights nearby. Not the most exciting work. But Spitz liked it.

"Traffic is a force of nature in this city," he would say to anyone who would listen (it was not a large crowd). "You listen to the weatherman. You listen to the newsman. You'd better listen to the traffic man. Traffic has a memory, it has a rhythm all its own. It might as well be a living thing."

At the moment, that living thing was sick. Paralyzed, in fact. Or maybe a better metaphor was that all its arteries were clogged.

Spitz sat at his computer screen, flipping from traffic camera video of various congested areas (which was all of them) and grid overlays that showed the entire network of freeways and surface streets. Most of them now flashed red, meaning they were jammed. Six different spots showed a starburst indicating a SigAlert—a major accident that caused a disruption of traffic service.

"Huh," he said as the big picture caught his attention. It wasn't unheard of to have six large accidents in the greater metropolitan area, but something about these six accidents intrigued him: the 405 Freeway at the Sepulveda Pass; the 101 Freeway at Cahuenga; the 10 Freeway just before the 110. *You know*, he thought, *if you were going to jam the freeways on purpose, these would be some of the best spots to do it.*

Darren Spitz called his supervisor.

5:41 P.M. PST
101 Freeway, Los Angeles

The helicopter came in low, swooping over the hoods of cars stretched on for miles. Jack saw it coming and got out of his car, leaving the keys in the ignition and the engine running.

"Hey!" yelled the driver behind him, but Jack ignored the call.

He jogged around and between the unmoving cars until he reached the edge of the freeway. There was a small park nearby and the helicopter made for it. Jack followed, and a few minutes later he ducked low beneath the propeller blades and slid into the passenger seat.

"Staples Center!" he yelled, and the chopper rose into the air.

5:47 P.M. PST
Staples Center

"Game time, baby," Chico D'Amato, the corner man, said. He tapped his fists onto the top of Jake Webb's gloved fists. "You ready for this?"

Jake Webb had never felt so ready in his life. He'd trained hard for the last four months. He'd hit his weight exactly, and then spent the last forty-eight hours bulking up on carbs and protein, a long-standing tradition among fighters who got to weigh in a day or two prior to the actual fight. He now weighed a good seven pounds more than his officially listed weight. He felt strong and he felt fresh.

Jake knew he was at his peak. He also knew that he matched up well against both Salvatore Silva and Ben Harmon. It didn't matter to him which one of them came away with the champion's belt tonight. He'd come after him and he'd take it. All he had to do was get through Kendall, who didn't look to offer him much of a problem.

"Your grandpa picked up his tickets," Chico told him. "He's out there. You gonna win for him?" Chico was an old hand at the fight game. He locked his eyes on Jake's and was content with the fire he saw there.

"I'm gonna win for him," Jake replied.

"Let me tell you what this boy's gonna do," Chico said. "He's gonna fight with a lot o' heart. You got to weather the first few minutes of the round. My guess is he'll fight tough then. Don't panic if he roughs you up, just stay in the pocket, keep your chin down. His ground game is good but it ain't great, so if he takes you down just stay calm. You watch, come the end of that round, his heart's going to go out a little bit. Doubt's gonna creep in. That's when you finish him."

"That's when I finish him," Jake repeated like a mantra.

5:51 P.M. PST
Staples Center

Zapata saw the four uniformed cops gather at the end of the corridor that led from the outer circle of shops and concession stands and into the seating area. He looked the other way and saw four more cops there. Once or twice, the police officers glanced casually up to his area, but they weren't searching. They were checking the Chairman and then glancing away.

The anarchist felt a pang in his chest, but he did not know if it was anger or fear. Could those policemen be here for the Chairman? Zapata looked across the arena to the entry corridors over there. No police officers. No police officers anywhere except near the Fed leader.

Casually, Zapata stood up and pulled out his wallet, checking his cash as though contemplating a trip to the hot dog stand. He walked to the nearest corridor and said "Excuse me" as he slid past the police officers. These men had no idea who he was or what he looked like, but there was no doubt in Zapata's mind that if these men had been told to come here, Agent Bauer was not far behind. Zapata went to a concession stand and bought a pair of binoculars. Then he walked around the wide circular hallway that girdled the Staples Center until he came to the far side of the arena. He climbed the outer stairs until he was up in the nosebleed seats on that side. Entering the seating area, he looked around for someone who seemed to be sitting alone, a muscled twenty-something in a T-shirt that said "Tap Out" on it.

Zapata showed the young man his ticket. "Don't ask," he said. "Just trade with me."

The man in the "Tap Out" shirt looked suspiciously at him. "I find out that seat's taken, I'm coming right back here."

"Deal," Zapata said. The man shrugged, took the much better ticket, and left. Zapata sat down in his new seat, as far from the Chairman as possible, and raised the binoculars to his eyes.

Agent Bauer could surround Chairman Webb with as many police officers as he wanted. It wouldn't matter.

At that moment, the entire arena darkened and deafening music blared. The fights were under way.

1 2 3 4 5 6 7 8 9
10 11 12 13 14 15 16 17
18 19 20 21 22 **23** 24

· ·

THE FOLLOWING TAKES PLACE
BETWEEN THE HOURS OF
6 P.M. AND 7 P.M.
PACIFIC STANDARD TIME

· ·

6:00 P.M. PST
Staples Center

It was not every day that a helicopter dropped out of
the sky and landed on the narrow plaza on the north
side of Staples Center. This chopper touched down
lightly and Jack Bauer jumped out, running low under the prop wash.

A moment later he reached the entrance. A large
crowd still hovered outside, composed mostly of late-
comers and fight dilettantes who didn't care about
the undercard fights. Jack pushed past them, ignoring
cries and complaints. At the glass doors he flashed his
badge.

"Okay," the teenage ticket taker said, waving him through. The metal detectors shrieked as Jack entered the Staples Center, but he flashed his badge again and the cop posted there let him pass.

6:07 P.M. PST
Staples Center

Peter Jiminez reached the Staples Center on a motorcycle, the only mode of transportation that had any chance of maneuvering in the paralyzed city. He left the bike in a motorcycle parking spot directly across from the entrance, jogged across the street, and got himself in much the same way Jack had.

Peter's heart was pounding. Bauer was a formidable opponent, and to hunt him would be dangerous. But Peter had one advantage: Jack had no idea that Peter was the hunter.

6:09 P.M. PST
CTU Headquarters, Los Angeles

Christopher Henderson opened his office door and looked down on the bullpen with its network of analysts' computers. What he needed to do now, he couldn't do from his own computer terminal. He walked downstairs and passed by Jamey Farrell's workstation. "Are you seeing that slow crawl data from server four?" he asked her.

Jamey lifted her head up from the screen. "Hmm? Oh, yeah, but it's nothing out of the ordinary."

Henderson looked dubious. "I'm going to check it anyway."

"We can have the techs do it," Jamey offered. "Or one of us."

Henderson smiled as warmly as he could manage. "Let's see if the old field hand can still work the fancy machines. I don't get much of a chance to be a computer whiz."

Henderson walked up the hallway to one of the tech rooms that housed CTU's massive servers. At certain times of day, techs and analysts turned this room into Grand Central Station, but at the moment it was empty and quiet. Henderson opened a panel that gave him direct access to the server's memory cards . . . specifically, memory cards that had to do with phone logs. If he accessed these memory cards from another terminal, the system would register his keystrokes and annotate his file with the fact that he had ordered the deletions. This way, the system would show that someone had accessed the panel, but that was Henderson's stated goal in entering the room, and Jamey would back him up.

Henderson popped a specific memory card out of its slot, then removed a small device with a tiny screen from his jacket. In moments, wires from the device were connected to the memory card, and he was reading its information. He scrolled down until he found a data file for his own telephone, including traces of his cell phone conversations inside the building. He deleted every one of them that went to Peter Jiminez. In moments, almost every communication between the two of them had been wiped clean.

Henderson purposely left a few lines of code in the file, specifically, those related to telephone calls and mobile intercepts of his calls to Smiley Lopez. These he did not erase. He altered them so that the source appeared to be Peter's phone instead.

Content, he replaced the memory card, closed the panel, and walked out of the tech room.

"You're right," he told Jamey with a wave. "Nothing there."

6:29 P.M. PST
Staples Center

Mark Kendall watched the opening fight on a television screen in his room. It was a bruiser. Neither fighter had much finish, but both were tough as nails. The fight had dragged out to the third of its three five-minute rounds, and neither fighter seemed willing to give up.

A handler for Professional Reality Fighting tapped on Mark's door and stuck his head in. "Let's go. This one's ending either way, and then you're up. Oh, and good luck."

Mark nodded. He stood and took a deep breath. This was it.

6:30 P.M. PST
Staples Center

Jack Bauer had reached the section where the Chairman was sitting. After showing his ID to the police officers, he scanned the crowd. No one nearby matched his memory of Zapata. If he planned to kill Webb, he was going to do it remotely. But how? A rifle shot seemed unlikely. There were metal detectors at every entrance, and even if Zapata had bought off one person, there were both metal detectors and checkers who opened every bag.

Jack walked over to the Chairman, immediately attracting the attention of the man next to him. Jack crouched low near Webb's seat. "Mr. Chairman, I'm Jack Bauer from the Counter Terrorist Unit!" Jack shouted over the cheers and jeers as the first fight ended. "I'm sorry to bother you, but I have reason to believe someone in this building wants to kill you. I strongly recommend you leave immediately!"

Martin Webb was startled. He checked the man's credentials again and glanced at Johan, who nodded starkly. "Who's trying to kill me?" he asked.

Cheers rose up for the winner of the first fight. A moment later, the crowd's roar dwindled to a low murmur. "I'm happy to explain in a safer venue, sir," Jack said.

Webb glanced around, as though he might find an assassin sitting in one of the seats nearby. "But there are all these police, and there's you, and Johan," he replied. "And I'm determined to watch my grandson." Bauer scowled and shook his head, but Webb insisted. "Sit with us, son. This'll be something."

6:40 P.M. PST
Staples Center

The Professional Reality Fighting shows were designed for maximum sport but also maximum showmanship. The two fighters both entered the fighting area via platforms that rose up from the basement training rooms. As they ascended, fireworks and flames shot up around them and music blared as the crowd cheered.

Mark Kendall heard none of it. He felt as though he was floating through the next few minutes as he moved down the catwalk connecting his mini-elevator to the actual cage. He was barely aware of the cheers and jeers. The referee stopped him to check his equipment and he nodded at the questions, but his mind was elsewhere. He was thinking of home. He was thinking of his daughter.

The next thing he new, he was in the cage, his bare feet gripping the canvas. Kominsky pulled off his shirt, and now he was wearing only knee-length fighting shorts. He saw his opponent across from him: Jake Webb, young, strong, and confident. He, too, wore only fighting shorts, and the muscles rippled visibly under his lean skin. Mark remembered being that young.

The ring announcer blared Mark's name: *"Intro-*

*ducing, in the red corner, the former PRF Heavy-
weight Champion, with a fighting record of 11–2,
weighing in at 238 pounds, Mark 'The Mountain'
Kendall!"*

The crowd cheered. Mark raised his hand in
acknowledgment.

*"And introducing in the blue corner, with a fight-
ing record of 5–0, weighing in at 239 pounds, Jake
'The Spider' Webb!"*

Thunderous applause assaulted Mark's ears. Well,
he knew whose side the crowd was on.

The referee called them out and gave them the
usual rules: no headbutts, no biting, no gouging, no
strikes to the groin. Pretty much everything else was
fair game. On command, Mark went back to his corner and waited. A moment later, the bell rang, the
crowd roared again, and Mark walked out into the
cage to save his daughter's life.

6:50 P.M. PST
Staples Center

Zapata watched Jack Bauer through the binoculars.
He'd seen the agent enter and speak with Webb, then
sit beside him. Bauer was scanning the crowd alertly.
Zapata felt an awkward mixture of annoyance, admiration, and pity for Bauer. The agent had clearly
deduced that Webb might be a target, but he had no
idea where the attack would come from. Even if he
were standing next to Kendall when he attacked, Za-

pata was sure the giant could snap Webb like a twig before Bauer could do anything about it.

Suddenly Jack Bauer stood up and walked away.

6:51 P.M. PST
Staples Center

Jack held the phone to his ear and, with the other hand, shut out the noise as he walked down the corridor. "What was that, Jamey? I couldn't hear you. Lot of noise."

". . . Jiminez!" Jamey yelled. "Jiminez needs to meet with you. Something about seeing Zapata. He's there, but downstairs, he said. All the way down. Take the stairs near the entrance."

"Got it."

Jack didn't like leaving the Chairman's side, but the truth was, he wasn't doing much more than acting as a bullet sponge, just sitting there. Someone else could do the job as well.

Jack walked back to the entrance and saw a doorway into the stairwell. The stairs went up to the higher levels, but Jack took it down.

6:52 P.M. PST
Inside the Cage

Three minutes into the fight. Kendall was drenched in sweat, but he felt good. He'd scored a couple of strong kicks to Webb's legs. The younger fighter had rushed in twice, strong as a bull, and tried to take him down. Kendall had stopped the attempts and landed two flurries of strong punches. He was sure one of them had rocked the young man. His heart soared.

Win it for them, he thought. Kendall saw an opening and attacked, throwing a fast combination of kicks and punches. He put all his power behind the punches, trying to smash through Webb's defenses. He ended his flurry, thinking of trying to take the fight to the ground.

Webb's right hand came out of nowhere and connected with his nose. He felt the cartilage give way and his chin press inward against his neck. The room spun around like a top. Another punch—a left hook? he didn't see it—caught him on the right side of his jaw. His body suddenly disconnected itself from his feet and he fell to one knee.

The bell rang for the end of the round.

6:54 P.M. PST
Staples Center Stairwell

Jack reached the bottom of the stairwell and pushed through double doors that read EMPLOYEES ONLY. Beyond was a huge storeroom the size of a football field with ceilings two stories high. There were metal shelves ten feet high on one side of the room, and on the other side were islands of storage crates covered in canvas sheets. Jack's footsteps echoed.

"Peter?" Jack called out. He pulled out his cell phone, but got no reception.

The bullet ripped through his left shoulder at the same time he heard the sound.

6:54 P.M. PST
In the Cage

"Shake it off," Kominsky was saying. That was the first thing Mark remembered after touching his knee to the ground. "You gotta fight!"

The bell rang for round two.

6:55 P.M. PST
Staples Center

Zapata watched the fight through his binoculars. The first round had gone as he expected. Kendall had dominated the first half on experience and sheer emotion, but he'd worn down quickly. Webb had landed the most powerful blows of the round just before its end. Kendall had been literally saved by the bell.

Now Kendall and Webb stalked each other. Webb looked more vibrant and eager. Zapata knew it wouldn't be long now.

6:56 P.M. PST
Staples Center

Jack dragged himself behind one of the stacks of crates. His left arm was all but useless now. Jesus! Two wounds to his right arm and now it was all he had left. He raised his gun, but a voice behind him said, "You're getting slow, Jack."

He whirled around, but Peter Jiminez grabbed his gun and dropped a knee onto his chest. He grinned down at Bauer. "I guess it's not so hard to kill you after all."

6:58 P.M. PST
Staples Center

Webb's kick caught Kendall on the right side, exactly on the liver. Kendall felt the world close in around him and nausea rush up into his stomach. His knees buckled again. The next thing he knew he'd been thrown onto his back. Webb was on top of him, straddling him, pounding him with knees. Webb's fists were smashing down on his face and skull.

1 2 3 4 5 6 7 8 9
10 11 12 13 14 15 16 17
18 19 20 21 22 23 **24**

. . . .

THE FOLLOWING TAKES PLACE
BETWEEN THE HOURS OF
7 P.M. AND 8 P.M.
PACIFIC STANDARD TIME

. . . .

7:00 P.M. PST
Staples Center Basement

"What the hell—?" Jack said, wincing through the pain in his shoulder.

"That's where you're going," Peter predicted. He put the gun to Jack's head. Jack jerked his head out of the way as the round went off, sounding like a cannon right next to his ear. He bucked his hips and Peter lost his balance, flying off. Ignoring the pain in his arm, Jack rolled on top of Peter, catching the barrel of Peter's gun in his right hand. Jack smashed his forehead down into Peter's face.

7:01 P.M. PST
In the Cage

Mark, underneath Jake Webb, tried to cover his face with his huge forearms, but Webb's punches were like pile drivers smashing through. He heard the crowd chanting, "Spider . . . Spider!"

Up in the stands, Zapata smiled satisfactorily. It was all going exactly as he'd predicted.

In the cage, Mark heard them chanting Webb's nickname again, and all his thoughts came in slow motion. They were chanting for Webb . . . as though he was the one fighting for his family. They should be chanting for him. They should be chanting for that little girl back home who lived in pain, and that woman who hurt for her baby girl. They should be chanting for him because he loved them so much and all he wanted to do was save her.

And in that moment he remembered again the thing he had learned the day she was born. His strength and his power and his huge heart, they were all given to him for one reason only: to protect that little girl, to keep her safe so she could grow up in the world. That was a father's job, that's what a father did, sacrifice himself for his little girl. And that's what he would do.

Mark Kendall bucked his hips up into the air so powerfully that all 239 pounds of Jake Webb went flying off. Kendall turned over and, like an avalanche, fell on Webb with elbows and knees. Webb absorbed four or five strong shots, then kicked Kendall away and stood up. The two giants squared off.

7:02 P.M. PST
Staples Center Basement

Jack landed two more headbutts, turning Peter's face into bloody pulp. Half blind, Peter reached up with his free hand and clawed at Jack's face. With one hand on the gun and the other arm out of commission, Jack had no way to stop Peter from tearing at his face and eyes. He tucked his chin and turned away, collapsing on the gun so Peter's arm was stuck beneath him. Then, with the gun arm trapped between the ground and his body, Jack spun and landed an elbow in Peter's face. Jack felt Peter's front teeth collapse into the back of his mouth.

7:03 P.M. PST
In the Cage

The round had ended. Kendall staggered over to his corner. His face felt stiff and his cheeks had swollen up, obscuring his vision.

"How bad's my face?" he asked as he sat down for a few seconds.

"Don't worry," Kominsky said, "you weren't handsome to begin with. Listen."

Kendall realized he was still hearing chanting . . . but now the crowd was calling out, "Mountain! Mountain!"

"That's for you," Kominsky said. "Go earn it."

7:04 P.M. PST
Staples Center Basement

It took Jack a minute to crawl to his feet. He was weak. Blackness crept in at the edges of his vision, then faded, then crept in again. He was holding Peter's gun in his hand. Peter was lying at Jack's feet, his face a bloody mess.

Suddenly Peter twitched, rolling for Jack's gun, which was on the floor. Even battered, he was fast. He almost got the weapon off the ground when Jack fired three rounds into his back.

7:05 P.M. PST
In the Cage

In the third and final round, Jake Webb came at Kendall hard. But Kendall didn't feel the blows anymore. He lunged forward, catching Webb in a bear hug and lifting him off the ground. Then he slammed Jake onto the mat. The crowd cheered.

7:06 P.M. PST
Staples Center

Up in the stands, Zapata watched in bewilderment. Mark Kendall was going to win the fight. He was on the verge of destroying his opponent. Zapata could not recall ever being so completely and utterly wrong before. He had miscalculated. He had not factored in some important variable. Some butterfly had flapped its wings somewhere and, chaos-like, had changed the course of his carefully laid plans.

A moment later it was over. Jake Webb, caught underneath Kendall and subjected to his vise grip, surrendered and tapped his hand to the mat. The referee jumped in, calling the fight, and Mark Kendall leaped to his feet, roaring in triumph.

Zapata fumed. He had never felt humiliation before, he had never felt embarrassment. He could not walk away from this mission. He was determined to finish. He would not be defeated by a has-been professional fighter and a stubborn government agent.

The anarchist left his seat and half walked, half ran the circuitous route to the far side of the arena. He ran to the planter near the concession stand and started to dig. Out came the package he had buried there. Inside was a short-barreled 9mm semi-automatic pistol. He had meant to use it to aid his escape if necessary. But now all he wanted was to complete his plan. He passed an exit onto the street and could have escaped, but he continued down the corridor toward his target. He was vaguely aware that he'd succumbed to pride, but he didn't care. Unpredictability was the essence of chaos theory, and he was surely acting unpredictably.

Most of the spectators were still in the arena, cheering the next round of fighters. Zapata arrived at Webb's section just as the Chairman was leaving, on his way to go make sure his grandson was all right.

Ten yards away, Zapata raised the pistol and fired.

Johan, the bodyguard and driver, had seen the motion and lunged in front of his boss. Three rounds embedded themselves in his chest and he fell. Zapata aimed at the Chairman again.

A bullet tore through the side of Zapata's neck, taking a thin strip of flesh. Zapata screamed and gagged. He saw Jack Bauer coming out of the stairwell moving unsteadily, aiming his firearm with one hand as the other hung limply at his side. The pain of the gunshot wound brought Zapata back to reality. *Idiot*, he thought. He dropped his weapon and ran.

Jack ran after him, pausing only to see that Chairman Webb was unhurt. People were screaming now. Inside the noisy arena no one had heard the shots, but the few spectators who were in the hallway to buy food had scattered. Jack ignored them. He wanted Zapata.

7:20 P.M. PST
In the Cage

Mark Kendall listened as the announcer officially declared him the winner. He heard people around him say words like "comeback" and "championship" and "lucrative contract." He stood there and let tears of joy stream down his face.

7:24 P.M. PST
Staples Center

Jack raced out the exit into nighttime Los Angeles illuminated by streetlights. Zapata was across the street already. Jack saw him hop onto a motorcycle and race away. Jack tucked the handgun under his useless left arm and stuck his hand in his pocket. He'd searched Peter's body before leaving it and found the motorcycle key. Hoping his luck would hold out, he followed Zapata's footsteps to the same parking area and saw another motorcycle. Hopping on, he started the engine. This was how Peter had gotten through traffic. And this was how Zapata had planned to escape.

By the time Jack drove onto the city streets headed for the freeway, Zapata was out of sight. He needed help. Keeping his right hand on the handlebars, Jack forced his left arm to work. Blood poured down his wrist and onto his mobile phone, but he dialed anyway.

"Jack!" It was Tony Almeida. "We just got back and heard what's happening at the Staples Center. Are you—?"

"Get a chopper in the air!" he shouted over the rushing wind. "Zapata is trying to escape on a motorcycle."

Jack wondered at Zapata's escape plan. It didn't make sense. Criminals had tried motorcycle escapes many times before in Los Angeles. No matter how fast they outran police cars, no matter how cleverly they used traffic congestion to block the black-and-whites, they couldn't outrun the eye in the sky. It was stupid, and Zapata wasn't stupid.

Jack got on the 110 Freeway headed north. It was as bad as before, although now in the darkness the stalled freeway looked like a river of orange and red lights.

"Chopper's up," Tony said. "We've got them . . . and you. You're behind him. We're trying to get units rolling, but this traffic—"

"It's his plan. He did it. We need to keep the chopper on him. Tony, there's more. Peter Jiminez tried to kill me. I don't know why. I had to kill him." Jack hung up and kept riding.

7:30 P.M. PST
CTU Headquarters, Los Angeles

Tony and most of CTU were on the monitors, watching a feed relayed from an LAPD helicopter. The chopper had been up in a minute and already had its spotlight shining on Zapata's motorcycle, which zigzagged and swerved around the cars essentially parked on the freeway.

Zapata reached a spot on the 110, just before that freeway hit the 101, where a strip of greenery, trees, and a fence separated the freeway from the surface streets. Zapata slowed down and then stopped.

"Is he giving up?" Nina asked.

On the monitor, they saw Zapata dismount, walk over to the shrubbery and pull out something long and metallic. He turned and looked upward at the LAPD chopper.

"RPG!" Tony yelled.

7:34 P.M. PST
110 Freeway

Zapata paused and took a breath, then fired the rocket-propelled grenade straight up, striking the side of the helicopter. The chopper instantly transformed into a ball of flame, for a split second lighting the freeway like a miniature sun. The shocked faces of the drivers imprinted themselves on Zapata's retina. He liked it.

The roar of the other motorcycle came on him too suddenly. He ran for his own bike, but just as he kicked it into gear, Jack Bauer roared up behind him, sacrificing the bike and himself as he rammed Zapata. The anarchist catapulted off the bike and into the dirt and grass. Bauer hit the ground hard, blacking out from the pain in his left arm. But he managed to hold on to his gun. By the time he stood, several minutes had passed.

Zapata had crawled through the shrubs and into a hole that led under the fence. Jack followed.

7:39 P.M. PST
CTU Headquarters, Los Angeles

CTU Headquarters was in chaos. Phones were ringing, data were pouring in, and the teams were struggling to keep up with it.

Nina, Tony, Chappelle, and Henderson were gathered in the conference room.

"This doesn't make sense," Nina said, examining one note. "Authorities at Staples Center say they have the body of Peter Jiminez. What was he doing there?"

"I don't know what Peter's been up to," Henderson said.

Tony had been holding a phone to his ear. "Jack again." He listened, his eyes widening in surprise. "Are you—? Okay, we'll do it." He spoke to the others. "Jack killed Peter. Jiminez was trying to kill him. Jack doesn't know why."

"He couldn't have been working for Zapata," Nina said. "What was he doing?"

Chappelle glowered. "Chris, have the analysts run checks on Peter's phone logs. Let's see who he's been talking to."

Henderson nodded.

7:45 P.M. PST
110 Freeway

On the far side of the fence, Jack worked his way gingerly down into a barranca filled with brambles. Now and then he stopped to listen. Over the random sounds of honking horns from the freeway back beyond the fence, he could hear Zapata out there somewhere, crawling away. Then the sounds stopped.

Jack hunted him slowly, methodically. But he guessed what Zapata was doing. After a moment, he turned back the way he'd come. The barranca was dark, but in the gloom Jack recognized the spot where he'd slid down into the ditch.

Zapata was there, just crawling out of the brush. "Nice try," Jack said.

The anarchist shrugged. "Doubling back is too predictable, but it was all I had left."

Jack looked down at him. Zapata was bruised and beaten, but even so, he looked too normal to have caused so much trouble. "You missed the Chairman," Jack said.

Zapata nodded. "A shame, too. It would have been interesting to see the infrastructure of this company collapse. Oh well, sometimes events are unpredictable after all." The anarchist's bruised face smiled at Jack. "You, for instance. You're quite a tool for your government. A loose cannon, right? A maverick. Unpredictable." He nodded appreciatively.

"Not really," Jack said. "The truth is I'm pretty predictable."

He shot Zapata in the head.

DON'T TAKE YOUR EYES OFF HIM.
NOT EVEN FOR A SECOND.

24 SEASON 5 AVAILABLE NOW

Loaded with hours of Special Features including DVD exclusive 11-minute short bridging Seasons 5 and 6. 23 Extended/Deleted Scenes and DVD-ROM Link to exclusive online content.

24 Season 5 Includes
Exclusive Season 6 Prequel
— Sponsored By Toyota

RAV4

TOYOTA | *moving forward* ▸